THE SHIELD OF KUROMORI

黒森

Also available

The Sword of Kuromori

Jason Rohan

THE SHIELD OF KUROMORI

A DIVISION OF EDC PUBLISHING

First American Edition 2016
Kane Miller, A Division of EDC Publishing

Original English language edition first published in 2015 under the title
The Shield of Kuromori by Egmont UK Limited, The Yellow Building,
1 Nicholas Road, London, W11 4AN

Text copyright © 2015 Jason Rohan
Cover illustration by Yin Yuming of Imaginary Friends Studios

For information contact:
Kane Miller, A Division of EDC Publishing
P.O. Box 470663
Tulsa, OK 74147-0663
www.kanemiller.com
www.edcpub.com
www.usbornebooksandmore.com

Library of Congress Control Number: 2015938823

Printed and bound in the United States of America
1 2 3 4 5 6 7 8 9 10

ISBN: 978-1-61067-356-3

For my father, who would have been proud.

1 —

"Hurry up!"

The covered truck rumbled along Honan Dori in low gear, heading east towards central Tokyo. Kenny Blackwood snatched at the outstretched hand and missed. He groaned and started running at full pelt after the vehicle.

Kiyomi leaned out over the tailgate and extended her arm farther. "Not this again!" she grumbled. "Move it!"

Kenny lowered his head, pumped his fists and threw himself forward to catch the departing truck.

"Oyama, *yukkuri shiro!*" a man's voice ordered from inside the canopy and the truck stopped immediately. Kenny, caught by surprise, thwacked into the rear bumper and bounced onto the asphalt.

"Ow. You could've warned me," he said, rubbing his bruised behind in the red glow of the brake lights.

"Are you hurt?" Kiyomi asked, jumping down and hauling him to his feet.

"Only my pride," Kenny said. "Where are we going?"

Kiyomi's father, Harashima, peered out of the truck.

1

"Kuromori-*san*, you're holding us up. Get in and then talk."

Kenny climbed into the back and nodded in greeting to the fourteen men who were waiting inside. Their faces were familiar from when they had all fought together to stop a crazed attack against America's West Coast barely two months ago. They were dressed in black, armed with automatic weapons and wore expressions of grim determination.

The truck picked up speed and Kenny found a space opposite Kiyomi. She leaned back, her eyes closed.

Watching her, Kenny felt his heart skip. She was still beautiful, but the deep shadows under her eyes and the creases on her forehead worried him. They had met only recently, but so much had happened in such a short time that it felt longer, like they had been friends for years. Only something had changed. Something was wrong. Kenny could sense it, deep in his core, though he couldn't pinpoint what it was.

He lightly bumped the toe of his shoe against Kiyomi's leather boot. Her almond eyes flicked open and she scowled at him.

"What now?"

"You're looking really tired," he said.

"Like, duh. Why do you think I'm trying to nap?"

"No, I mean – Is everything OK with you? You haven't been the same since . . ."

"Why does everyone keep going on about that?" Kiyomi snapped. "Yes, I'm tired. Yes, I'm hacked off.

Yes, I'm sick of everyone tiptoeing around me like I'm made of glass. Get over it, will you?"

Harashima stood up, gripping a nylon strap for support in the swaying truck. A flash of concern crossed his face as he took in Kiyomi's rant, but he set his jaw and addressed his men: "Not long ago, we fought together in Kashima to stop an atrocity. Akamatsu, fool that he was, sought to tip the balance through his control of the dragon Namazu."

Heads nodded and feet shuffled. The ripple of discomfort came as no surprise to Kenny. Many of the passengers in the truck had been injured that day, and some had buried friends.

"But, with the help of Kuromori-*san*, champion of Inari, we succeeded." Harashima nodded towards Kenny, who smiled sheepishly. "However, before we set off for Kashima, we were exploring the sewers beneath Tokyo, hunting for the dragon's lair."

"Yeah, that was your bright idea," Kiyomi muttered to Kenny. "Genius move."

"We know now that we were searching in the wrong place, but we did find something before we left," Harashima said. "Here." He handed out a thin dossier which each man flicked through and passed down the line.

When the folder came to Kenny, Kiyomi leaned over to observe. It took a moment for Kenny to register what he was seeing – and then he fought the urge to be sick.

3

"The first picture was taken back in July," Harashima said. "The others are more recent."

"Let me see that," Kiyomi said, taking the folder from Kenny's limp fingers.

"As far as we can tell, those are the remains of three men," Harashima continued. "Probably homeless, taking shelter in the outflow tunnels."

"But, sir," Kenny said, struggling with the words. "One of them . . . it looked like . . . he was bitten in half?"

"That's right."

"What could do that?"

Harashima softened, seeing the revulsion on Kenny's face. "There are many things, Kuromori-*san*, that live in darkness and feast on human flesh. You have met some of them already."

"And we're going . . .?"

"North to Kasukabe, to the Shutoken Gaigaku Hosuiro, the world's largest drainage system, also known as the G-Cans Project."

Kenny knew he was going to regret the answer, but he had to ask. "Why are we going there?"

"Because tonight the hunter becomes the hunted. A *yokai* has crossed the line and it is our sworn duty to stop it."

Kenny's gaze swept around the back of the truck. "No offense, sir, but do you have enough men for this?"

Harashima smiled. "Of course, Kuromori-*san*. We have you."

*

Ninety minutes later, Kenny's footsteps echoed in the narrow stairwell leading into the depths of the Earth.

The truck had pulled up at the entrance to the G-Cans Project and the chief engineer had greeted them. Harashima made the introductions and, while Kenny could only understand a few words of Japanese, he heard the name Sato mentioned. Kiyomi's uncle was with the Japanese Secret Service; if anyone could get a group of armed men into a government facility with no questions asked, it would be him.

"Oh, wow," Kenny said, looking out over the low concrete wall adjoining the stairs. "You've got to see this." He placed his hands on the damp stone and took in the view, while Kiyomi inched her way down. She was taking her time, moving with uncharacteristic reluctance. Kenny sympathized; after all, the last time they had ventured underground, it had cost Kiyomi her life. Anyone would think twice about clambering into the cold, wet darkness, not that Kiyomi would admit to any misgivings.

"Is that a cloud? Underground? Inside a room?" she said, standing alongside Kenny.

Stretching out before them was an enormous concrete-walled water tank, as long and as wide as Westminster Abbey and as tall as Buckingham Palace. Immense concrete supports thrust upward, like columns in a vast cathedral. Water lapped the pillars and vapor swirled in ghostly wreaths.

"Looks like it," Kenny said, continuing downward. "This place is big enough to have its own climate." He shivered in the damp. "Where are the others?"

"If your Japanese was better, you'd have heard Papa explain. There are five other water tanks, connected by over three miles of pipe, each thirty-six feet wide. We're putting two guys in each tank and the rest are checking the tunnels. We've all got motion trackers, locator beacons and radios. The plan is to find the thing, summon help and get out fast."

Kenny pondered this and his eyes grew wide. "Whoa. You mean we're on our own?" His voice echoed back, sounding no less worried.

"What? Are you scared? You're the one with the sword."

"Yeah, it's just . . . You've seen *The Lord of the Rings*, right? This place is just like the dwarven halls, when all the goblins come creeping down from the ceiling." Kenny squinted up into the darkness, scanning for any sign of movement.

"Thanks. Like this isn't creepy enough already?" Kiyomi shuddered. "I *hate* being underground." She dug out a flashlight and thumbed the switch, sending a powerful beam into the haze.

Kenny splashed down into the chilled, waist-deep water. "Ugh. Wrong day for sneakers," he groaned.

Powerful spotlights shone down from above, each trained on a giant pillar. The reflections off the pale, rounded stone made it seem like stalactites of light were piercing the low mists.

"This is all your fault," Kiyomi grumbled as they waded into the chamber.

"What have I done now?" Kenny said, his teeth clenched to keep them from chattering.

"If you hadn't sent Papa's men down here, looking for Namazu, then they wouldn't have found the . . . you know. Leftovers."

"How does that make it my fault?" Kenny protested. "It's not like I knew this was here." Annoyed, he changed the subject. "What's the point of this place, anyway? It's just a drain."

"What do you mean, 'just a drain'? Do you have any idea how important this facility is?"

Kenny switched on the handheld motion tracker, which resembled a GPS. "Uh, actually, no."

"You know what a typhoon is? A hurricane with wind speeds of at least seventy-five miles per hour and up to three feet of rain in a day. Tokyo used to flood regularly and thousands drowned, so this was built. The five giant cans take the extra water out of five rivers, like a massive storm drain. This tank we're in now is the final overflow. From here, the floodwater gets pumped into the Edo River. Without it, parts of Tokyo are underwater, so it does matter."

"Fine, OK, I get it," Kenny said, stooping to sniff the shimmering surface. "So this is basically just rainwater, right? No sewage or floating stuff to worry about?"

"No, not unless you get so scared – *YAAAAAHH!*"

Kenny jumped so hard, he nearly dropped the motion tracker. Kiyomi's flashlight picked out a furry lump disappearing back into the fog.

"What was that about?" Kenny gasped.

"A rat," Kiyomi said, shivering in disgust. "Ugh. A big one too."

"So why didn't it show up on this thing?" Kenny held up the tracker. "Is it broken?"

"No, it's calibrated for large objects only, otherwise every rat and roach would set it off."

"Big things? What, like this blue blob here?"

"Let me see that." Kiyomi snatched the tracker from Kenny's grasp. "Oh, crap. Kenny, we're out in the open. Get back – fast!"

"Why? What is it?"

From out of the mist, a shallow surge rippled forward. Behind it came the frantic squeaking of hundreds of rats.

"Oh, no." Kiyomi threw herself into the water and was gone.

Kenny spun on his heel, ducked down and felt tiny feet and claws scramble over his back, shoulders and head as the wave of screeching rodents broke over him. Still cradling the motion tracker, he opened one eye and squinted at it while the rats dispersed and swam away in all directions, leaving a large blue blob closing in on him from behind.

Kenny whirled around as the water exploded before him. With a thunderous roar, a huge white shape launched itself out of the mist, its cavernous jaws edged with long jutting teeth.

2 =

Time froze as Kenny's brain recognized what he was seeing, but simultaneously refused to accept it. The effect was paralyzing and the shadow of a giant albino crocodile slid over him as its jaws snapped at his chest.

Leaping from the water, Kiyomi flung herself at Kenny, barging him aside. The shock of cold water snapped Kenny back into the moment. He kicked out frantically and swept his arms in long strokes to put distance between himself and the monster reptile, stopping only when he reached the nearest pillar.

"Kiyomi!" he yelled into the void.

"Over here," she responded, shining her flashlight from behind another support.

"What do we do?" Kenny shivered in the cold, eyes searching the dark waters. "Where is it?"

"Probably circling for another att– *Look out!*"

Kenny reacted without thinking. Leaping backward, like an Olympic gymnast, he launched himself twenty feet into the air. The giant reptile thrashed beneath, pushing out a great bow wave, and vanished again.

With an ungainly splash, Kenny sprawled in the water. His mind's eye had captured a snapshot of the monster, white as bone, with dead eyes and rows of tiny ivory pyramids along its back.

"A plan would be good right about now," Kenny said, summoning forth Kusanagi, the sacred sword. The blade felt good in his hands.

"OK. You keep it busy. I'll do the rest." Kiyomi flicked off the flashlight, vanishing into the gloom.

"What kind of plan is that?" Kenny yelled. "Why don't *you* keep it busy while *I*...?" He waved the sword in front of him. "Kiyomi? Oh, great." He peered into the darkness, scanning for telltale bubbles or ripples. "Here, fishy fishy. Come to Kenny. I've got a surprise for you."

The hairs on the back of his neck prickled and Kenny spun around, pushing away from the massive column. The crocodile surged past, but a swipe of its powerful tail whacked Kenny off his feet. Instinctively, he let go of the sword as he fell into the water. The monster cruised around a pillar and churned towards him again. Kenny scrabbled for the sword in the black water. The crocodile's jaws gaped wide and it almost seemed to smile as it honed in.

"Kenny, now!" Kiyomi cried, leaping from a support to land on the creature's back, *tanto* in hand. She raised the short sword to strike a killing blow.

In the same instant, Kenny abandoned his search and channeled his inner spirit – his *ki* – into his right hand.

11

Ribbons of energy laced his knuckles. The crocodile was so close he could feel its rank breath.

"*Chikara*!" Kenny cried. He sidestepped the onrushing jaws and slammed his fist down, punching a crater clean through the crocodile's skull. It stopped as suddenly as a car hitting a wall and its body somersaulted, pitching Kiyomi across the chamber.

Kenny sighed, extracted his arm, shook off the greasy brain tissue and went in search of Kiyomi. He needn't have bothered.

"You idiot!" she screamed, rising from the water. "I had it! I was about to kill it and then you – you went and did that!"

"I dropped the sword. What else could I do?" Kenny said, holding his hands out in apology.

"And you're lucky I dropped mine, otherwise I'd gut you right now," Kiyomi snarled, shoving him aside as she headed for the stairs.

"Jeez, what's all that about?" Kenny muttered under his breath. "And since when can you see in the dark?"

"That was a trap!" Kiyomi railed, thumping her fist on the table for emphasis.

"What makes you so sure?" Harashima asked. "I'm confident that our information was good."

"Oh, come on, Papa, don't tell me you've fallen for that whole crocodile-in-the-sewer urban myth?"

They were back at the Harashima residence, in the

main room, two hours after leaving Kasukabe. Kenny was sitting in a bathrobe, sipping a hot chocolate, and trying to keep up with the exchange.

"One, crocodiles are cold-blooded. There's no way it could live for long in that water. Two, it would need a lot more food than it could find in the river." Kiyomi held up her hand while counting off the reasons. "Three, how would homeless guys find their way into the G-Cans Project to end up as dinner? And, four, what are the odds of *us* finding the ugly sucker when no one else could? It was definitely a setup."

Harashima turned to Kenny. "Kuromori-*san*, what do you think? Was this creature natural or *yokai*?"

Kenny pursed his lips. "It seemed normal enough, although Kiyomi's right, this whole thing stinks."

"Very well." Harashima nodded. "I will have the body recovered and we will look closer." He clapped a hand on Kenny's shoulder. "You did well, Kuromori-*san*, very well indeed."

"Hey, what about me?" Kiyomi snapped. "I saved Kenny's butt – again – *and* I was ready to finish off the croc until Mr. Show-off here decided to get cuddly with it."

"Cuddly?" Kenny retorted. "What, are you jealous because I'm better at this magic stuff than you are?"

"Hah! Me, jealous of you? In your dreams!"

"Enough!" Harashima barked. "Kiyomi-*chan*, go to your room. Now."

Kiyomi glared before storming out. Harashima closed

his eyes, took a deep breath and held it. After ten seconds, he exhaled slowly.

"I put you two together today for a reason," he said to Kenny. "How would you describe Kiyomi-*chan*'s . . . emotional state tonight?"

"Uh, well . . ." Kenny ran his fingers through his damp hair to buy time. He didn't want to get Kiyomi into any further trouble with her father, but at the same time, she had been acting really weird.

"As I thought," Harashima said. "She has anger-management issues, as they call it these days."

"You can say that again," Kenny agreed. "She's always been a bit fiery, but lately it's been off the chart."

"Something is wrong, Kuromori-*san*," Harashima said, his brow furrowing. "You know that my family is sworn to hold the balance, to keep the forces of chaos from dragging Japan backward, to keep the *yokai* in check."

"Yes, sir," Kenny said.

"I do not know how I can do that if my own family is tearing itself apart. Kuromori-*san*, I want you to make me a promise."

Kenny had a sneaking suspicion he wasn't going to like what came next, but nor could he refuse. "OK."

"If anything was to happen to me and I could no longer lead this organization, I would want you to take over as commander to my men."

Kenny blinked. "I-I can't do that, sir. I'm just a kid. I'm a *gaijin*. They'd never accept me. Surely your brother is a better bet. Besides, nothing's going to happen to you."

Harashima gave a low bow. "Kuromori-*san*, sooner or later, everyone's time comes to an end. My hope was that Kiyomi-*chan* would take my place, but as she is now . . ."

A quiet tap on the door signaled that Kenny's ride home was waiting.

By the time Kenny got back to the two-bedroom apartment in Shibuya he shared with his father, it was midnight. He slipped the key into the lock and opened the door gently.

"Kenny? That you?" his father called from the main room – a combined living and dining area with a kitchenette.

"Yeah, Dad." Kenny kicked off his soggy shoes and went inside.

Charles Blackwood stood up from his computer desk in the corner, stretched and came over to give his son a hug.

"Whew, you're damp," Charles noted. He sniffed Kenny's hair. "And you smell like a swamp. You should have a bath before bed."

"OK, OK." Kenny yawned. "And I've got school tomorrow."

"Is your homework done?"

"Not yet. I'll do it on the train in the morning."

"That's hardly ideal. You want anything to eat? Hot drink?"

"No, I had something over at Kiyomi's."

Charles folded his arms. "So? How was work?"

"You know I can't talk about that, Dad. For your own safety."

"Well, what can you talk about?" Charles appraised his son's disheveled appearance. "Kenny, don't take this the wrong way, but you look awful."

Kenny laughed. "Wow, good thing you cushioned that one."

"I mean it. I'm not dismissing the importance of what you do, but . . . you're making it very hard for me to be a father to you, which is kind of the whole point of you being here. I hardly see you. If you're not at the Harashimas, you're in school. When do we get some time together?"

Kenny slumped in the doorway. "Yeah, I know. Tell you what, Dad, I've got soccer tryouts tomorrow after school. Come see me try out for the team and then we can go for food afterward."

"You're on. I'd like to see you play."

"Thanks, Dad. Oh, and one other thing."

"Yes?"

"Is it just me or are all girls nuts?"

Charles chuckled. "What's Kiyomi done this time?"

"Nothing, it's just . . . I'm worried about her, Dad. There's something wrong. I can feel it."

Charles frowned. "What do you mean?"

Kenny's voice was small, as if he was afraid to say the words. "It's like with Mum. I think she's ill. Really ill, as in . . . maybe dying."

3 ☰

Kenny carried his tray to an unoccupied table in the school lunchroom and sat down. He'd been the new kid at school enough times to know how it worked. Everyone was nice enough, but they still waited to size you up. Who were you going to be: the clown; the nerd; the smart aleck; the sporty one; the cool kid; the punching bag; the teacher's pet? Every class had its own cliques and factions. Kids in those didn't need anyone new; their groups were self-contained. That left the outsiders, those who had to fend for themselves. They would gravitate towards any new student, hoping to find an ally.

The problem was that Kenny had learned to be on his own. He had stopped trying to make friends long ago because what was the point? You always had to move on. Better not to have any at all and avoid awkward good-byes. Except this time was different. Now he was enrolled at the American School in Japan and it was meant to be for a few years. That was going to take some getting used to, but he had been told – by a goddess no less – that he had to reach out to others or he would be emotionally stunted and never fulfill his potential.

"You want to hear a joke?" A girl's voice interrupted his thoughts. "What did one horse say to the other horse?"

Kenny looked up to see blonde highlights, a tan complexion and a dazzling smile. "Huh?"

"Why the long face?" A giggle like bubbles popping on a sunny day. "Stacey Turner," she said, balancing her tray on one hand and extending the other.

Kenny half stood and shook her hand.

"Are these seats taken?" Stacey asked, eyeing the empty chairs.

"No, no. Please, be my guest."

"That's so sweet." Stacey set her tray across from Kenny's and parked her jeans. "You're the new guy, aren't you? And from your accent I'd say you're Australian, right?"

"No. I'm from England actually."

Stacey's eyes grew even wider. "That is so cool. I just love English accents. Quick, say, 'Would you like a cup of tea?'"

Kenny sat back. "I really don't think that's –"

"Oh, you're blushing! That is so sweet." Stacey wriggled around in her seat and waved to another table. Chairs scraped and three other girls hurried over, squeezing in around a bewildered Kenny.

"This is Julianne, that's Nikki and here's Sarah," Stacey said, making the introductions. "Girls, this is the new guy. He's . . ."

"Uh, Kenny," he said. "Kenny Blackwood." He felt awkward, thinking how much easier it had been facing the giant crocodile.

"He's so cute!" Julianne said.

"Look, he's blushing!" Nikki observed.

"From England, you say?" Sarah added.

"I have a confession to make," Stacey said to Kenny, shushing her friends. "Nikki bet me a thousand yen I wouldn't come over and talk to you, but I'm going to let her off."

"Why's that?" Kenny ventured.

"Because you're so cute, that's why!" The girls rocked with laughter in their chairs while Kenny's cheeks burned. "Aww, you were looking so miserable all by yourself, so I came to cheer you up," Stacey said. "It's what we do. We're the cheer squad."

"You're cheerleaders?" Kenny finally realized.

"Yep." Stacey put a warm hand over his. "Say, do you play soccer?"

"A little."

"You should try out for the team tonight. We'll be there too."

"Well, uh, I was planning to –"

"That's so great! We'll see you later."

"And we'll be checking out your legs!" Julianne added with a wink.

Kenny picked up his tray, no longer hungry.

*

Once afternoon classes had finished, Kenny hurried to the locker room. He pulled on his soccer gear and jogged out onto the grass for a warm-up, remembering to stretch first. He glanced up, scanning the faces of the few parents who had come to watch, more in hope than expectation.

Coach Heagney checked off the list of names and put the ten prospective players through a series of drills, having them dribble around cones, through arches, playing quick one-twos and keep away, while the team trained nearby.

"I want to see you do as many kick ups as you can in two minutes and then I'm going to give you all a practice match. There are two places up for grabs, so you'll need to impress me, if you want to make the team," Heagney said, chewing a wad of gum.

"Hey, Kenny! Kenny!" Stacey's voice rang out from the sideline. Kenny groaned and tried to ignore the four cheerleaders shaking their pom-poms and working on synchronized dance moves.

"Wow, nice legs!" Julianne added, laughing.

Kenny concentrated on keeping the ball in the air. He got as far as twenty-eight before a voice brayed, "Sorry I'm late, Coach. I had detention."

Heagney scowled. "Again? Don't make a habit of it, Brandon. I don't want you missing any matches for me."

"Whatever." Brandon snapped a mock salute and dropped to do fifty push-ups in front of the cheerleaders.

Coach Heagney gathered the hopefuls together and

handed out training bibs. He stopped in front of Kenny. "What's your name, son?"

"Kenny, sir."

"I've been watching you. You're looking pretty sharp. You played before?"

"Yes, sir. Center midfield."

Heagney nodded to himself. "OK, boys. I've got the team here." He waved towards ten players in school jerseys, lining up on the side. "You'll be playing five-a-side in two games. That way, I get to see you play against every member of the team. Any questions? OK, grab a drink and we'll start."

Kenny was taking a glug from a water bottle when he felt a tug at his shoulder. A tall, skinny kid from the team was beside him.

"I'm Dionte," he said. "You're the new kid, Kevin, right?"

"Close. It's Kenny."

"Kenny." Dionte repeated, making a mental note. "You've got some nice moves. You any good?"

"I'm OK," Kenny said.

"Well, don't be too good, if you know what I'm saying." Dionte lowered his voice. "You see that big guy over there? That's Brandon, the coach's son. He's the star player on the team and he likes it that way. Watch out for him; he's got a mean streak."

"Let's go, ladies," Heagney called, signaling for the start.

The first match was a tough 5–5 tie, with Kenny scoring twice and setting up two goals for his team of newcomers. He came off to a round of whoops from the cheer squad.

For the second game, Kenny found himself facing Brandon at the kickoff. "Think you're something special, huh?" Brandon muttered, towering over Kenny. "We'll see about that."

The match kicked off with Brandon passing the ball forward to Dionte on the left wing, before surging past Kenny and administering a hard shove as he raced by. Kenny hit the grass hard, but rolled as Kiyomi had taught him, springing back to his feet. It was too late. Dionte crossed for Brandon who steamrollered two defenders to nod the ball home, past the flailing goalkeeper.

The team immediately scored again from the restart. Brandon clattered into a player attempting to dribble past, collected the ball and fired a long pass into the box, for a teammate to smash goalward.

"We're getting murdered here," one of Kenny's players grumbled. "The ref isn't giving us anything."

"I've got an idea," Kenny said. "You two, make a run down the wings, draw the defenders to you. You and you, drop back in case of a counter. Leave me space in the middle."

"You sure about this?" someone asked.

"What do we have to lose? We're two down already."

Coach Heagney signaled for the kickoff. "You guys ready?" He put his whistle to his lips.

Kenny closed his eyes and remembered his training: all

matter was composed of energy and that energy could be harnessed and shaped by will. He'd been encouraged to practice, so why not now?

PHEEEEEP! Dionte touched the ball forward and Brandon charged towards it like a thundering rhinoceros. Kenny reached the ball first, flicked it up with his left toe and then hammered it on the volley straight upward with his right, while falling backward. The game stopped as everyone stared at the ball rocketing higher and higher into the peach-hued sky.

Coach Heagney squinted upward, his chewing gum falling from his open mouth, as the ball vanished from view. He shook his head, then spluttered, "What was that? Did you just lose the ball?"

Kenny sauntered over to stand by the goalpost.

"You! Blackwood! Didn't you hear . . .?" The coach's voice trailed off as the ball reappeared and dropped out of the sky. It didn't have time to bounce as Kenny tapped it into the goal with the side of his foot.

"You have got to be kidding me," Heagney muttered.

"That's not fair!" Brandon screamed. "The ball was out of play. The goalkeeper wasn't even in the goal."

"Two–one," Heagney called, holding up his fingers to show the score. "Final play. Next goal wins."

"You are dead meat," Brandon snarled into Kenny's face.

BZZZT! Kenny's wrist tingled. With a scowl, he checked the screen on his smartwatch. It had buzzed to indicate the arrival of a message from Kiyomi.

The text was typically blunt: MEET ME OUT FRONT – NOW. WE'VE GOT TROUBLE.

Kenny grimaced. This was not good. "Coach? How much time do we have left?"

Heagney peered at his battered stopwatch. "About three minutes."

"Great," Kenny muttered to himself. He'd have to make this fast.

The whistle blew. After a quick exchange of short passes, Kenny received the ball and bore down hard on goal. He skipped past two challenges and was about to shoot when a large shadow from the corner of his eye signaled Brandon was flying in. Kenny sensed a two-footed, studs-up lunge, coming for his shins. Without breaking stride, he flicked the ball upward, back-heeled it over his head and dived past Brandon's incoming legs.

Kenny's palms hit the turf; he hunched his shoulders, tucked his head in and dropped his elbows to complete a forward roll. Then he sprang forward at full stretch to connect with the ball, heading it past the astonished keeper. Behind him, he heard a lumbering Brandon hit the ground.

"AAAAH! My ankle!" Brandon rolled around, clutching his foot.

"Can I go now, sir?" Kenny asked.

"Wha –? How the –? Yes, you can go, Blackwood." Heagney snatched up his first aid bag and raced over to where Brandon lay, wailing.

Kenny sped away from the soccer field.

"Kenny! That was amaz– Hey! Where are you going?" Stacey yelled, as he sprinted past.

"I'm a superhero. I'm off to save the world," Kenny called over his shoulder.

"Kenny Blackwood, you get back here!" Stacey threw down her pom-poms.

Kiyomi was waiting on her super-advanced motorcycle, tapping one foot on the ground and revving the engine softly. She was wearing her black biker leathers and the mirrored visor of her helmet was up, reflecting a vapor trail in the golden sky.

Kenny's heart fluttered, as it often did when he saw her. He slowed and ran a hand through his hair to tame it.

Kiyomi glared at him. "What took you so lo–?" Her eyes widened and she struggled to stifle the smile stealing over her lips. "Why are you wearing . . .? No!"

"Yep." Kenny spread his arms in surrender. "I reckon I made the team. The coach said we had to impress him and I was so good I impressed myself."

Kiyomi arched an eyebrow. "Still as modest as ever, I see." She thumped the seat behind her. "We've got to go. *Oni* on the move."

"In broad daylight? How many?"

"At least two. Papa suspects there's something bigger going on, so we're to observe and report."

Kenny climbed onto the back of the bike. "Only

watching? Are you able to do that?"

"Don't push your luck. I'm still mad at you for last night. And for making me wait." Kiyomi flipped her visor down.

"You're always mad at me," Kenny muttered, and the motorcycle slipped silently away.

4 四

Kiyomi swung a left out of the school gates, then made another, cutting down a leafy backstreet, bordered on one side by utility poles linked with black cables. Kenny clung on, the manicured shrubbery and wide green spaces of Nogawa Park zipping by on his left.

Kiyomi pulled the bike over at a gas station.

"Why have we stopped?" Kenny asked.

Kiyomi tapped the touch screen display on the dashboard. "They should be here any minute. I got Poyo to plant a bug on the vehicle. They're heading east."

"Since when do *oni* hitch lifts? And in what?"

A large cream-and-turquoise delivery van rumbled past. The logo on its side was a black cat carrying a kitten in its mouth.

"In that," Kiyomi said, throttling hard and leaving smears of rubber on the forecourt.

The van hugged the grassy central reservation and signaled a right at the next crossroad. Long shadows stretched in front as the sun began to dip below the horizon. Kenny squinted at the road sign ahead with its

English lettering below Japanese symbols.

"Ajinomoto Stadium? Are they going to watch a game?"

Kiyomi shrugged. "The airport's that way too. Who knows?"

After about half a mile, the delivery truck left the road, turning right onto a strip of red asphalt. Kiyomi pulled over to the curb.

Reading the road sign overhead, Kenny said, "Kokuritsu Tenmondai? What is that?"

"It's the National Astronomical Observatory," Kiyomi replied. "As in telescopes and stargazing."

The delivery van squeezed between two stone pillars, each with a globe light on top, and paused by a security cabin on the right.

"Now what?" Kenny said. "Do we follow them in there?"

"Too obvious. We're meant to be watching only."

The van driver handed a parcel to the guard and drove into the compound.

"I can ditch the bike and sneak in," Kiyomi said, eyeing the thick tree cover and low perimeter railings.

"What about me?" Kenny said.

"No chance. You're wearing soccer gear. Talk about conspicuous."

Kenny scowled. "Thanks for nothing. Why did you bring me along then? How about I just –?"

His remaining words were ripped away by a blast of scorched air as an explosion tore through the security hut. A ball of fire billowed upward while chunks of debris rained down.

"No way!" Kenny cried out. "Move!" He pointed to the gates.

"We're only supposed to observe!" Kiyomi shouted back.

"People are getting killed. Let's go!"

Kiyomi revved the engine. "Remember, this is your idea. Hang on tight!"

The motorcycle blazed through the mangled iron gates. The entrance to the main building was partly screened by a roundabout, which was planted with a stand of palm trees encircled by tall sculpted bushes. Kiyomi wrenched the handlebars to the left, skidding to avoid the obstacle.

"There they go!" Kenny said, pointing at the van, which was disappearing behind a plum-colored building on the right.

"Where are they going?" Kiyomi wondered aloud, cranking the throttle. "This doesn't make any sense."

She hurtled past a small parking lot and rounded the same three-story building. Ahead, at the end of a short avenue, was a white circular structure with a metal-paneled dome roof.

The delivery truck screeched to a stop beside the staircase leading into the observatory and the rear doors were flung open by a pair of huge hulking figures.

"Two *oni*," Kiyomi growled, eyes narrowing. "Let's –"

A blinding flash of light cut her short. Kenny barely

had time to flinch before a searing wall of hot air slammed them both off the bike, as a section of the nearest building erupted with a deafening roar.

The evening sky wheeled crazily overhead and tree branches clutched at Kenny's clothing as the blast flung him high into the air. He crashed down onto a small shrub and slowly rolled to his feet, his ears ringing. Printed pages fluttered around, many edged with orange flames.

"Kenny!" Kiyomi was already up and heaving her motorbike to a standing position. She pointed at the fractured building. "People are trapped in there. You go help them. I'll deal with the *oni*." She swung a leg over the bike.

Kenny opened his mouth to protest, but Kiyomi cut him off.

"Don't argue. You're better at that stuff. I can handle two *oni*." She sped away towards the domed building, zigzagging her way around the chunks of rubble strewn across the road.

"*Tasukete! Tasukete kure!*" a woman was shrieking, her voice barely audible above the jangle of fire alarms.

The cry came from above and Kenny made out two fists pounding against a cracked windowpane on the top floor, leaving red smears on the glass. An orange glow flickered from behind her while plumes of oily black smoke belched from fissures in the creaking, sagging roof.

Kenny took a deep breath, backed up a few paces and then sprinted towards the burning building. As soon as he hit the curb, he bent his knees and leapt into the air, his brow furrowed in concentration. A sudden, powerful gust of wind thrust him upward and he landed on the windowsill, some twenty-five feet above the ground.

"Get back!" Kenny warned the woman, summoning Kusanagi, the Sword of Heaven. The blade shimmered into his hand and Kenny swept it around the frame, slicing through the glass as easily as if it was plastic wrap. The panes collapsed inward and Kenny dived into the building, having dismissed the sword. The Japanese woman stared at him in disbelief.

"Come on!" Kenny shouted above the alarms and the crackle of fire. "We've got to get out of here before the roof caves in."

"Go? Where?" the woman said, her eyes darting around.

Kenny ran to the door and recoiled as the intense heat from the burning corridor forced him back. The building groaned, like a huge wounded beast, and Kenny felt the floor shift beneath him.

"The window! Now!" he yelled, throwing his arm around the woman to propel her forward, but it was too late.

With an angry bellow, a section of floor yawned open, collapsing under Kenny's feet. He tumbled downward, into the smoking ruins of the floor below, followed by half of the roof.

*

31

Kiyomi crept along the dark passageway leading into the observatory. Guttural voices echoed within the musty dome ahead, at first indistinct, then gradually becoming clearer.

"*Urg-ra n'guh-n-hak ra-rar ng gah* – with this stupid thing?"

"How would I know?" the other *oni* replied. "I've learned not to ask too many questions. Give me that pole. Not that one; the one behind you. It's numbered."

Kiyomi heard the hollow clang of metal against metal.

"Is this even going to work?" the first *oni* said. "How heavy is that thing anyway?"

"Seventeen tons, more or less."

"And the frame is going to take that?"

"It only needs to hold till we cut the mounting."

"Where are the others? They're late. What's keeping –? Wait . . ." The *oni* let out two loud snorts.

"What is it?"

"I thought I smelled a human in here."

Kiyomi froze, pressing herself against the wall.

The *oni* sniffed again. "Huh. It's gone now."

"You're just smelling your own backside. Where's the cable?"

Amid the clank of metal and the grunting of *oni*, Kiyomi crept closer to the end of the passage, which led from the front stairs. The ogres had entered through a ground-level access and were in the equatorial room, the huge circular chamber which lay beneath the sixty-five-foot-high dome.

The room itself was dominated by an enormous cream-colored, double-barreled telescope, forty feet long and almost three feet wide. It sat at a 45-degree angle on a complex mounting system of wheels, gears, pulleys and levers, all poised on a single massive, white-painted column of solid steel.

Wooden beams radiated from the center of the ceiling like the ribs of a giant umbrella, arching high overhead to form a vaulted roof, connected by thousands of interlocking planks.

"Careful, careful . . . Got it!"

Kiyomi craned her neck to observe the two *oni* working on the floor below. One was brick red with a single horn growing from his forehead; the other was sky blue with a chipped tusk. Red was supporting a steel tube A-frame, while Blue positioned the legs against the concrete outer wall. Scaffolding poles and heavy steel cables spilled out of canvas bags by their feet. Both *oni* wore silvery overalls.

"Hurry it up. Five minutes left to complete the hoist," said Red, propping the scaffold against another A-frame to form two sides of a pyramid, its apex above the telescope mounting.

"They'd better be here soon with the cutting gear," Blue grumbled, bolting the sections together.

Double doors crashed open behind Kiyomi, making

her jump. She whirled around and saw two burly shadows filling the doorway: more *oni*.

"The party don't start till I walk in," boomed the one in front. "You can hit the music now."

Kiyomi muttered under her breath; two *oni* were a challenge, but four were deadly – and she was caught in the middle.

The two newcomers stomped down the passage towards her.

"Can't . . . hold . . . this . . . much . . . longer," Kenny said through gritted teeth.

The woman coughed and waved a hand to clear the dust-filled air. Her streaming eyes widened at the sight of a hunched teenage boy in soccer gear, knees bent and arms outstretched, holding a structural support beam over her head.

"*Muri, da*," she mouthed.

"I've . . . got leverage . . . but this . . . still . . . weighs . . . a ton," Kenny said.

The woman pulled herself up onto all fours and assessed the damage. The top two floors had partly collapsed, dumping tons of rubble inward, but the outer wall remained intact. A faintly glowing square marked a window. She began to crawl towards it.

As soon as she was clear, Kenny twisted, dropping the steel joist and the section of concrete floor attached to it, letting it slam into the floor with an earsplitting crash. He placed his hands on the small of his back and straightened up, his silver complexion giving way to normal pink as his body reverted from the near-invulnerable metallic state he had adopted.

"No good," the woman said, banging her fist on a twisted beam in frustration.

Kenny picked his way through the wreckage to join her. They were almost at the window but a fallen girder barred their path.

"Stand back," Kenny said, summoning his sword. It materialized into his hand and, with one slice, the beam fell away in two pieces. "Let's go."

He dismissed the blade once more and helped the woman out through the shattered window frame onto the grassy strip outside, where they gulped in deep lungfuls of fresh, sweet air.

"Who *are* you?" the woman said. "How can you . . .? And where is sword?"

Kenny ran a hand through his filthy hair and shrugged. "It's a long story."

The shriek of sirens announced the arrival of ambulances from the neighboring Hasegawa Hospital, and groups of white-coated laboratory staff ran from the main building, first aid kits in hand, to assist bloodied survivors. The woman was swallowed up by a mob of her colleagues, all talking at once.

Kenny slumped on the grass and allowed himself a satisfied smile, but it wasn't to last.

An explosion ripped through the remains of the top floor, showering onlookers with broken glass. Kenny jumped to his feet and squinted up at the ruined building. A third of it had fallen in and smoke billowed from the top-floor windows. The twisted remains of a metal fire escape dangled from a wall. And then he heard the screams of people trapped inside.

The building groaned again and swayed slightly, threatening to collapse at any moment.

With no time to waste, Kenny started running.

5 五

Kiyomi was trapped; two *oni* were bearing down on her, while two in front were working in the equatorial room.

Fortunately Kiyomi had instinct and training to fall back on. Her gut said to hide, but the passageway was short with no recesses; her schooling said to take the initiative, to change defense into attack. Her training prevailed.

"*Kiiii-aiii*!" she screamed, bursting from cover. The red *oni* froze as Kiyomi flung herself forward, planted her palms on the floor and pushed off from the handspring. She tucked her knees in hard, somersaulted over the *oni*'s head and landed with feline grace on the horizontal mounting of the telescope.

The blue *oni* reacted immediately. With a roar, he leveled the steel pole in his hand, then swung it straight at Kiyomi to squish her like a bug.

"NO!" barked one of the newcomers. Something flashed in his hand, thunder echoed through the dome and Blue's head exploded like a water balloon. Kiyomi froze, one hand tucked into the gap between the two tubes.

The blue *oni*'s twitching body crumbled to dust and the huge gun barrel swung in her direction. The hand holding it glinted in the dim light.

"I thought I made myself perfectly clear," the newcomer said to Red, whose complexion was draining to a weak pink. "There is to be no damage to the telescope. Speaking of which . . ." CLICK-CLICK. His thumb ratcheted back the hammer on the heavy pistol and he took aim at Kiyomi's chest. "Move. Now."

Kiyomi didn't wait for a second request. She sprang up, arms outstretched, caught hold of the partly assembled metal frame above her head and vaulted onto the circular walkway, which doubled as a viewing gallery where the wall ended and the dome began.

"Stay up there, out of my way, and I won't kill you," warned the *oni* with the gun. "Agreed?"

"Agreed," Kiyomi said. She wasn't sure, given the distance, but the new *oni* seemed to be wearing a silver mask.

The *oni* in the passageway behind him, a lavender-hued brute with one arm longer than the other, set down the oil drum he was carrying and picked up the fallen scaffolding pole. Handing it to Red, he said, "What are you waiting for? *Shogatsu*? Hurry it up."

Crouched down on the walkway and watching the *oni* below, Kiyomi reached for her phone. She had two thoughts: *What are those* oni *doing?* and *Where's Kenny when I need him?*

*

Orange flickers illuminated the top floor of the gutted building. The metal stairs and platforms of the fire escape hung like modern art sculptures on the wall. Kenny listened intently, trying to filter out the incessant shrill of the fire alarms and approaching sirens.

THUMP-THUMP-THUMP! It was unmistakable: someone was pounding on the fire escape door, trying to break it loose from its warped frame. Kenny scoured his surroundings. People were trapped on what remained of the top floor and, with time running out, he had to help them down – but how?

KRAKK! Kenny looked up. The sound had come from one of the many tall trees around him. This one was sagging inward, close to a blazing window. Its leaves had shriveled in the heat and a heavy branch had split as the moisture inside had turned to steam and expanded. Staring up at the tree, Kenny had an idea.

He stood directly beneath the fire escape door – high above on the third floor – and marched away from the building, counting the distance in paces. Satisfied, he stopped and selected a large pine tree, about seventy feet tall and half a foot wide.

"Here goes," he said to himself and, hefting the sword, he cut a deep notch into the trunk with two diagonal swipes, one down and one up. A wedge of trunk fell out. Kenny waited. Nothing happened. He cut again, making the cleft deeper. Still nothing.

"Oh, for goodness' sake!" He stepped back from the

tree, took a running jump and drop-kicked the trunk as high as he could. The pine shuddered and, with a series of cracks as loud as gunshots, it began to topple.

"Yes, yes!" Kenny cheered, watching it swing towards the building. Then "No, no!" as it begin to twist away.

Fists clenched and eyes screwed shut, Kenny concentrated his will. Two blasts of wind caught the upper branches on each side, holding the treetop for a moment. It rolled and then began to fall again. The tip smashed in the fire escape door and the long straight trunk settled at a 45-degree angle.

Kenny punched the air and began clambering up the trunk. He wove his way around the first few branches, then called Kusanagi and lopped away the thicker foliage. The trunk tapered at the top, where it rested on the sill. "Hello in there!" Kenny called through the battered door. "You've got to leave now."

A bespectacled Japanese man gaped at him from the doorway, eyes as wide and bulgy as a goldfish. "*Shinji rarenai*," he said.

"Come on!" Kenny extended his arm. "Let's go."

The man shook his head and backed away. A younger man, wearing a fire marshal's reflective vest, pushed past him. "The tree," he said. "It's not safe."

"Of course it is. Look." Kenny jumped on the trunk. It creaked and shook. His foot slipped and he landed with a thump on his rear, dislodging a bird's nest which shattered on the ground, far below. "OK, tell you what. I'll make it easier." Kenny took Kusanagi and, with a quick cut down and across, he fashioned a shallow step.

He moved back and cut a second. "Stairs," he said. "Will that do?"

The fire marshal nodded once and stuck a cautious leg out. He reached back, held the hand of a secretary and guided her out. Kenny continued working his way down the trunk, cutting out steps for the office staff to follow. There were eight workers in all, holding hands in a human chain, all helping each other. The tree shuddered as a burst of flame coughed from the open doorway above. A woman screamed and stumbled, her shoe tumbling to the ground.

"It's OK," Kenny called up. "You're doing great."

BZZZT! Kenny's wrist vibrated.

He carved out the last step and jumped down to check his smartwatch. TRAPPED IN DOME WITH 3 ONI AND MORE ON THE WAY. BE CAREFUL. Kenny blinked. Since when did Kiyomi ever warn him to be careful? It was usually the other way around. How bad was this?

He took a quick look to make sure that the office workers were safely clear of the blazing ruin and then made for the short road leading to the observatory. Rounding the trees, he saw another delivery van whiz past, followed by the earthshaking bulk of a container truck. Both ground to a halt outside the domed building.

Kenny's feet pounded the asphalt as he drew nearer.

The back doors of the van flew open and a gray *oni* jumped out. It was hunched over, carrying something. Kenny slowed down, trying to make out what it was. One hand supported the weight, the other gripped a handle. Was it a leaf blower? A hedge trimmer? A chain saw?

The *oni* strode away from the vehicles and leveled the object in Kenny's direction. His blood turned to ice as he made out six long tubes in a circular arrangement.

Kenny had played enough video games to recognize a M134 Gatling Minigun when he saw one – and this one was aimed right at him.

SQUEEEEEEEE-AAAAAWWW! The screech of the circular saw changed pitch as it bit into the metal of the telescope mount, bearing down harder and spraying an arc of golden sparks across the floor. The lavender *oni* leaned in, pressing down on the spinning disk.

"Easy does it. You don't want to snap the blade," warned the silver-masked team leader. He hummed a tune to himself while he inspected the gantry assembled around the telescope. Scaffolding poles crisscrossed in a steel web and heavy cables were draped around the huge instrument.

Kiyomi sat up at the sound of doors opening. Eleven pairs of heavy boots clomped into the room and took up positions around the perimeter. Eleven *oni* – four dressed as drivers, plus seven passengers – add the three in the room . . .

42

"We've got company," one of the drivers said to the lead *oni*.

"I know," the chief replied, pointing a claw up at the gallery. Kiyomi raised her middle finger in acknowledgement.

"No, outside. Some stupid-looking *gaijin* kid in shorts. He can see us."

The mask raised its eyebrows. "Kuromori? Hmm. Nothing changes. We stick to the plan. If he gives us any trouble, I'll take care of him."

"Here it goes!" said the *oni* with the saw.

"Quickly! Take up the slack," ordered the boss.

Moving as one, the *oni* all took up positions, some grabbing hold of the telescope, others bracing the frame and the remainder taking hold of the cables. The giant instrument pivoted on the last of its mounting before, with a final cut, it lurched free. Cries and groans filled the dome as the *oni* struggled to support the weight. Kiyomi watched the gantry buckle outward, but it didn't break.

"Steady . . . steady!" called the chief. "Lower it gently. Six and Eight, move into position."

Two *oni* ran forward to situate themselves at each end of the telescope and it was lowered onto their shoulders.

In well-drilled, practiced movements, the monsters arranged themselves around their prize, six on each side, like coffin bearers, and proceeded to shuffle towards the lower exit, led by the one with the saw.

Silver remained in the room. His glowing red eyes

picked out Kiyomi, hunched on the walkway, her arms around her knees.

"So you're the girl who likes to kill *oni*," he said.

Kiyomi glared back at him. "Put down the gun and let's find out."

Silver chuckled and reached into his uniform pocket, extracting a sausage-shaped metal tube.

"Now what?" Kiyomi pressed. "You're going to shoot me and run away like the coward you are?"

The *oni* flipped the cap off the tube and tapped a cigar into his hand. He bit the end off and stuck it between his fangs. "Hey, you kill *oni*, I kill humans. It's what we do." He snapped his fingers and a flame jumped up from his hand. He waved the cigar tip over the flame and sucked, inhaling deeply. "Oh, man. That's good. As I was saying, it's nothing personal, just business, right?" He leaned down and tore the cap off the large steel drum. "No? OK – for you, it's personal – but still, we're not that different. Am I right or am I right?"

He tapped out a beat on the lid of the drum before picking it up and, humming again, he poured gasoline onto the floor and splashed it up the walls. The gasoline fumes wavered and swirled high into the air, making Kiyomi's eyes sting from the sweet, sickly odor.

Silver set the drum down again and pressed the back of his palm against his forehead by way of a salute. "Well, it's been nice talking to you. Who knows? Maybe I'll see you in Hell one of these days."

And with that he turned on his heel and headed for the exit, tossing the cigar over his shoulder. It bounced once, rolled – and nuzzled a puddle of fuel.

Kiyomi barely had time to scream before – WHOOOOMPF! – a blue flame rolled across the floor, igniting the remainder of the gasoline. In seconds, the interior of the dome was ablaze. Fiery tongues leapt high into the air, licking at the vintage wooden ceiling.

6 六

Kenny hurled himself to the ground as the world exploded around him. Blistering chunks of high-velocity lead chewed up the asphalt, grass, bushes, trees – everything.

BRRRRRRRRRRRRRR! The Minigun roared, disgorging over twenty rounds per second through a fiery halo which hovered in front of the spinning barrels. Spent cartridges cascaded to the ground, clinking like a slot machine paying out a jackpot win. Chips of asphalt pelted Kenny's body and wooden splinters stabbed into his hands, which were shielding his head. *Move!* his brain screamed, but his legs weren't listening.

"Me see you!" the *oni* bellowed above the roar of gunfire, and adjusted his aim.

Kenny centered his *ki*, imagining a thick heavy wall and threw an arm up.

"Huh?!" he heard the *oni* cry, and he opened his eyes. A low bank of soil had risen up from the ground, shielding Kenny from the *oni*'s weapon. The beat of thudding bullets stopped. "Not fair!" the *oni* bellowed and Kenny heard the thumping of its boots approaching.

This time, his legs scrambled into action, propelling him headlong into the nearest stand of trees. Foliage detonated once again on all sides as the *oni* resumed firing.

"Where you hide, boy, if no trees left?" the *oni* said.

Kenny crouched behind a thick, sturdy Japanese cedar, three feet wide at the base. He was pinned down, with valuable seconds ticking away.

"Hey, stupid!" he yelled. "Reckon you can chop down *this* tree?" Kenny poked his head around for the *oni* to see.

"*Oni* not stupid!" the *oni* said.

Kenny dropped to his knees and ducked his head as a flurry of bullets ripped into the tree. The smell of burning wood stung his nostrils and splinters rained down.

"Hah!" the *oni* said. "Me tell you. No tree, no hide. You die now."

K-RAKKK!

Kenny peered upward, saw the huge tree start to lean over – and smiled.

"Hey, what so funn–?" The *oni*'s yellow eyes widened as the massive trunk crashed down, driving him into the ground like a hammer pounding a nail.

Kenny was trying to think of something smart to say when movement caught his eye. The three delivery vans were pulling out from the observatory, followed by the forty-foot container truck. The *oni* were leaving, but where was Kiyomi?

Edging forward for a better view, Kenny saw a wisp of black smoke rising from the observatory dome. With an icy ball of dread in the pit of his stomach, he began to run.

Kiyomi shrank from the sea of fire below; with the floor now a blazing inferno, there was no way down. The heat was as intense as a sauna and growing hotter by the second.

The flames jumped higher, licking at the wood beams of the roof, while a burst of confetti sparks danced in the air. Kiyomi buried her face in the crook of her arm and blinked furiously. It was only a matter of time before the wooden dome caught and, even if she could survive the fire, the roof would cave in and crush her.

Kiyomi sprang to her feet. Ignoring the steam rising off her leathers and wiping sweat from her eyes, she scanned the inside of the dome, searching for a telltale sign of movement within the pall of smoke. There! A faint stirring about a third of the way up. Kiyomi ran around the gantry until she was in line with the disturbance.

She reached into her boots and drew a short dagger from each one. Gripping them tightly, she stepped up onto the searing handrail, balancing on the narrow beam like a gymnast, with her back to the raging flames. She took a deep breath, focused her will and crouched down. She then launched herself upward, kicking off with her toes, arms stretched high over her head.

She soared aloft, into the smoke, keeping in line with one of the heavy, rib-like support beams that curved overhead. As soon as the joist was within reach, Kiyomi stabbed the blade tips into it, one on each side, skewering the wood. The tungsten-carbide points bit deeply and held. She dangled for a second, feeling the ligaments in her arms and shoulders stretch, while the beams above creaked and popped, expanding in the rising temperature.

Kiyomi blinked her stinging eyes and searched again for the tiny crack in the planks through which she had seen eddying smoke escape. There it was – where two panels overlapped: a split, barely half an inch wide. She let go of the blade in her right hand, so her whole weight was supported by her left.

Ignoring the rising ache in her lungs, she drew back her free hand and smashed the heel of her palm into the crack. The impact jarred through her arm. Sweat ran down her left wrist and she felt her grip loosening on the dagger. Kiyomi slammed her palm against the wood again.

Spots danced behind her eyes, but she refused to give in. If only she had a hand free to perform the correct *kata* and trace the power symbol in the air, to channel her *ki* . . . But then Kiyomi found herself wondering: *What would Kenny do?* The goddess Inari had chosen him as her champion because of his ability to think differently. If Kenny couldn't find an answer, he changed the question.

And then it came to her – though it was a long shot

and the timing would have to be perfect. Ribbons of flame danced along the support beams, like heralds announcing that the dome was now ablaze. She was out of time.

Kiyomi let go of the dagger in her left fist and whipped the same hand across, down, up again at a diagonal and then down again, writing a *kanji* character in the air as she fell.

"*Chikara*!" she yelled, exhaling in a single gasp. At the same time, her right fist streaked through the smoke and connected with the split in the wood. *KAH-RUUNCH!* Her strike tore through the plank as easily as if it was paper, punching out the external metal tile. The fire quickened, as if sensing the loss of its quarry, and flames reached towards her. Kiyomi thrust her other arm into the hole, pulled up and wriggled her shoulders through.

"Kiyomi!" Kenny stared, struck with numb horror at the flames spewing out of both entrances of the observatory. Even from where he stood, the heat was blistering, and the awful truth was that anyone inside would be incinerated. Kenny wiped a grimy knuckle across his stinging eyes and prepared to direct the anger and grief welling inside. He had created water once before. Now it was time for –

BZZZT!

Kenny blinked in bewilderment. He checked his smartwatch and read: GET OUT OF THE WAY.

"Huh?" He stumbled backward. The next thing he knew there was a scraping, sliding sound from above, a blur of movement and a black-leather-clad figure dropped to the ground directly in front of him, landing on all fours, with steam rising off its shoulders.

Kenny was speechless. Kiyomi wasn't.

"Where have you been?" she demanded. "I'm trapped in there with a whole army of *oni* turning me into barbecue and you're out here – sightseeing."

"What? You told me to go rescue people, and that's what I was doing, until this *oni* turned up with a Minigun and shot down half the trees."

Kiyomi took in Kenny's appearance – clothes smeared with dust and soot, splinters in his hair, knees grazed, small cuts across his face – and softened. "OK. He's clever, I'll give him that."

"Who?"

"The *oni* in charge."

"I thought you said before that all *oni* are stupid." Kenny glanced back at the fallen tree.

"This one's different. He created a diversion, blew up two buildings and then set us a trap."

A loud splintering sound came from the dome and a section of roof fell inward, sending a shower of sparks into the twilight sky.

"We should go," Kiyomi said. "Fire and ambulance are here already; it won't be long before the police start asking questions." She set off towards a large shrub.

"Let's start with why," Kenny said. "Why go to all this trouble? Why burn down half the observatory?"

Kiyomi reached into the bush and grabbed a pair of handlebars. "Best way to cover your tracks," she said. "Set a fire and destroy all evidence."

Kenny frowned. "Evidence? Of what?"

"Ken-*chan*, they just stole a seventeen-ton telescope."

Kiyomi wheeled her motorbike out of its hiding place and waited for this to sink in.

"They stole a honking great telescope?" Kenny repeated.

"Uh-huh." She pulled on her crash helmet.

"Why?"

"I don't know. Let's ask them." Kiyomi sat astride the bike and powered up the engine.

"How are we going to do that? They're long gone."

Kiyomi switched on the dashboard display screen. "Yeah, but they're stuck in rush hour traffic, heading south on Route 123."

Kenny smiled. "You planted a bug? Then why are you wasting time talking to me?" He jumped on the bike behind Kiyomi. "Let's get after them!"

Kiyomi flipped her visor down. "Hang on tight. This might get rough."

She spun the bike around, its rear tire spraying up a geyser of dirt, and cut through the trees behind the burned-out building, before streaking out of the front gate.

Two police cars were stationed outside the National Observatory to control access. One of them reversed slowly, to permit another fire engine to pass through, when a silent motorcycle blitzed past, hurtling out of the gates. It swerved right, narrowly avoiding a number 91 bus, and headed south on Route 123.

Cars crawled along the road, bumper-to-bumper. Kiyomi consulted the dashboard display once more and swung out into the center. Keeping both wheels on the orange line in the middle, she followed the curve of the road, eating up the distance.

"They haven't gone far," she called back to Kenny, who was hanging on for grim life. "They're at the next traffic lights, by the primary school."

"Won't they see us coming?"

As if on cue, a boxy delivery van pulled out into the opposite lane and parked at a right angle, blocking the road.

"That's not good," Kenny warned. "Better slow down."

Kiyomi sped up. "No way. I'm not stopping for those clowns."

"Are you nuts?"

"Hold on tight!"

Kenny saw the leer of triumph on the face of the *oni* in the driver's seat change to befuddlement as Kiyomi eased off the throttle for a split second, leaned forward, then hit the power and snapped her arms back.

The front of the bike lifted in a perfect wheelie and Kiyomi veered left, bringing the wheel down with a thump on the back of a yellow taxi. Before Kenny could object, she opened up the throttle again and the motorbike lurched over the stationary vehicle, nosed down over the hood and onto the trunk of a Toyota sedan in front. Kenny felt his stomach heave up into his chest and drop down again while he clung on to Kiyomi.

The *oni* watched the motorcycle ride up and down over the row of waiting cars, passing around the back of the van.

"NOOO! You come back – now!" he roared, shaking both fists.

With a final burst of speed, the motorbike leapt off the roof of a Honda wagon and touched down on the asphalt, streaking it with black rubber. Ignoring the shouts of angry drivers, Kiyomi continued down the center line, leaving the *oni* behind.

BEEP! Kenny whipped his head around at the sound of smashing metal and tinkling glass. Behind him and closing fast, the delivery van was tearing down the road on the wrong side. The few cars heading north swerved onto the wide sidewalk and screeched to a stop, out of its way.

The *oni* behind the steering wheel grinned and stomped the accelerator to the floor.

"Kiyomi!" Kenny shouted.

Kiyomi's eyes flicked to the handlebar mirrors. "I can't outrun him, or we'll miss our turn," she said. "You slow him down."

"Me?" Kenny said. "How?"

"In the pannier on your right. Grab the *tetsubishi* spikes and throw them on the road."

Kenny reached into the box. "Ow! I just stabbed my thumb. Forget it. I've got a better idea."

Kenny peered ahead, ignoring the van, which was now barely ten feet behind. The drill tower of a fire station flashed by on the right and a four-way intersection lay ahead.

"Get as close as you can to the curb," Kenny said, as Kusanagi materialized into his hand.

The van's front bumper was closing on the motorbike's rear wheel. "Me crush you like bag," the *oni* bellowed through the open window.

"It's 'bug,' you dope, as in 'crush you like a bug,'" Kenny said. "Oh, never mind." He lashed out with the sword, slicing through the bulk of a roadside utility pole. The concrete column wavered for a moment, before it fell, ripping loose thick black electrical cables, which whiplashed through the air.

The *oni* caught a glimpse of movement in its side mirror before the pole smashed onto the top of the cab, amid a shower of sparks. Lightning crackled around the van, which rolled to a stop.

"Nice shot," said Kiyomi.

"Not really," Kenny said. "I wanted it to drop in front of him, like a roadblock."

The bike hurtled over the slim ribbon of the Nogawa River, and Kiyomi turned right onto a side road which ran past scrubby farmland and small industrial units.

"I don't see them ahead," Kenny said. "Have we lost th– Look out!"

The second delivery van charged out of a builder's yard on the left and barreled straight at them. Kiyomi yanked the handlebars sharply to the right, skidding the bike through a gap in the safety rail which lined the road and onto the narrow sidewalk. Kenny held his breath as Kiyomi slalomed her way past trash cans, utility poles, vending machines and pedestrians, all obstructing the sidewalk.

The delivery van roared alongside the bike, separated only by the railing. "Hah! Me catch you!" barked the *oni* driving.

"Red light ahead," Kenny warned, his voice rising, as they approached a 3-way intersection.

"I'm not blind," Kiyomi said through gritted teeth. "*You* might want to close your eyes, though."

Traffic in front moved in both directions. The motorbike shot off the sidewalk, blasted through the pedestrian crossing, slipped between two cars and swung a wide left, hugging the center line once more. The rear tire skipped sideways with a *VIP-VIP-VIP* sound. Kenny looked back and groaned; the light had turned green at the last moment and the van was still in pursuit.

Kiyomi crossed the orange line and powered down the opposite lane. It was free of cars and Kenny saw workers ahead clearing the ditch which ran alongside the road. The van followed, zipping past the commuter cars on the left.

"He's gaining on us," Kenny said.

"That's because I'm letting him," Kiyomi said, whizzing past red plastic cones lining the curb.

And then Kenny saw why their lane was clear: a large bulldozer was trundling towards them, holding up traffic and blocking the lane.

Kiyomi opened the throttle and ripped towards it.

"No! You're not . . ." Kenny started.

"Yes, I am," Kiyomi replied. "Hold on tight."

Workmen scattered at the sight of the accelerating vehicles; two dived headfirst into the ditch, and one abandoned the wheelbarrow he was pushing up a plank on a large mound of earth, grabbing his hard hat instead with both hands and ducking.

Kiyomi took one last glance in her mirrors, to see that the *oni* was right behind, and adjusted her course by a fraction. The bike hit the plank, shot upward and soared high into the air.

Kenny wanted to scream but he was holding his breath too tightly. He saw the bulldozer pass beneath in a yellow blur and braced himself for the landing. The bike jolted down on the center line and Kenny flinched at the impact, shutting his eyes for a moment. It felt like a giant had just kicked him up the backside. The motorcycle skidded and wobbled before Kiyomi brought it back under control.

Behind them, the *oni* wasn't so lucky. The van smashed into the front scoop of the bulldozer, flipped upward and somersaulted over the line of cars – right towards Kenny and Kiyomi.

"Down!" Kiyomi slammed her arm across Kenny's chest, throwing him off the bike, and dived after him. The van crashed into the asphalt, missing them by inches, and clattered end over end.

Kenny grinned up at Kiyomi, who was lying on top of him. "You know, if you wanted a kiss, you could've just asked me," he said.

"Ugh," was the reply. Kiyomi sprang to her feet and yanked the motorbike upright. She shot Kenny a look. "Are you going to lie there all day?"

Kenny stood up, aching all over. "I thought you were tracking the van. Now that it's trashed, how are we going to find them?"

"I put the tracker on the telescope when I landed on it. That's what we're after. These guys are just slowing us down."

"Ohhh. So where is it?"

Kiyomi squinted at the touch screen display. "Oh, crap." Her shoulders sagged. "I should've seen this coming."

"Why? What is it?"

Kiyomi pointed across the road. "See those cars and low buildings over there?"

"Yeah."

"That's Chofu Airport. They're flying it out."

Thirty seconds later, the motorcycle shot up the curving access road, past the IBEX Aviation building. A twin-propeller Dornier 228 droned overhead, its landing gear extended. Kiyomi drifted through the parking lot, scanning the rows of Cessna and Piper Cub aircraft that stood on the apron of the runway.

"I'm not seeing them," she said. "Maybe they're in a hangar."

"With a forty-foot truck? What's the reading say?"

Kiyomi consulted the display again. "Weird. It says they're moving . . . and they're out here. But where?"

Kenny's eyes swept the airfield. "What's wrong with this picture?" he said. "Look."

Kiyomi followed his outstretched finger and saw a heavy, squat airplane with twin jet engines taxiing towards the runway. "What are you showing me?" she said.

"Duh! That's a military transport plane."

"So?"

"Clue number one: military plane at a civilian airport.

Clue number two: its cargo bay is big enough to fit a truck inside."

"The truck's already on the plane?" Kiyomi watched the jet trundle into its final takeoff position. The engines howled as power built up.

"That'd be my guess. So now what? Do we phone – Hey!"

The bike leapt forward, almost throwing Kenny off before he grabbed Kiyomi's shoulder to steady himself. She speed-shifted through the gears in seconds, launching the motorcycle down the access road which looped to the south of the runway.

Engines roaring, the Kawasaki C-1 transport began its takeoff. It shuddered forward, picking up speed.

"Please tell me you're not going to do what I think you're going to do!" Kenny yelled in Kiyomi's ear.

"Ken-*chan*, these freaks just hurt a lot of people. I'm not letting them get away with it." As if to underline the point, Kiyomi twisted the throttle harder, pushing the RPM display into the red.

The tail of the transport jet loomed into view and towered overhead, its triangular silhouette blotting out the evening stars as the aircraft continued to accelerate.

"Come on!" Kiyomi yelled at her motorbike, urging it ever closer to the undercarriage. The airplane continued to advance, steadily pulling away from the bike.

"We're not going to catch them! They're too fast!" Kenny screamed, straining to be heard over the thundering jet engines.

Kiyomi ignored him, reached into a side pouch on the bike and brought her feet up, setting the soles of her boots onto the seat. She crouched for a second, like a jockey on a racehorse, and then let go of the handlebars, straightening up.

Kenny dared not breathe as Kiyomi balanced on the seat, afraid that any movement from him would topple the bike. Her right hand shot out, a flash of metal glinted in the plane's lights and the *kaginawa* grappling hook soared over the airplane wing in front.

The wheels of the C-1 jet left the runway and rose into the air. Kenny saw the cord snap taut in Kiyomi's hands and she jumped. Instinctively, Kenny dived for the weighted end of the remaining line and grabbed it, looping it around his wrists. The motorcycle slipped away from beneath him and he half expected to be smeared into paste on the tarmac.

Instead, he was hauled upward and pounded by the air rushing over the wing. The nylon cord cut into his wrists and hands and the roaring wind of the slipstream buffeted and pummeled him, making it hard to see or breathe. Below, the illuminated runway dropped away at a sickening speed and Kenny knew he couldn't hold on for much longer. Unless . . .

He closed his eyes, forced the panic from his mind and centered his *ki* once more. Since he was being battered by the wind in front, what he needed was a counterforce, to even it out . . .

A powerful gust of air from behind propelled him forward towards the wing. Kiyomi hauled in the line, hand over hand, reeling them in to sprawl on the metal surface. The air was thinning and an icy chill blasted through Kenny's thin soccer clothes. The C-1 continued to climb. Far below, the night lights of Tokyo sparkled like jewels scattered on velvet.

"Great plan," he yelled in Kiyomi's ear. "Are we meant to freeze, suffocate or fall off now?"

A crack of light split open in the body of the plane and a harsh neon glow spilled out. Kenny craned his neck around and saw that a door had opened just behind the wing. Standing in the gap was the unmistakable shape of an *oni*, leveling a large handgun at them.

"Kenny!" Kiyomi screamed. "We're sitting ducks out here!"

The *oni* took aim and pulled the trigger. *BLAMM!*

SKING! The bullet ricocheted off the sword in Kenny's hand. The *oni* fired again, sending two more rounds Kenny's way. Kusanagi bucked in his hand, deflecting the heavy-caliber slugs.

"*Nar-gu-rah uk-kru n'gak-rak,*" the *oni* barked, reaching back inside the plane.

"Ken-*chan* – he's getting a rocket launcher!" Kiyomi yelled.

Kenny didn't need telling twice. He raised the sword high over his head and swept it down, slicing through the metal structure of the wing. It fell away, spinning through the sky, with Kenny and Kiyomi clinging to it like two surfers on a board.

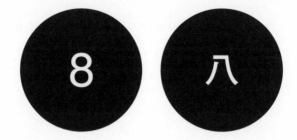

The detached wing flipped, throwing Kenny and Kiyomi into free fall. Kenny rolled over and over before, intuitively, he thrust out his arms and legs in a star shape to increase resistance. The wind whipped at his flimsy clothes and the uncontrolled tumbling motion slowed before settling into a semi-glide.

It was a strange sensation: on the one hand, Kenny felt like he was floating; on the other, the rush of air surging past left him in no doubt that he was falling – and falling fast. Above, fraying clouds hung low in the purple sky. Below, amid Tokyo's glittering expanse, lay a splotch of darkness.

Kiyomi drifted down, twisting her shoulders and knees to maneuver through the air. She drew opposite Kenny, locked her hands on to his wrists and pulled him closer, until her forehead touched his.

"You're an idiot!" she screamed.

Her words were lost in the rush of wind, but Kenny could lip-read. He nodded downward. "What's the black area down there?" he yelled, exaggerating the shape of each word.

Kiyomi craned her neck in each direction to fix her bearings before answering.

"That's Saitama, near Tokorozawa. It's a reservoir, either Lake Sayama or Lake Tama."

"Trust me!" Kenny shouted.

The city lights below were brighter now and he could make out details: a Ferris wheel, a covered stadium and another airfield. Closing his eyes, Kenny pictured a powerful updraft whooshing from the ground like a geyser. He focused on the image, feeling the air between his fingers, throwing it upward like splashing water from a pool.

He opened his eyes again and his stomach heaved. The moonlit surface of the lake was rushing towards him at almost one hundred fifty miles per hour. Kenny screwed his eyes shut, clenched his teeth so hard that he thought they would break, and summoned every trace of willpower he had. He knew he could do this, but more importantly he had to believe it.

"I trust you."

Kiyomi's words sparked like a firefly in the blackness of his mind. Something flared deep down in the core of his consciousness and power surged through him. Kenny braced for the impact; hitting water at that speed and height would be like slamming into concrete.

Nothing happened.

He waited, not daring to open his eyes.

"Uh, Ken-*chan*." Kiyomi's voice was quiet, as if afraid to disturb him. "You can set us down now."

Kenny blinked and gasped. He and Kiyomi were suspended six feet above the lake. The autumn air was motionless around them and they floated, as if gravity had ceased.

"I – I don't know how . . ." Kenny began to say, before a whisper of doubt crept into his mind. *This can't be real.*

SPLASSHH! The shock of the chilled lake water slapped him back to reality and he swallowed a mouthful before kicking up to the surface. Kiyomi bobbed alongside him, treading water in her soggy leathers. Fury blazed in her eyes.

"I know, I know," Kenny spluttered, before she could speak. "I'm an idiot. But at least we're not dead."

"Urgh! No thanks to you."

"What? It wasn't my idea to jump onto a moving plane."

"And it wasn't mine to cut the wing off."

An orange light flashed in the mountains to the west and the muffled crump of an explosion rolled towards them.

"You can thank me later," Kenny said, and began the long swim to shore.

A circular intake tower with a green conical roof, like a medieval turret, stood some fifty feet clear of the water.

Connecting it to the mainland was a suspension bridge and the industrial lights of a pumping station shone like a beacon, guiding Kenny and Kiyomi to shore. They pulled themselves up the shallow bank and flopped, panting, onto a forlorn patch of grass.

Kenny breathed in deep chestfuls of air and waited for his drumming heart to slow. His limbs were leaden and he wanted nothing more than to fall asleep on the dirt, except the chattering of his teeth would have kept him awake.

Kiyomi unzipped her phone from its waterproof pocket and made a call.

"How long before our pickup?" Kenny asked, sitting up and hugging himself to keep warm.

"About half an hour," Kiyomi replied. She wrapped her arms around her knees and shivered.

"And how long before hypothermia kicks in?"

Kiyomi rolled her eyes. "You're such a wimp. It isn't that cold."

"Easy for you to say. This soccer jersey isn't exactly warm."

"You try swimming in leathers. At least you'll dry off quickly."

Neither spoke for the next few minutes. The only sounds were the whisper of leaves on the breeze, wavy ribbons of distant music from an amusement park, frogs chirping and the occasional plop of a fish.

"This is silly," Kenny said and slid over to squeeze next to Kiyomi.

"What are you doing?" she asked, with undisguised suspicion.

"Jeez. It's basic survival," Kenny said. "We're both cold and wet. We've got nothing dry to change into, so the next best thing is to share bodily warmth. That or light a fire, and I don't see anything to burn."

"All right," Kiyomi agreed, "but don't try any funny stuff."

"Yeah, right, because you're really appealing right now." Kenny regretted the words as soon as they left his lips.

"What's that supposed to mean?"

"Oh, uh, just . . . well . . ."

Kiyomi's elbow landed in Kenny's ribs. "Come on, spit it out."

"All right then. It's just . . . you've been . . . such a pain in the butt lately."

"*Me?* What about you? You've been the most useless –"

"No." Kenny held up a hand to stop her. "Hear me out. Listen. Ever since . . . you know . . . happened, you've been really angry, all the time. OK, I'm used to you being a bit feisty, and it was kind of cute, but now . . . now, you're like the flipping Hulk – a total rage monster. Tonight just caps it all off. You could've gotten us killed, what, four times, at least. Reckless is one thing, but this . . . this is like you just don't care."

Lights flashed behind Kenny's eyes as the back of his head slammed into the earth and the air was driven from his lungs by Kiyomi's knees on his chest. He tried to breathe in, but her fingers drilled into his throat, cutting off his airway.

"Who are you to call me reckless?" Kiyomi spat. "I ought to rip your stupid throat out and . . . and . . ."

The mask of rage faltered. Kiyomi's eyes widened from angry slits and her twisted snarl changed to a gasp of distress. Her hands flew to her mouth and she pushed away, tears brimming in her eyes.

Kenny sat up, a hand to his bruised throat, and drew in ragged gulps of air. "You . . . see?" he wheezed. "That's . . . what . . . I . . . meant . . ."

"Ken-*chan*, I'm so sorry," Kiyomi sobbed, dropping to her knees beside him and throwing her arms around his shoulders. "I don't know what . . . I would never . . . You're my friend."

Kenny felt the warmth of her tears against his neck and cupped his hand over hers.

They were in the same position when the powerful headlights of the limousine swept over the shore and Oyama strode towards them with a blanket in each ham-sized fist.

Kiyomi was first in the house, tugging off her sopping boots in the entryway. She paused at the sight of a pair of polished black loafers which didn't belong to her father.

"Kiyomi-*chan*," Harashima said, standing at the door to the main room. "I need to speak to you and Kuromori-*san*."

Kenny arrived and, seeing Kiyomi's father, bowed. "*Konban-wa*, Harashima-*sama*," he said.

Harashima nodded in acknowledgement, but kept his gaze fixed on Kiyomi. "Now," he said.

Kiyomi shook out her damp hair. "But Papa, can't I have a shower first? Look at me. I'm soaked. And hungry."

"Oyama will bring you a fresh towel and some hot soup. What I have to say will not wait." Harashima turned and went back into the room.

"Uh-oh. He seems cross," Kenny whispered, kicking off his sneakers and reaching for house slippers.

"You have no idea," Kiyomi muttered.

She stepped into the room and yelped in surprise. "*Ojisan! Bikkuri shita!*"

Kenny followed and was greeted by a familiar face. "Sato-*san*!" He remembered to bow to Kiyomi's uncle. "*Konban-wa.*"

"*Konban-wa*, Kuromori-*san*." Sato returned the gesture. "Your Japanese is improving."

Kenny blushed. "That's not hard when you're starting from zero."

Oyama appeared with two bathrobes. He handed them out and took his leave, sliding the door closed.

Sato sighed and turned to Kiyomi. "Unfortunately, this is not a social visit. Your father called me."

Harashima had both hands clasped behind his back. "Kiyomi-*chan*, I am very, very disappointed. You were under strict instructions not to engage the *oni* under any circumstances."

"Sir," Kenny said, "it was my idea. Lives were in danger."

"Including yours," Harashima snapped. "You are too valuable to take stupid risks like this."

"We're fine," Kiyomi protested. "We saved people – and we stopped *oni* stealing the telescope."

"Did it never occur to you that we might have wanted them to steal it, so we could follow them and find out why they wanted it?"

"That doesn't make any . . ." Kiyomi's words trailed off.

"Instead, what do we have?" Sato said. "Burned-out buildings, downtown explosions, a plane crash near the American Navy base, a fallen utility pole, dented car roofs, and witnesses speaking of a fair-haired boy in soccer clothes waving a sword. Do you have any idea how difficult it will be to suppress this? As far as the world media is concerned, we've just had a major terrorist incident."

"Sir," Kenny said, measuring his words, "isn't that the point?"

Sato raised an eyebrow.

"I mean, surely that's what the *oni*, or whoever it was that sent them, want everyone to think. They blew up two buildings as a diversion, tried to steal a giant telescope, torched everything to cover their tracks and then planned to fly it away. That would all have happened, even if we hadn't been there. The question is, why?"

Harashima pursed his lips.

A pot scraped in the kitchen. Frogs chirped outside.

"Very well," he said. "I want you two to tell us everything that happened this evening. Leave nothing out. Any detail, even the most insignificant to you, might be critical."

Sato nodded. "There's definitely something big happening, since they're not afraid to show themselves so publicly. We need to work out what it is, before it's too late."

9　九

"This makes no sense," Harashima said, once Kiyomi and Kenny had finished their debriefing.

"Tell me about it," Kiyomi added, stretching and yawning.

Sato drummed his fingers lightly on the table around which they were all seated. "Everything you describe is wrong. *Oni* don't work in organized groups. They have limited intelligence."

"Yep, and they don't wear uniforms or drive vans," Kenny said. "We know."

"Not to mention using guns, explosives, pulleys, winches, scaffolding, cutting gear, gasoline . . ." Kiyomi said.

"So what are we left with?" Harashima said. "Either these are not *oni* or . . ."

"Or this is a different kind of *oni*, one we've never seen before," Sato finished.

The door slid open and Oyama entered, bearing a tray of refreshments which he set on the table. He was about to depart when Kiyomi tugged the sleeve of his kimono and whispered in his ear. Kenny saw a hairline crease appear in the wide brow before the big servant bowed and left.

"Kiyomi-*chan*, from what you have described, the one with the mask is in command," Harashima said. He poured himself a steaming cup of green tea.

Kiyomi nodded. "Yeah. Silver mask and gloves. Really weird. The others all seemed scared of him."

"It wasn't a mask," Kenny said, taking a rice cracker. "I saw him too, in the doorway of the plane. His mouth moved. Masks don't do that."

Harashima glanced at Kiyomi. "You spoke with him, yes?"

Kiyomi frowned, recalling the conversation. "It wasn't clear, with me being up on the walkway, but I'd swear it was a mask."

Sato placed a hand on Kenny's shoulder. "It's all right, Kuromori-*san*. The mind can play tricks. It would have been difficult for you to see at night."

Kenny shrugged the hand away. "I'm telling you, it wasn't a mask."

"And I'm telling you," Sato said, "*oni* come in many shapes, sizes and colors, but silver is not one of them."

Kenny looked to Harashima for support. "Sir, you said it yourself, maybe this is something new, something you haven't seen before."

"A silver *oni*? With advanced intelligence? A leader, who commands the others and uses modern technology? I think if such a creature existed we would know of it by now. You're mistaken."

"I know what I saw."

WHAM! Kiyomi's fist slammed onto the table, rattling the tea set. "Kenny, you are so . . . so *ganko*!" She stabbed a finger against her temple. "Your head, it's like a stone! Nothing goes in."

Sato and Harashima exchanged a look. The government man leaned back, stroking his chin, lips tight.

"Let's go back a few steps," Sato said. "This started with a tip-off, yes?"

Oyama returned with a covered tray, set it down beside Kiyomi, bowed and withdrew again.

"Yes," Harashima answered. "We received word that some *oni* were gathering for a raid. That's why we followed them."

"But their operation was planned with absolute precision," Sato mused. "Such carelessness does not fit."

"You think they wanted us to find them?" Kenny asked.

"It is possible. After all, you both walked into a trap and they were prepared for you."

Kiyomi uncovered a plate of *sashimi* and a bowl of chopped steak topped with a raw egg. She took up her chopsticks and began to eat. A frown flickered over Sato's face.

"The thing I don't get," Kenny continued, "is why steal such a massive telescope in the first place?"

"Maybe they're amateur stargazers," Kiyomi said, a

red slab dangling from her chopsticks.

"Then they could just buy a good one in Akihabara," Kenny said. "It doesn't have to be seventeen tons."

"How do you know it weighs seventeen tons?" Sato asked.

"I heard one of the *oni* say it, while they were building the scaffold," Kiyomi replied.

"Did you now? That's interesting," Sato said, nodding to himself. "*Ak-gu-harak n'ka ga-hruk?*"

Kiyomi shrugged. "I don't know. I was hiding at the time. I think it was the blue one with the chipped tusk. Why?" She set down her chopsticks. "What? Why are you all staring at me?"

"Stay calm," Sato said. "Take a deep breath and place both hands on the table, palms down."

"Papa," Kiyomi appealed to her father. "What's going on?"

"Just do as your uncle says." Harashima stood up and moved to block the exit.

"Kuromori-*san*," Sato said to Kenny, "your neck is bruised, but nothing you have said explains that."

Kenny looked away. "Oh, that. Uh, my collar got snagged by a tree while I was running away. Stupid thing half strangled me."

Sato's gaze was fixed on Kiyomi. "An admirable lie, Ken-*san*, but trees do not leave finger marks. Kiyomi-*chan*, hands on the table. Now!"

Kiyomi's nose wrinkled as her pout curled into a snarl.

She leapt to her feet, throwing the table over. "Nobody tells me what to do, least of all you, *oji*."

"Kiyomi-*chan*, listen to me!" Sato said. "Think about it. You're tired, right? You've been having bad dreams? Nightmares?"

The snarl wavered. "How could you know?"

"Your temper has been very short. You get angry, quickly and easily, yes?"

Kiyomi's eyes flickered around the room, like a cornered animal seeking an escape. "Yes," she agreed, her voice anguished.

"And, let me guess, you've been eating steak tartare and *basashi* just now? And if I was to ask Oyama, I'm sure he'd tell me that raw meat has gone missing from the refrigerator."

Kiyomi clasped her hands over her ears. "How do you know – What's happening to me?" she gasped.

Sato strode over and pulled Kiyomi's hands away from her head. "And when did you learn to speak *oni*?"

"No!" Kiyomi's right foot landed in Sato's chest, slamming him against her father and sending both men sprawling.

The door slid open and the mountainous figure of Oyama filled the frame. Kiyomi ducked under his outstretched arms and dived between his legs, wriggling out into the hallway before dashing out of the front door.

Kenny stared.

"We mustn't let her get away!" Sato said, scrambling to

his feet. "We have to find her – before she does something foolish."

Harashima pressed the intercom button. "Lock all the gates and activate the motion sensors," he said. "She won't get far."

"Sir, let me deal with this," Kenny offered. "Please. I know where to find her."

Harashima studied the agonized look on Kenny's face. "Very well," he said. "But be careful."

Kenny knew the garden well enough to navigate the paths, even at night. He hurried to the octagonal wooden summer house which served as a *dojo*. He and Kiyomi had spent many hours there that summer and it held a lot of memories.

"Kiyomi?" he called, stopping at the threshold. "We need to talk. I know you're in there."

No answer.

"Look, what just happened back there was really freaky. I mean, it freaked me out. Question is, what do we do now?"

He perched on the top step and leaned his back against a post, directing his words into the black void beneath the roof.

"I'm not a doctor, but I'd say what you need most right now is a friend. I know I do and, since you're the best friend I've got around here, I hope you don't mind if I just sit and talk. Is that OK?"

Still no response.

"I have nightmares too," Kenny said. "Not all the time, but often enough. Sometimes, it's me and Namazu, replaying all that. Other times, it's Hachiman, or me being chased by *nukekubi*. My dad says it's post-traumatic stress; my brain's way of making sense of something by revisiting it until it's no longer threatening. But the worst nightmare . . . is when I find you, cold and still . . ."

Kenny paused to dab his eyes on the sleeve of his bathrobe, before continuing.

"When you . . . it was like a hole had been cut into my chest. A chunk of me . . . died with you, and the thought of going on . . ." He sighed. "You don't remember any of this, but I went a bit nuts. I'd lost my mum . . . and I wasn't going to lose you too. I was crazy. Desperate. I remembered something Inari had told me, about choosing life and not setting limits. I had this loony idea that I could swap my life for yours, and I would have done it too. Better for you to live with the loss than me, I guess. Pretty selfish, I know. Anyway, that's when Taro stepped in and sacrificed himself instead. That's what this is all about, isn't it? Your soul is an *oni*'s and that's why you're changing. Your uncle figured it out pretty quick."

"Ken-*chan*?" Kiyomi's voice was barely a whisper in the darkness.

"Yes?"

"Kill me."

"What?"

79

"Please. I'm begging you. Use the sword. Kill me. Send the *oni*'s soul where it belongs. It's the only option."

"No. There has to be another way."

Kiyomi inched closer. "Ken-*chan*, you've seen it yourself. I tried to kill you. I'm a danger. I'm becoming a monster, an *onibaba*. Killing me would be a mercy."

"No," Kenny said. "You're sick, like my mum was sick. The difference is that this is my fault. I did this to you."

Kiyomi stepped out into the starlight. "Don't blame yourself, Ken-*chan*. You tried to cheat death, but death always wins in the end."

Kenny sprang to his feet. "Don't speak like that, Kiyomi. This isn't over, not by a long shot." He held out his hand. "You once made me promise to do whatever it takes to save lives. OK, that promise still holds, only this time it's your life. I swear to you that I will find a way to put this right, to undo the mess I made – no matter the cost."

"Kenny, don't make promises like that. You don't know –"

"I set my limits, no one else. Do you remember the very first words you ever said to me?"

Kiyomi nodded. "Yes."

"You said, 'Trust me,' and I did, and you saved my life. Now it's my turn. Trust me."

Kiyomi reached out and took Kenny's hand. "All right."

10 +

Oyama was waiting in the doorway with a selection of sandwiches which he offered to Kenny.

"It's what he does when he's worried," Kiyomi whispered, catching the puzzled expression on Kenny's face.

"Oh, uh, thanks," Kenny said, taking the plate into the main room. He set it down on the table, now upright again.

On seeing Kenny and Kiyomi, Sato finished the call he was making.

Kenny picked up a sandwich and lifted one end; it was filled with potato salad. He put it back, hoping no one had noticed.

Harashima came to the door and embraced Kiyomi as she entered. "Thank the gods you are safe," he said. "Please, don't ever run away again. I couldn't bear the thought of losing you."

Kiyomi pressed her lips tightly together and nodded.

"Thank you, Kuromori-*san*," Sato said. "You have done well. Kiyomi-*chan*, I have sent for someone who may be able to help. He will be here in the morning. In the meantime, you should rest."

"Sato-*san*," Kenny said, "what about the *oni*? The ones tonight."

"I've made some enquiries about the airplane," Sato said. "A transport plane like that will have been chartered by someone, probably from a shell company owned by another one. It will take some time, but if we can find out who hired the plane, that will be a start."

Harashima nodded. "Kuromori-*san*, Oyama will take you home now."

Kiyomi walked Kenny to the front door. He handed her the damp bathrobe and pulled on his soggy shoes.

"Ken-*chan*, about what you said . . ." Kiyomi began.

"I meant every word," Kenny said, taking her hands in his. "I'm responsible and I will find a way to put this right – or die trying."

Oyama dropped Kenny off on Honan Dori and he walked the remaining half block to his apartment building, a nondescript thirteen-story lump of concrete and glass. He took the elevator to the seventh floor, plodded down the corridor and let himself into the apartment.

"Hi, Dad," he said, standing in the doorway to the living room.

Charles looked up from his corner desk, beside the balcony. He was tapping away at a keyboard, images from the flat screen television on the opposite wall reflecting in his rimless glasses.

"Kenny." Charles removed his spectacles and rubbed his eyes with the heel of his palm. "It's late. Have you eaten? There's pizza in the fridge."

"Pepperoni?" Kenny asked, hoping for something more promising than a potato salad sandwich.

"Tuna and corn, with potato and mayo." Charles saw Kenny's face fall. "It's not as bad as it sounds."

"I'll be fine," Kenny said. He opened a cupboard and rummaged around for a Cup Noodles.

Charles muted the TV and brought an empty coffee cup over to the counter. "Where have you been?"

Kenny shrugged.

"I did make it to your school," Charles said. "I was a bit late but I thought I'd catch you at the end."

"Sorry about that," Kenny mumbled, topping up the teakettle and putting it on the stove.

"Good news though. You made the team." Charles watched his son closely, trying to read his mood. "So how was practice? It looks like it got rough."

"Oh, yeah. You could say that." Kenny stuck a finger through one of the many tears in his soccer jersey. "Even my aches have aches. You haven't been watching the news, have you?" He leaned over to catch a glimpse of the TV and spotted footage of a rocket lifting off.

"No, I've been working. I'm doing a piece on the space program, specifically the effects of the geo-engineering project on national pride." Charles spooned coffee granules into a mug. "Why? Has something happened?"

Kenny sighed. "It's complicated, Dad."

A plume of steam whistled from the spout of the kettle and Charles poured boiling water into the containers.

"This would be . . . your grandfather's business?" he said, stirring his coffee.

"Yeah. I know we don't really talk about that, but . . ." Kenny pushed the block of dried noodles under the water with his fork and watched a cluster of bubbles rise.

"Kenny . . . son . . . if something's bothering you, you *can* talk to me. I may not be able to help, but you might feel better just sharing it."

Kenny pulled up a stool and sat at the counter. "OK. Here's a question. When Mum was sick, what would you have done to save her? If you could?"

"Oh, wow. You know how to ask the big ones, don't you?" Charles grabbed a stool. "You know, when your mother was first diagnosed, I asked them what it would take, to cure her. They said a bone marrow transfer, from a suitable donor."

Kenny pushed his noodles away.

"So we did all the tests," Charles continued. "I was first. I prayed that I'd be a match, that I'd be the one who could save your mum."

"And?"

"I was not even close." Charles closed his eyes for a

moment and shook his head. "I don't know if I should tell you this bit . . ." He sighed. "You, on the other hand, were perfect."

Kenny blinked "I was? So why didn't we –?"

"You were three. Nowhere near old enough. We only tested you in case she lived long enough." Charles stared down into his coffee, steam misting his glasses.

"That sucks."

"Yeah. It pretty near killed me. Imagine watching someone you love slowly die, knowing that the power to save them is in your hands, but you can't use it." Charles looked away, staring at some far-off point.

Kenny studied his father's face before he spoke. "It's funny. This is going to come out wrong, but I always used to think of you as being weak – you know, with the drinking and everything. But you're actually a lot stronger than I thought; to have gone through all that and to still be here."

Charles reached over and ran a hand through Kenny's hair. "Maybe that's where you get it from. I still think of her every day . . . and every time I see you." He slipped his glasses off and wiped his eyes.

Kenny reached for the noodles, plunged in his fork and twirled it around. "Thanks, Dad."

"This is about Kiyomi, isn't it?" Charles put his glasses back on. "About what happened in that cave."

"Yeah." Kenny nodded. "It is. Wait, that reminds me. You know a lot about Japanese myth and folklore, right?"

Charles smiled. "Try growing up in our house and not learning that."

"Have you ever heard of a silver *oni*?"

After a long pause, Charles said, "No, not silver. I think I've come across every shade in the rainbow, plus a few weird combinations, but never a metallic one. Is it important?"

"Very."

"I'll look through my notes tomorrow and ask around the faculty. You should eat." He got up and took the coffee cup back to his desk. "And Kenny? I meant what I said about us needing to spend more time together. We have a lot of catching up to do." He turned the volume back up on the TV.

Kenny slurped his noodles and watched a computer simulation of a satellite taking up position in orbit, but his eyelids were heavy and his mind drifted back to his conversation with Kiyomi.

With a shudder, a terrible truth came to him and goose bumps prickled his arms. The *oni* self growing inside Kiyomi was, in its own way, like a cancer. Left unchecked, it would consume her, leaving an empty shell inhabited by a monster. If that happened, he would be forced to end her life, both to stop her suffering and to protect others from the beast she would become. Kenny would have no choice other than to kill her.

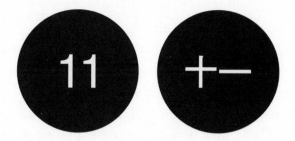

The squawk of emergency sirens and excited commentary from the television jolted Kenny from a fitful sleep. He rolled off the futon and sat up, yawning and stretching his aching limbs. Shuffling across the hall, he stumbled into the bathroom and splashed cold water on his face before emerging into the living room.

His father was already up, dressed and sliding two perfectly fried eggs out of a frying pan onto a plate alongside two rashers of bacon.

"Morning, sleepyhead," Charles said. "I thought I'd cook you a decent breakfast to make up for last night's dinner. Pancakes?"

"Sure." Kenny took a seat at the counter and blinked at the television. The morning news was on, flashing dramatic scenes of burned-out buildings, wrecked delivery vans, long traffic jams and a plane crash in a forest.

"Other teenagers get drunk and write graffiti," Charles said, with a sly smile. He took two fat, fluffy pancakes out of the toaster oven and balanced them on the plate.

"How do you know that was me?" Kenny drizzled

syrup over his pancakes and dug in.

"I didn't, until they mentioned a *gaijin* kid wearing soccer gear. They've got some blurred CCTV pictures, but nothing definitive. What were you doing?"

"You know I can't tell you, Dad. For your own safety."

"Well, you must have done something right. One of the survivors was saying that a blond-haired angel flew up to save her."

Kenny's cheeks burned.

"Just promise me you'll be careful, OK? I'm very proud of you." Charles slid a glass of orange juice next to Kenny's plate. The news switched to a story about a satellite launch.

"Dad, isn't that what you were working on last night?" Kenny asked, eager to change the subject.

Charles looked up. "Yeah, the *Hoshi no Kagami* Project."

"What's that about?"

"Don't they teach you anything in school these days?"

"I know it's a global warming thing. They're going to cool down the planet, right?"

Charles glanced at his watch. "We call it 'climate change' now. OK, very quickly, an American astro-physicist named Lowell Wood calculated that if we could somehow deflect away just one percent of the sunlight which reaches the Earth, it would restore world climates back to how they were before we added all the greenhouse gases."

"Right, and they're putting a giant pair of sunglasses up there."

"Don't be silly. Everyone thought it was a crazy idea – too expensive and impractical – but once the UN's Intergovernmental Panel on Climate Change endorsed it, scientists started to take it seriously."

"And Japan took the lead." Kenny washed down his bacon with a gulp of juice.

"Yes, but only as a proof of concept experiment. Japanese scientists, using graphene rods to support a film of – Are you listening?"

"Mm-hm. Test me afterward if you don't believe me."

"It's like a giant parasol, thirty miles wide, with sodium foil filling the gaps. The plan is to test it over Japan, to see how feasible it is."

"And that's what all the rockets are for, right? Lots of launches to assemble the thing up there."

Charles nodded. "It's a big deal, you know. There's a lot of money and national pride at stake. This is one of the world's biggest engineering projects."

Kenny rolled his eyes. "I know."

"The final piece goes up in the next couple of days. You might even get a national holiday out of it." Charles checked his watch again. "I'm running late. Wash up when you're done, leave the place tidy and let me know when you'll be back. I'll see you later." He grabbed his laptop bag and dashed for the door.

Kenny reached for the remote and turned the TV off.

TONK-TONK. A hollow tapping sound came from near his father's desk.

Kenny mopped up the last of the egg yolk with a forkful of pancake and padded over to investigate. The sound seemed to be coming from beneath the desk. He dropped to all fours and crawled under for a closer look.

BLAM! Two furry paws slammed on the picture window and a raccoon-like face smushed up against the glass, with huge eyes and a pink lolling tongue.

"Poyo!" Kenny yelled at Kiyomi's pet. "You scared the life out of me." He opened the balcony door and waved the dumpy *tanuki* into the apartment. "We're seven floors up," he scolded. "Care to tell me how you got here?"

Poyo sat on his haunches and shrugged, then sniffed the air. He licked his lips and waddled towards the kitchen.

"I've finished breakfast, so you're too late," Kenny warned.

Poyo climbed up a stool and pulled himself onto the counter where he picked up the frying pan. He dipped a paw into the bacon grease and licked it greedily.

"So, is this a social visit?" Kenny asked.

Poyo paused and shook his head, flinging a string of drool onto Kenny's plate.

"Business then. Do you have a message?"

The *tanuki* nodded, then pointed at Kenny.

"Me? OK. Do what?"

Poyo sat back, held two fists up and rocked them side to side in a circular motion.

"If that's supposed to be driving a car, it's not very good."

Poyo farted.

"That's one way to respond to criticism, I guess." Kenny smiled, in spite of himself. "So where am I traveling to?"

Poyo labored up onto two legs and flattened the fur on top of his head, drawing it down. He then puckered his lips and made a smooching noise.

"Very funny," Kenny droned, no longer amused. "I'm to see Kiyomi, is that it?"

Poyo nodded and resumed licking the frying pan.

"Next time, she could just send a text," Kenny muttered, heading to his room to get changed.

The journey to the Harashima residence took about forty-five minutes by public transportation and involved three trains and a short walk.

The *yakuza* guards on duty waved Kenny through the dragon gates, onto the driveway leading to the house.

"Kuromori-*san*," a familiar, high, clear voice rang out.

"*Sensei*!" Kenny spun around and was delighted to see a tall, ancient-looking figure on the path behind him.

"You have been busy," Genkuro said. "Come. Walk with me. Let us enjoy these beautiful gardens."

"Uh, OK." Kenny fell in beside his former teacher while Poyo lagged behind.

They wound along a narrow gravel path, through stands of sculpted azaleas and rhododendrons. Shafts of sunlight speared through deep purply-red maple leaves overhead.

Genkuro stopped at a tall clump of bamboo. He reached out and touched a spindly stem, the top of which rustled high above. "Tell me what you see, Kuromori-*san*."

Kenny squinted upward. "A stick of bamboo," he said. "It grows in sections, it's really tall and the leaves are at the top."

"Anything more?" the elderly teacher asked. "About its nature?"

"It grows very quickly. And we can eat the shoots." Kenny racked his brains for anything else. "Oh, yeah. It's a type of grass."

Genkuro smiled. "So often, the young look but they do not see."

Kenny bristled. "It's bamboo, a kind of grass that grows very tall. What else is there to say?"

"Bamboo never stops growing. It appears weak, but its roots are strong. It is almost unbreakable, because it bends under pressure. It lives long and endures much hardship. Perhaps you should learn from it."

"That's a trick question," Kenny retorted. "You didn't ask me what bamboo was like, only what it is."

"Is there a difference?"

Kenny scowled at the bamboo, as if it was mocking him.

"Snow falls in winter," Genkuro said, holding out his hand for a spotted butterfly to explore. "It lands on the bamboo, gathers and weighs it down, so low the leaves touch the ground. The snow melts, falls away and the bamboo springs back up. What would happen if the bamboo did not yield?"

"It would break."

"Indeed. Misfortune would follow." Genkuro looked expectantly at Kenny, as if waiting for understanding to dawn.

"What?" Kenny said. "I don't get it."

"Kuromori-*san*, there is a time to resist and a time to yield. You do not yet know when to do these."

"Meaning what?"

"Meaning Kiyomi-*chan*'s body surrendered her spirit. Death came to her, as it comes to us all. Except you resisted. Your feelings overcame your sense and you brought her back."

Kenny's eyes narrowed. "Inari said I had a choice: to accept fate or to change it."

"Some fates are not for changing. Now you know why it is forbidden."

"Why? Because death finds another way? That sucks. I'd rather deal with it on my terms than on someone else's."

Genkuro watched the butterfly flit away.

"My mistress has a lot of faith in you, Kuromori-*san*. Your weaknesses give you strength, but your strengths are also weaknesses. You should speak with her."

"No thanks. I don't need someone else saying, 'I told you so,' when all I did was save a life."

"Unfortunately, that was not all you did." Genkuro began walking back towards the house. "You took a life to pay for a life, but you used stolen currency to do so. That is why Kiyomi-*chan* is changing, and why it is your doing."

12 +=

"The airplane was hired by Sugawara Material Exports," Sato reported to Kenny and Harashima, back in the house. He pointed to a map on the bank of TV monitors which covered a wall. "An engineering company. They submitted a flight plan to Kagoshima Airport."

"Where's Kagoshima?" Kenny asked.

Sato zoomed out the map and stuck a finger on a blob at the southwestern tip of the Japanese mainland, not far from South Korea. "It's down here, on the island of Kyushu."

"And how far is that from Tokyo?" Kenny wondered.

"Around six hundred miles," Harashima answered.

"Isn't that a long way to fly with a stolen telescope?"

"It's a coastal area," Sato said. "Perhaps they intended to smuggle it out by sea."

"It's the closest point between Japan and China," Harashima added. "Almost a straight line across the East China Sea."

Kenny pursed his lips in thought.

Sato continued. "As we suspected, Sugawara is a small business which has changed hands many times. I have a team working to find out which is its true owner."

"Maybe I should go to Kagoshima," Kenny suggested. "See if I can find out anything about the pickup. I mean, someone must have been waiting for the plane to arrive."

"Out of the question," Sato said. "It's bad enough that you destroyed half of Tokyo last night. Now you want to travel south, not knowing where you're going or what it is you're looking for?"

"Why not?" Kenny said. "You got a better idea?"

"Haven't you caused enough damage already?" Sato said. "Look at what happened the last time you went off and followed your own desires?"

"Are you going to keep throwing that in my face?" Kenny's voice grew louder. "Does everyone forget that I actually did something right last time? That we won?"

"At a cost," Harashima said, his voice low. "Always at a cost."

The door slid open and Genkuro bowed before entering the room. "Kuromori-*san*," he said, fixing his steely gaze on Kenny. "It would help considerably if you chose not to shout."

"I'm sorry," Kenny said. "How is she?"

Genkuro turned his gaze to Kiyomi's father. "*Oni* are creatures of passion; they thrive on powerful feelings such as anger, rage, jealousy. We have had a small measure of good fortune. First, the *oni* Taro, who sacrificed himself, was not as savage as many of his kind. Second, Kiyomi-*chan* has not been under too much stress since. These things have helped to slow the change. However, the fact remains that, with each day, her *oni* self grows stronger. It is merely a matter of time before it takes over completely and the human self is no more."

Harashima pressed his knuckles against his mouth, anxiety clouding his face. "How long do we have?"

"That would depend on how much emotional stress she is forced to bear. The greater the intensity of the feeling, the stronger the *oni* self becomes."

"So lots of quiet rest and peaceful calm is required?" Sato said.

"That would be advisable."

"Can I see her?" Kenny asked. "Please?"

"As long as you cause no disturbance."

Kenny tapped on the *shoji* screen door.

"Who is it?"

"Me. Kenny."

The door slid open a crack. "Go away."

Kenny leaned close to the gap. "What have I done now?"

"It's not you. It's me. It's what I might do, what I'm capable of."

Kenny stroked his throat. "That isn't you. It's that . . . thing inside you. And I put it there."

The gap widened a little more and a trace of Kiyomi's

perfume drifted out on a cushion of warm air. Kenny breathed it in deeply.

"I've already told you," Kiyomi said, "you can't blame yourself for anything that happened. If you hadn't . . . done what you did, we wouldn't be having this conversation at all."

"That's not how it seems to me. Everyone's acting like I messed up by saving you. I mean, how was I to know?"

"They're just worried, that's all."

"And you? Are you worried?"

"No. I'm not worried; I'm too busy being terrified."

Kenny chewed his lip. He had never thought of Kiyomi as being scared of anything before, and here he was feeling sorry for himself.

"What are we going to do?" he asked.

"I don't know," Kiyomi said. "Just stay here and wait, I suppose. Try and delay things for as long as possible."

"That's stupid," Kenny said. "You can't just shut yourself away in the dark and hide. That's not you."

"What makes you such an expert?"

"I know a little bit about depression," Kenny said, closing his eyes. "The worst thing is to give up hope. It's a vicious circle: you feel low so you don't do anything, and then, because you don't do anything, you feel low. Don't give in to it. Otherwise, you might as well be dead anyway."

Kiyomi closed the door. "Well, thanks for stopping by to cheer me up."

His eyes still closed, Kenny slumped against the wall and thumped his head against it three times.

The door swept open and Kiyomi joined him in the hallway, jacket in hand and bag on shoulder. "You should be careful doing that," she said. "You've suffered enough brain damage already."

Kenny grinned and straightened up. "I thought you were hiding in your cave."

"What, like an *oni*?" She put two fingers up, one on each side of her head, to form a pair of horns. "Not yet. So where are you taking me? I know – Tokyo Disneyland! I haven't been there for ages."

"Yeah, right. Roller coasters, crowds, lines? It's supposed to be stress free. How about . . . an aquarium? They say watching fish is good for relaxation."

The limousine pulled away from the drop-off point and Kiyomi grabbed Kenny's arm as they walked along the wide avenue leading towards Tokyo Bay. A huge red-and-white Ferris wheel sat on the horizon like a stained glass rose window set against the sky.

"We're here, so now you can tell me," Kiyomi said. "What did you say to my dad?"

"Well, first I told him that being cooped up wasn't your thing," Kenny replied.

"Let me guess. He said, too bad, it was for my own good?"

"Yep, but then I said being shut in your room was

going to cause you more stress, not less."

"Smart move. Turning the situation around."

"And then I hit him with the one weak spot every Japanese parent has."

"Which is?"

"Education. I told him that since I'd skipped school to come around today, the least he could do was allow us a field trip to study marine biology."

Kiyomi laughed. "You really said that? And he agreed?"

"Uh-huh. I think he was looking for an excuse to let you out for some air. Plus, I promised it'd be stress free. Although he said he'd quiz me when we got back."

Kiyomi spread her arms out and wheeled in a circle, eyes closed, the sun on her face. Her long hair fanned out behind her.

"Careful, you'll get dizzy," Kenny warned.

Kiyomi stopped. "And if I fall? Who's going to catch me?" She stumbled in Kenny's direction and collapsed against him.

"You know I will." He propped her up.

Kiyomi brought her mouth close to Kenny's ear and whispered, "Thank you."

"For what?"

"For everything. For bringing me out today. For not giving up on me. For being a dork. For being a friend."

"Uh-oh. You're not going soft on me, are you? I'm not sure I could cope with you being nice."

"Hah! Don't worry, I can still kick your butt anytime."

"In your dreams."

"It's not your butt I'm kicking in my dreams."

A blue sign showing a fish holding an arrow directed them left, towards a glass dome rising above the trees. Fixed to a nearby wall were the words "Tokyo Sea Life Park."

The path led through the admission gate and onto a wide circular plaza, dominated by an enormous octagonal glass-and-steel dome, sitting on pillars. To Kenny, it looked like a cross between a greenhouse and a spaceship. Children's excited voices bounced off the inside, while white-gloved security guards directed visitors towards an escalator leading downward.

Kiyomi stopped and turned back, shivering.

"What's up?" Kenny asked.

"I'm cold," she whispered.

Kenny pulled off his jacket and draped it around her trembling shoulders. "You know, we don't have to do this," he said. "Underground isn't my favorite place either. Not after . . ."

Kiyomi closed her eyes tightly and dug her fingers into Kenny's arms, as if she was in danger of being swept away. She took a deep breath and held it.

"Let's go outside," Kenny said. "We can walk through the park."

"N-no," Kiyomi insisted. "I can do this." She breathed in deeply again. "I'm a warrior. Fear is not real, it's only

101

in my mind." She took long careful breaths, counting each one in and out.

Kenny waited and watched, a frown twisting his eyebrows.

"I'm fine," Kiyomi said, handing Kenny his jacket. "Really. Come on, let's go see the fish. Nice and calm."

The escalator descended into darkness. Kenny felt Kiyomi's hand clutch his with a fierce grip. Blue light rippled against the walls and ceiling, and a shark glided silently past.

They stepped off the escalator into a room where one wall was the transparent front of a huge tank teeming with life. A shoal of sardines shimmered and danced in the sunlight streaking down, while scalloped hammerhead sharks drifted in lazy circles beneath.

"There, that's not so bad, is it?" Kenny whispered.

Kiyomi gave him a weak smile. "Don't forget to take notes. This is homework, remember?"

A party of rowdy schoolchildren led the way down a staircase, past another huge tank, before splitting up to explore lots of smaller displays, representing different seas of the world. Kenny and Kiyomi followed, stopping to admire species as diverse as angelfish, perch, wrasse, sea cucumbers, ratfish, porgy, plaice, butterfly fish and dozens of others.

"That one looks like you," Kiyomi said, pointing to a particularly ugly grouper nosing the glass.

"Very funny," Kenny said. "I'll find your twin in here. He who laughs last –"

"Doesn't get the joke," Kiyomi quipped.

Kenny smiled. It was almost like old times again. He allowed himself a moment of satisfaction; this had been a good idea.

The hallway opened onto a circular room, surrounded on all sides by a huge doughnut-shaped tank, some hundred feet in diameter, which stretched to the ceiling. The schoolchildren pressed against the glass, hypnotized by the sleek silvery shapes inside. Kenny stopped to track the bluefin tuna zipping through the water in a wide circuit, propelled by their small boomerang-shaped tails.

"Hey, Kiyomi," he whispered, "what does *oishii* mean? Everyone keeps saying it, over and over, when they're looking at the fish."

"It means, 'yummy,'" Kiyomi replied with a grin. "Fancy some sushi later?"

The final exhibit was a new attraction: a gigantic tank, bigger than all the others put together and taking up an entire wall. Sky-blue light filtered from the viewing window, making silhouettes of the schoolchildren transfixed by the scene. Inside the tank, two whale sharks crossed paths with giant manta rays, yellowfin tuna, sharks, bonito, barracuda, dolphinfish and many other species.

Kenny tapped on the glass.

"It's acrylic," Kiyomi said, reading from an information card. "Plastic. Two feet thick. This tank holds 7,500 tons of water, about three Olympic-sized swimming pools."

"Wow. That's some serious engineering," Kenny said. Movement caught his attention; something sinewy inside the tank. "Did you see that? Over there, under that rock?"

"Uh-uh. I was watching the shark."

"I think it was a tentacle."

"It was probably just an eel. They're allowed to have them in here, you know."

They stood and watched the seascape play out before their eyes; it was like being at the bottom of the ocean. Fish of all shapes, colors and sizes wove intricate patterns.

Kenny looked away at last. "That's funny," he said. "Everyone else has gone."

"You mean we've got the place to ourselves?" Kiyomi murmured. "How romantic." She raised an eyebrow at Kenny.

Kenny swallowed hard, then scowled, distracted by something. "Wait a minute. I thought Japanese kids were all well behaved and didn't dump litter."

"Yeah? So?"

"Well, some little runt's left a big lump of chewing gum on the glass over there. Look."

Kiyomi saw the fist-sized gray blob stuck to the glass – and a metal tip sticking out of it.

"Kenny, that isn't gum!" she screamed. "It's –"

The plastic explosive detonated with a flash and a

deafening blast. Kenny cried out in pain and clapped his hands to his ears.

A web of cracks crawled across the viewing window – and the plexiglass wall exploded, allowing thousands of tons of water to crash into the room.

13 +三

With no time to think, Kenny raised his hands as if warding off an attacker, eyes tightly shut and breath held, bracing for the impact. Water surged into the room, roaring like breaking surf, bringing with it the dark shapes of struggling sea creatures.

A crushing, cold wetness flowed up Kenny's legs and the force of the current almost swept his feet from under him.

"Kenny!" Kiyomi's voice rose above the thundering tide. "Whatever you're doing, don't stop!"

The lightness of his own body told Kenny that power was coursing through him, but how? He hadn't had time to focus his will, or even to picture any action, yet he was using his *ki*, purely on instinct – to do what?

He opened his eyes and his knees almost buckled. A huge section of tank wall had ruptured and water gushed from the edges – but most of the liquid wavered and shimmered, held back by an invisible barrier of energy emanating from Kenny's outstretched hands.

"What do I do now?" Kenny yelled, fighting down a wave of panic.

"Hold back the water long enough for us to get out," Kiyomi answered. "If we can go up one floor . . ."

"That's not going to work," Kenny said through clenched teeth. "This is getting . . . harder and harder to control. You should go now. Run!"

The force field bowed under the weight of the tide; the top edge curved downward, resembling a giant frozen wave.

"I mean it," Kenny said. "Get out – now!" Blue shadows rippled and churned over his head.

"I'm not leaving you," Kiyomi said, splashing towards him. The water swirled waist deep in the room.

"And you call me stubborn? Go!" The energy barrier continued to bulge inward.

"I won't leave you. You didn't give up on me and –"

Kenny's raised hand was yanked away by something; at the same time, his feet were torn from under him. As he toppled backward, into the flood, his eyes widened in horror; with his concentration broken, the force field collapsed and the full weight of the water came hammering down.

A gun-metal-gray torpedo shape sliced through the water towards him. Kenny caught a nightmarish glimpse of row upon row of serrated teeth set into cotton-candy-pink gums. He summoned Kusanagi to his hand and pulled his arm back to strike the onrushing bull shark – but his arm wouldn't move. Whatever had grabbed hold of him was not letting go.

Kenny twisted and kicked, trying to get out of the shark's way. It was almost upon him when it changed trajectory and, flashing its pale belly, surged past him, in Kiyomi's direction.

More sharks, rays and a host of other fish spilled from the breach. Kenny felt something tighten around his legs and chest. Only his left arm was free and he flailed around, squirming to try and reach the sword in his right hand. In doing so, he saw a long, slender, rust-colored coil unfurl, its underside studded with white disks. It reached up to wrap itself around Kenny's throat. He grabbed for the tentacle, dug his fingers in and pulled hard, bringing his face around to stare into a yellow eye with a horizontal slit pupil.

The giant octopus adjusted its grip, leaned back and maneuvered, bringing the nexus of its legs and body directly above Kenny's face. It was like staring into a strange compass, with knobbly arrows indicating the directions. At the center was a small opening, from which emerged a black, parrot-like beak.

Kenny dared not scream, knowing he would lose what precious little air remained in his lungs, but the more he struggled, the tighter the creature held him. The beak snapped open and shut before it bore down on Kenny's face. He jerked his head away, but with his limbs bound, there was little else he could do. The beak was half an inch from his face. It opened wide.

Silver flashed in the water and the tentacles loosened all at once, falling away from Kenny in slack loops. The saclike body of the octopus floated upward, trailing clouds of blue blood and black ink, while the heavier limbs drifted down. Kiyomi adopted a fighting stance, an empty Pringles can in one hand, her *tanto* short sword in the other. A bubble of air enclosed her head, like an old-fashioned diving helmet, and she pointed upward.

Kenny took a moment to create an air pocket of his own, breathed deeply, then ducked as a large shadow cruised overhead. The bull shark snapped up the dead octopus and sailed on, before something caught its attention. It twisted its head and powered back towards Kenny. He looked down at the cuts and scrapes on his hands from the night before, and remembered something he had read years ago: that a shark could detect one part blood in a million parts water.

The bull shark was well named, barreling through the water with powerful thrusts of its thick tail. Kenny saw its yawning mouth, edged with razor teeth, and brought his sword up to meet the charge.

"Kenny! Look out!" Kiyomi's voice was muffled, but her warning was clear. Kenny kicked to the side, away from the shark – and into the powerful grip of two large hands which grabbed him from behind.

The bull shark whirled away and Kenny cried out as his wrist was wrenched, forcing him to drop the sword.

"Not so tough now, boy?" a voice bellowed in his ear.

Kenny reacted at once. He concentrated for a second; the water around his hands bubbled and hissed to a boil.

"Oww!" the voice yelped, and the hands released their grip.

Kicking backward, Kenny planted his feet against whoever was holding him and pushed away. He rolled in the water and rounded on his attacker. The bull shark continued to circle, watching and waiting for an opportunity to strike.

The creature facing Kenny was almost ten feet tall. It was human in shape, but with thick trunk-like arms and legs, massive shoulders and a sleek, pointed head which sprouted from its chest, with no discernible neck. Its gray sandpaper skin, dull, dead eyes and massive mouth left Kenny in no doubt that it was some kind of shark-*oni*.

It stamped a huge clawed flipper onto the fallen sword and roared a challenge at the boy in its shadow. "Me know you, Kuromori," it rasped. "Without sword, you nothing. Here, in water, you weak, me strong. Now, you die!" It grinned, exposing evil rows of triangular teeth.

"You're forgetting something," Kenny said. "I need air to breathe. You don't." He thrust his hands out, launching a stream of tiny bubbles in the shark-*oni*'s direction.

"Hah! Me not scared of bubbles," the *oni* said, taking a stride towards Kenny.

"Oh, yeah?"

The tiny globules of air clustered around the shark-*oni*'s head and then coalesced into a single large bubble, which slipped down like a wide silvery collar, coming to rest on its shoulders and over its gill slits.

The shark-*oni* gasped and stiffened, its hands clawing at the silvery doughnut of air. "Help!" it wheezed. "Can't . . . breathe . . ."

Spotting an easy kill, the circling bull shark accelerated towards the stricken monster.

"Please . . ." croaked the shark-*oni*, one hand outstretched.

"I've got this!" Kiyomi said, gliding into the path of the shark. It snapped its huge jaws at her, but she twisted away, grabbed hold of its dorsal fin and drove the short sword down into its brain. A plume of blood drifted up like red smoke and the shark slammed into the floor. Kiyomi plunged the sword into its head, again and again.

Kenny recoiled in horror, then remembered the suffocating *oni*. "Who sent you after us?" he asked it. "Last chance."

"They'll . . . kill . . . me . . ." the shark-*oni* pleaded.

"Hello? Isn't that a bit late now?"

The creature nodded and slapped the floor in defeat. "*Ei . . . ein . . . no . . . yo . . .*"

Kenny waved and the large bubble dissipated into froth. The shark-*oni* coughed and spluttered.

"Kiyomi," Kenny called, retrieving his sword. "Kiyomi!"

She seemed not to hear him, her face twisted in fury as she stabbed the *tanto* repeatedly into the dead shark. Kenny swam over and placed a hand on her shoulder. Kiyomi spun around, lashing out with the short sword.

Kusanagi jumped in Kenny's hand, parrying the strike, and sliced through the blade as if it was gossamer. Kiyomi blinked at the stub of handle in her fist and slapped a hand over her mouth to stifle a sob.

"It's OK," Kenny said. "We should get out of here." More sharks were circling, drawn by the scent of fresh blood.

Kenny kicked upward and swam for the surface, passing a majestic whale shark and dodging a manta ray. His head broke the water and he looked up to see a square glass ceiling and, beyond it, the entrance dome.

Minutes later, Kenny and Kiyomi dripped and squelched their way along a curved, tree-lined access road, heading back to the pickup area.

"This is nuts, you know that?" Kenny said, wringing out his hoodie for the third time. "I mean seriously nuts, with the emphasis on serious."

Kiyomi nodded, her eyes fixed on the ground.

"That's twice now, in two days, they've almost killed us," Kenny continued. "Yesterday, it was bombs and bullets. Today, it was the old *oni*-disguised-as-a-schoolboy trick. I mean, come on. They dropped a freaking ocean on us. What does that tell you?"

"Ken-*chan*," Kiyomi said quietly.

"It means something serious is happening, that's what, and they want us out of the way first. These guys have been one step ahead of us –"

"Kenny!"

He stopped, mid-rant. "Yes?"

"It's me. I'm the common link."

"Huh? What do you mean?"

"I've been thinking about it. We came here today for a break, right? And what happens? Only the worst thing imaginable at an aquarium. It's like they're not content just to kill us. They want to subject us to the maximum danger and stress in the process. That way, even if we don't die, they accelerate my . . . my change and they win in another way."

"Wow. I thought I was being paranoid. Why would anyone want you to become . . . a you know?"

"Because it throws us off. If you have to spend all your time preventing me from wreaking havoc, it frees them – whoever *they* are – to do what they want."

Kenny narrowed his eyes and thought about this. "So, if you're right, they're watching us the whole time and keeping us on the back foot, to slow us down and distract us?"

"They've come prepared for us on every occasion."

"True." Kenny trudged on, hands in pockets, his mind turning over the problem. He sighed heavily.

"What's the matter?" Kiyomi asked.

"There is something we can do," Kenny said. "I don't want to do it, but it's the one thing that can get us ahead of these guys."

"Which is?"

"There's someone I need to speak to. Someone who can give us some answers, fast."

14 十四

"Nearly there," Kiyomi said to Kenny, gazing out of the limousine window at the blur of apartment buildings and small shops that lined the stretch of Metropolitan Route 4, more poetically known as Aoume Kaido, or "Green Plum Highway."

"Already?" Kenny twisted around in his seat. "I thought Inari's shrine was in Kyoto. This is . . ." He peered out, looking for a road sign.

"Nishi-Tokyo," Kiyomi said. "The west side. You need to see Inari in a hurry; here we are."

Kenny shook his head. "I don't get it."

"Kyoto is the main shrine, the mother of them all. There are another thirty thousand Inari shrines all across Japan."

"So why are we going to this one?" Kenny checked his watch; they had been driving for an hour. "Isn't there anything closer to the aquarium?"

"In 1929, Inari transferred some of her spirit from Kyoto to this shrine. Think of it as the official Tokyo branch."

"And because Inari's housed here, it's just as good?"

Oyama turned right onto a narrow, unassuming side street. A tall red *torii* gate rose into view and the car pulled up alongside.

"I won't be long," Kenny said, reaching for the door handle.

"Wait, I'm coming with you," Kiyomi said.

"No, I think it's best I do this on my own," Kenny said. "Besides, you might not be too welcome . . . in your current state . . ."

Anger flashed in Kiyomi's eyes before she crossed her arms and slumped back against the leather.

Kenny stepped out and looked up at the *torii* towering above, marking the threshold between the material and the spiritual worlds. He took a deep breath and walked under it, past sculpted bushes and up two flights of stone steps. At the top was a roofed gate, with a guardian fox statue on either side. Each wore a red bib and held in its mouth an object: one a key; the other a jewel.

Past the gate, a long courtyard led to the *honden*, the low building which served as home to the patron deity. Kenny remembered enough etiquette to find the purification stand, and rinsed his hands and mouth as he'd been taught, drawing water with a bamboo ladle. Finally, he approached the barred entrance to the *honden*, bowed twice, clapped twice and bowed once more.

"Hello?" Kenny called. "Anyone home?" He looked around, confirming his suspicion that he was the only visitor. He leaned closer to the entrance, peering past the offering chest into two smoked-glass windows. His reflection squinted back from under the visor of his cupped hands.

"It is customary to cross the hands over the chest before the final bow," a voice said, making Kenny jump. "Perhaps you would care to try again."

An old Japanese man in the vestments of a Shinto priest – white robes, black hat, purple trousers and black shoes – swept an open palm towards the *honden*.

"OK, sure, whatever," Kenny grumbled under his breath. He repeated the supplication, this time crossing his arms.

"My mistress will see you now, Kuromori-*sama*," the priest said. "She has been waiting for you."

The smoked-glass doors opened inward, roiling a thick fog of incense which spilled out over the steps. Kenny shrugged at the priest and stepped into the cloud.

The heady scents of rose, sandalwood, cedar and clove gave way to a fresh autumnal breeze. Birdsong came from all around and Kenny shielded his eyes from bright sunlight in a clear, blue sky. Instead of *tatami*, his feet pressed down on perfectly manicured grass. An ancient, twisted cherry tree spread its boughs overhead and mountain peaks gleamed on all sides.

Straw mats formed a picnic square by the base of the tree, and a woman wearing a dazzling white kimono sat there on her heels, eyes closed, palms resting lightly on her lap.

Kenny faltered and stopped to wipe his face on his damp sleeve and flatten his salt-sticky hair. He was so grubby and disheveled that he felt as conspicuous as chocolate sauce on a wedding dress.

Inari opened her amber eyes. "Kuromori," she said. "You have disappointed me."

"I have?" Kenny squelched closer. "How come? I thought I did pretty good."

Inari blinked slowly. "That is because you are still a child."

Kenny's lips tightened. "See? I knew I'd be getting this. This is why I didn't want to come here."

"Please be seated." Inari busied herself with an iron kettle resting on a charcoal brazier in front of her.

Kenny sat, cross-legged, on the *tatami* and watched the goddess scoop boiling water into an earthenware cup using a bamboo ladle. She rinsed out the cup and then added more hot water to some powdered green tea. She stirred it briskly with a bamboo whisk and presented it to Kenny, all with smooth, controlled movements.

He smiled to himself. "It's funny. The last time I was at a tea ceremony, I was stinking and wet too."

Inari's face betrayed no emotion. "Kuromori, I invited you to be my champion and it was not an ill-considered choice. I know of no one else who would think to suffocate a fish."

Kenny grinned. "It seemed a good idea at the time." He bowed, took the cup in his right hand, set it on his left palm and rotated it clockwise three times before sipping the bitter green froth. He reversed the movements and handed the cup back. "Thank you. I'm more of a PG Tips man myself, but this is good."

Inari sat back on her haunches. "Do you know why I am displeased with you?"

Kenny sighed. "That's easy. Because I messed up and brought Kiyomi back. I violated some big – No? That's not it?"

Inari had shaken her head; it was little more than a flutter. "Try again."

"Because I didn't kill Namazu? I haven't been practicing with Genkuro-*sensei*? Uh . . . I haven't been flossing regularly?"

"You made me a promise: that you would serve me, without fail and without question."

"I remember that," Kenny said quietly.

"You swore to carry out my will in the mortal world, to act with honor, and to place duty before your own needs."

"Yeah, like a knight, or a samurai."

"Yet you have not done this."

"I haven't done that badly. I beat Hachiman, I got the sword, I took on this ridiculously huge dragon . . ."

"You are still so young. Your grandfather was a man and thus much easier to reason with. You are but a child."

118

"Can you lay off with that? I'm fifteen. That's hardly a child."

"Maturity comes in three stages: first the body; then the mind; finally the heart." Inari took a deep breath and let it out slowly. "Kuromori, many of my brethren think me foolish for placing so much trust in a *gaijin*. They feel you are arrogant, impetuous and ill-disciplined."

Kenny rubbed his brow. "Well, nobody's perfect. I get the job done."

"Indeed. I tell them that these things are true, that you are stubborn, impulsive and proud, but you are also brave, resourceful and you have *gaman* – persistence, endurance. That same resolve which means you will never surrender, whatever the odds, is both your greatest strength and your greatest weakness."

"How can that be?"

"If you insist you are right when others think you wrong, it is a strength – provided you are correct. Do you know why the Harashima girl was meant to die?"

"Huh?" The sudden change of direction caught Kenny by surprise.

"To free you. Your soul is divided. Where you should serve me, your heart longs for her. Kiyomi's presence holds you back and keeps you from becoming a true warrior."

Kenny flushed scarlet, first with embarrassment, then with annoyance. "Wait. You said before that I had to let go of the past, to forgive in order to heal . . . and that . . . feelings were part of that."

"I did, and that took you to the next step. But you were also to let go of these things, lest they hold you back and be turned against you."

"You're saying that Kiyomi was meant to die so I could go on and become this super warrior of yours – and that I messed it up by bringing her back?"

Inari's beautiful face remained impassive.

"That's nuts!" Kenny exclaimed. "You said I had a choice: to accept fate or to change it. What if I don't want to be what you want me to be? Did you think of that?"

"Kuromori, we can but delay our fates. Kiyomi is still slipping away, is she not? And that is the only reason you have remembered me: because you desire my help. It is not duty that has brought you here today, but your feelings for the girl."

"She's a friend. And I owe her my life. That's all it is. I pay my debts."

Inari's gaze lingered over Kenny. "You know I can see your thoughts."

Kenny reddened again. "So help me. It's the least you can do. I saved millions of lives for you when I stopped Namazu. Doesn't that count for anything?"

"You care for the girl so much that you would bargain for her life?"

"Read my mind and you know I'd trade my life for hers. How badly do you need me?"

Inari smiled. "The young are so full of passion. It is . . . refreshing. Very well. You will resume your service to me and, in return, I will tell you how to save Kiyomi."

"Really? You know . . .? OK. Yes, you have my word. Thank you. What do I have to do?"

"Hachiman is not the only one with a grudge, or the followers to exact revenge for a perceived slight. We gods have long memories and time holds no sway over us."

"Meaning that if it takes a thousand years to get even, that's nothing?"

"That is so. I foresee a time of darkness coming to us all, and have reason to believe that a scheme is already under way that will end all life on these islands."

Kenny sat up. "They'd hurt Japan?"

"A person in pain will lash out, even at loved ones. For some, it is preferable to destroy that which they cannot possess."

"Is that what this *oni* business is about?"

"You must travel to Mount Chikurinji in Okayama. There is another star-watching instrument there, larger and more powerful than the one you destroyed. An attempt will be made to steal that one as well. You must stop them."

"Why? What do they want with a telescope?" Kenny asked.

"I do not know, but it is important to them. That is reason enough to prevent their having it."

Kenny nodded. "All right. Now, about Kiyomi?"

"You must understand what you did. Kiyomi died, from injuries caused by the *ushi-oni*. Her spirit, her soul, her *ki* left her body and began the journey to Yomi, the Land of the Dead. But, before her essence had fully arrived, you drew some of it back and used the soul of an *oni* to make up the rest. The *oni* spirit is stronger than that of a human, so it is taking control."

"What can I do to stop it?"

"You would need to find the missing part of Kiyomi's spirit and restore it to her body."

"And her soul would be in Yomi?"

Inari raised a hand in warning. "Beware, young Kuromori. My brother, Susano-wo, rules the underworld and he is to be feared."

"His name is Susan? You're kidding me."

"Listen to me, Kuromori. Susano-wo is not only among the most powerful of the gods, but he is also cunning, unpredictable and insane. He is not to be trusted."

"How bad can he be?"

"He commands storms, slays dragons for amusement, and once he skinned a horse and threw the bloodied corpse into his elder sister's house."

"That's bad."

"Put aside any thoughts of bargaining with Susano-wo for Kiyomi. No good will come of it. You have delayed the girl's fate, but you have not changed it. Go now to Mount Chikurinji and do your sworn duty."

Kenny bit his lip and nodded. "One last question. The shark-*oni* said something to me, when I asked who had sent him. He said, '*Eiein no yo.*' Does that mean anything?"

Inari pondered this for a moment. "The correct translation would depend on the context, but it could mean 'forever world,' 'eternal night' or even 'the everlasting four.'"

"That's no help. Is it the name of an organization, or a clan or something? A code word?"

"I do not know, but whoever it is, they want you dead."

15 十五

"How far is it to Okayama?" was Kenny's first question when he jumped back into the limousine and slammed the door.

Kiyomi raised her head, killing the music on her phone and unplugging the earbuds. "Okayama? That's in Chugoku, about four hundred miles away. Why?"

"Inari wants me to go there. Something about another telescope."

Oyama started the engine and the car pulled out.

"Really?" Kiyomi's fingers fluttered over the touch screen on her phone. "Found it. The Okayama Astrophysical Observatory, up on Mount Chikurinji. That the one?"

Kenny nodded. "Yeah, she said the *oni* were going to try again."

Kiyomi continued reading the web page. "72-inch telescope, largest in Japan –"

"Six feet? That's tiny," Kenny scoffed.

Kiyomi rolled her eyes. "That's the lens size, you dummy. The telescope is thirty feet long and weighs fifty tons. They're going to need a lot of *oni* to get that out, and it won't be easy at twelve hundred feet above sea level."

"That's to avoid light pollution?"

"Yep. Clearer skies, thinner air, better view of the stars. Did Inari tell you why they want it?"

Kenny shook his head. "No, only that it must be important to them if they're going to all this trouble."

"Kuromori-*san*, I am very disappointed in you," Harashima said, hands clasped behind his back. He was facing the bank of television screens in his office, all set on mute but showing chaotic scenes of emergency services rushing to the Sea Life Park. "You promised me that a visit to the aquarium would be a calming, relaxed day out. Instead, we have international news coverage, again reporting terrorists loose in Tokyo. What were you thinking?"

"Sir, it wasn't my fault," Kenny protested. "It was a trap. We were followed and someone blew open a fish tank. It got messy."

Kiyomi came in, a deep-red, half-chewed hunk of raw steak in her hands.

"Kiyomi-*chan*, must you do that?" her father said.

"Sorry, should I get a plate?" Kiyomi said, tearing off a fresh bite.

"You see? This is what you have done," Harashima muttered to Kenny.

"Don't blame him, Papa," Kiyomi said. "Ken-*chan*'s doing his best."

Harashima's mouth twisted like he was sucking a pickled plum. "Is that so? Kuromori-*san*, what is the scientific name for the giant Pacific octopus?"

"Uh . . ."

"Come on, Papa, everyone knows it's *enteroctopus dofleini*," Kiyomi said. "Ask another one."

Once the rebuke was over, Kiyomi accompanied Kenny out onto the front driveway.

"Thanks to you, I'm grounded," she said. "Virtual house arrest – for my own good, of course."

Kenny sighed. "You know the story of King Midas?"

"The dude who turned everything into gold?"

"Yeah. I'm the reverse Midas. Everything I touch turns to poop."

Kiyomi laughed. "We could probably get you a job at a fertilizer plant. That should keep you out of trouble."

"I don't know. You have some seriously weird monsters in this place. Are you sure a giant poop isn't one of them?"

"Not that I know of. Although if there is one, I'm sure you'll be the first to find it."

Kenny's smile faded. "If you're grounded, how are you going to come to Okayama with me?"

Kiyomi shook her head. "I'm not. Papa's sending my uncle with you."

"Sato?"

"Yep. He's supposed to keep you on track, make sure

you do your duty."

"Is that how it works? I go from being their secret weapon in this war to just another pet monkey? That didn't take long."

"Ken-*chan*, it's not like that."

"Maybe not, but it sure feels like it." Kenny kicked at the gravel. "When can I . . .?" He coughed and cleared his throat. "Uh, you and me . . . should, er, hang out again sometime. Soon. When would be good for you?"

Kiyomi cocked her head and looked quizzically at Kenny. "Mr. Blackwood, are you asking me out?"

"No, I didn't – Well, not exactly . . . it's just, uh . . . we work well, as a team, you know, like mixed doubles in tennis."

"You're asking me to play tennis?" Kiyomi sounded annoyed.

"Never mind. I'll call you. I'm allowed to do that, right?"

"What makes you think I'll pick up?" And with that, Kiyomi turned on her heel and stamped back into the house.

"Now what have I done?" Kenny said, glaring up at the afternoon sky.

The limousine scrunched to a stop beside him and Oyama opened the passenger door.

"All right, all right, I can take a hint," Kenny grumbled and climbed in.

*

Half an hour later, Oyama deposited him on Honan Dori and Kenny trudged the remaining distance to his apartment building. He pushed open the glass doors and was halfway across the lobby when someone called his name.

"Kenny! I knew it."

"Huh?" He spun around to be confronted by Stacey Turner, his cheerleading classmate. She was clutching a pile of textbooks and chewing gum furiously.

"Ooh, you're a naughty boy," she said. "But that's OK, I like bad boys." She winked at him. "Apparently, you're off sick today, but when no one phoned in I figured you were cutting class." She arched an eyebrow at him. "Well?"

Kenny shook his head to clear it. "Stacey? Wh-what are you doing here? How do you know where –"

"I'm not stupid. I went to the office, offered to bring you your homework, so you wouldn't fall behind, and they were so grateful that they gave me your address. Here." She held out the stack of books, all neatly marked with color-coordinated Post-it notes.

Kenny took the pile, still dumbstruck.

"Here's where you say, 'Thank you, you're such a good friend, bringing me my homework.'" Stacey blew a pink bubble while she waited.

"Uh, this isn't a good time," Kenny mumbled.

"That'll do. You're welcome. So, what's the hurry? Your girlfriend coming around?"

"What? I don't have a girlfriend."

The eyebrow went up again. "Oh, silly me. So when you ran off yesterday, that was a *taxi* waiting for you. With two wheels, tight leather and a fat butt."

"Hey, Kiyomi doesn't have a fat b–"

"Gotcha! She has a name, you're defending her and you've checked her out."

"Stacey, what is this about?"

Stacey pulled a rolled up newspaper from the back pocket of her jeans and brandished the front page like a wanted poster. "This! I know this is you, so don't try denying it."

Kenny took the Japanese newspaper with its jumble of text and pictures. He was unable to read any of it, but the grainy CCTV picture of a sandy-haired boy running through smoke in soccer gear was hard to miss.

Stacey blew another bubble in triumph, then wrinkled her nose. "Ooh, you need a shower. You smell like . . ." Her eyes widened and she took a step back. "The aquarium today! That was you as well."

Kenny looked around to check that no one else was in the lobby. "Stacey, listen to me. You mustn't tell anyone anything."

"Let me guess: or my life will be in great danger? You're such a jerk. Like I'm going to fall for that. I thought you'd get enough attention around here just for being a blond *gaijin* without having to lay on the whole secret agent routine. Boys are such dogs."

"I haven't done anything! Why are you picking on me like this?"

"I'm not picking on you. I'm just . . . curious. I saw the news last night and I thought a fire at the observatory was a bit weird, what with it being near the school, and then when they mentioned a mystery kid in soccer gear . . ."

"It's not me," Kenny said, fixing his eyes on the marble floor.

"Uh-uhh!" Stacey tut-tutted and waved a finger at him. "I went online, pulled up all the news pics, ran them through Photoshop to clean them up and that's definitely a Newcastle United logo on the front of the shirt. How many of those are you going to find in Tokyo?"

Kenny's shoulders slumped in defeat. "What is it you want?"

Stacey arched her eyebrows. "Kenny! That is so . . . rude. I don't want anything. I'd just like to get to know you a little better, that's all. Come on, you have to admit it is unusual and it certainly livens things up a bit."

"Believe me, you're better off not knowing. For your own good."

"My choice. I can take it."

Kenny clenched his jaw. "I'd like to say thank you for stopping by, but . . ."

"You're honest. I like that." Stacey patted him on the cheek. "So I'll see you in school tomorrow. We can talk some more then."

"Wait." Kenny remembered his manners. "Are you

going to be OK heading back? Do you want me to walk you to the station or anything?"

"Aw, that's sweet. Such an English gentleman, but I'll be fine. I've been in Tokyo for six years now. I can take care of myself." She patted her backpack.

"OK . . . but be careful anyway." Kenny watched Stacey leave, then turned to the elevators. He barely had time to press the button before a girl's scream from outside pierced the air.

Kenny dropped his books and ran for the door.

16 十六

Kenny shoulder-charged the glass door while summoning Kusanagi to hand.

The screaming came from a side street around the corner and he dashed towards the sound – to be greeted by howls of laughter as Stacey doubled over, clutching her sides.

"Oh, the look . . . on your face . . . !" she gasped between guffaws. "Priceless! I knew it . . ." Her eyes grew wide. "Wow, cool sword. Where were you hiding that – up your butt?" She collapsed again in a fit of giggles.

"This is not funny!" Kenny hissed, dismissing the sword. His face and ears were burning.

"Ooh, wook at the gwumpy face," Stacey spluttered. "So it's true. You are some kind of superhero dude? Hey, where'd the sword go? You were holding a *katana* a moment ago."

"I thought you were in trouble," Kenny muttered. "Thanks for nothing." He turned on his heel.

"Wait! Kenny! I was only messing with you. Jeez.

Talk about a sense of humor failure."

The side street was narrow, with a pair of vending machines on the corner, one selling cans of coffee, the other dispensing alcohol. Kenny was striding back towards the lobby door when the thrum of a powerful car engine made him stop and turn. A sleek lipstick-red Lamborghini convertible slid to a stop beside him. The top was down and two young women waved to him. The passenger was wearing a white surgical mask to filter pollen and she held up a Tokyo street map.

"*Sumimasen*," said the driver, beckoning Kenny over.

"You've got to be kidding me," Stacey said.

The driver climbed out of the bucket seat, flashing a long slender expanse of thigh. She wore a black leather jacket, micro-miniskirt and designer shades. Her thick glossy hair was so long it almost swept the floor.

"*Mayotte shimaimashita*," she said to Kenny. "*Nihon daigaku e no michi o shitte imasu ka?*"

Kenny stopped staring, swallowed hard and looked to Stacey for help.

"She's lost," Stacey said, her fists on her hips. "When you're done salivating, she wants to know how to find Nihon University."

The passenger climbed out and slunk over on dangerously high heels. She was dressed in a similar manner to the driver and could have been her sister. She held out the map.

"Uh-buh-duh," Kenny burbled. "I, uh . . . ahem." He pulled at his T-shirt collar. "*Gomen nasai. Nihongo o wakarimasen.*"

The two women looked at each other and giggled.

"*Kawaii, da ne?*" the driver said to her friend.

Stacey mimed putting two fingers down her throat. "Oh, please. This is ridiculous." She took a step closer. "Hello? *Nihongo o hanashimasu. Tasukeru koto ga dekiru?*"

The Japanese girls pointedly ignored her offer of help. Kenny backed up a step and felt the glass door behind him. Both of the women were stunning and he felt seriously out of his depth.

The one wearing the mask tugged playfully at the elastic behind her ears. "*Watashi . . . kirei?*" she asked in a teasing voice.

"Great. First they think you're cute. Now she's asking if you think she's beautiful," Stacey translated. "What am I? Chopped liver?"

"What do I tell her?" Kenny said, bewildered.

"How do I know? You can't even see her face," Stacey said.

"*Kao o mitai?*" the masked lady purred again.

"Do you want to see her face?" Stacey said, pulling on her backpack.

"Uh, OK," Kenny said.

Long-nailed fingers whipped the face mask away and it was Kenny's turn to scream. Where the woman's mouth should have been was a raw, gaping slash stretching from ear to ear. Jagged, triangular teeth filled the gash and a long serpentine tongue flickered back and forth.

In that same blood-chilling moment, the driver's luxuriously long hair sprang to life, snaking up in prehensile coils to twist and spiral around Kenny's arms, legs and throat. The color drained from Stacey's face.

"*Glkkk!*" Kenny gurgled, unable to speak as the lashing whips of hair tightened around his neck.

The slit-mouthed woman reached out, taking his face in her hands, and moved in, as if for a kiss. Spots danced before Kenny's eyes and his head felt light. He knew he had to focus, to channel his *ki*, but he was about to faint. The ragged teeth drew closer and the mouth opened impossibly wide.

"Kenny! Close your eyes!" Stacey yelled.

Kenny screwed his eyes shut, heard the sound of running feet, a *pfft-pfft* squirting sound and shrieks of agony rang out.

"*AAAAAAHHH! Itai! Itai! Me ga itai!*"

Kenny felt a few scattered drops touch his face and his skin burned as if scalded. The tresses around his throat loosened and he sucked in a chestful of air.

"Back off, sister! I'm warning you," Stacey said.

Kenny opened his streaming eyes and saw Slit Face stumbling along the sidewalk, her hands clamped to her face and bawling in pain. Her companion was advancing on Stacey, who was brandishing a small deodorant-sized canister. The woman's hair moved constantly, undulating as if under water. It fanned out and clumped into long whiplike tails.

"*Tomare*," was Stacey's final warning.

Whip Hair smiled and a coil of hair reached up to remove her sunglasses, revealing eyes as black and dead as those of a shark. Stacey gave an involuntary shudder and, in that instant, the treacherous locks of hair shot out, curling around the girl's wrist and tearing the container from her grasp.

Kenny wiped his eyes and sprang into action as he saw the ends of the hair solidify into wicked, needle-shaped points.

"*Ima, shine!*" Whip Hair cried and the stiletto points pulled back, ready to strike like a dozen arrows.

"No!" Kenny yelled, throwing his sword like a spear.

With lightning speed, the snakelike tendrils of hair reacted, adjusting direction to pluck Kusanagi from the air.

"Oh, crap," Kenny said.

Whip Hair smiled and turned to face him, with one lock of hair aiming the aerosol at him and another wielding the sword.

"Stacey, run!" Kenny said. "I'll slow her down."

"Not if she nails you with pepper spray," Stacey said, rummaging through her backpack. "Here, use this." She tossed Kenny a can of ultra-hold hairspray.

He reached out, but another tentacle of hair lashed out and intercepted the can.

"Hey! No fair!" said Stacey.

"Stay out of range," Kenny said, circling Whip Hair, an arm raised to shield his eyes. She lashed out with the sword and he jumped backward.

A scream and a muffled thump came from Slit Face as she bumped into the sports car and fell into the passenger seat.

Kenny racked his brain, quickly running through his limited range of options. He had some control over the elements – air, water, fire, earth and metal – but Kusanagi could cut through anything he might summon.

"Quick," Kenny said, keeping his distance. "Throw me something else."

"Huh? OK. Catch." Stacey hauled out a heavy math textbook and lobbed it in Kenny's direction. A loop of hair grabbed the book, bending under the weight.

"Perfect," Kenny said. He concentrated on the book.

It burst into flame, toasting the hair around it. With a shriek of alarm, Whip Hair flung down everything she was holding and beat her smoking hair against the ground to extinguish the flames. Kenny moved in, holding his breath to avoid the stench of burning hair. He kicked the hairspray across to Stacey and retrieved his sword. Stacey snatched up the spray can, took aim and sent a heavy mist in Whip Hair's direction. The hair immediately began to clump together in sticky lumps.

"*Nandayo?*" the woman wailed.

Kenny grabbed a burning page of algebra and touched it to the nearest trailing lock. *WHOOF!* It ignited instantly and Whip Hair screamed as flames engulfed her head. Kenny waited a few seconds before sending a blast of wind to extinguish the fire and clear the air of roiling smoke.

Whip Hair gingerly patted her hands over her smoldering scalp, which was now bald and patchy. "*Kami ga nai!*" she gasped in horror.

Kenny leveled the sword at her, touching it against the monster's throat. "Get out of here," he said, "and tell whoever sent you that I got the message."

Whip Hair nodded, hobbled to the Lamborghini and drove off, with Slit Face's legs kicking up from the passenger seat.

"You owe me a copy of *Advanced Calculus*," Stacey said, gathering up her things. "What was *that* about?"

Kenny picked up the charred textbook. "It's a long story."

Stacey folded her arms and sighed. "That was a *harionago* and the *kuchisake onna*," she said. "They're both *yokai*. My question is, why are they after you?"

Kenny gaped. "How do you know –?"

Stacey rolled her eyes. "Oh, please. Give me credit for having a brain, will you? I'm half-Japanese. We grow up with these stories. I've just never seen one until now, and they were definitely after you, not me. By the way, you're welcome."

"Huh?"

"In case you didn't notice, hero boy, I just saved your butt."

"I wouldn't have had any problem if you hadn't faked being attacked, remember? I was minding my own business."

"Where's that sword gone?"

"Look, I'm kind of Public Enemy Number One for these . . . things, OK? I can see them, even when they don't want to be seen, and they really hate that. I attract them. I'm a magnet for freaks and that's why you're better off not getting too close to me, all right?"

Stacey tilted her head and watched Kenny. "That's funny. I'm hearing brave words, but what I'm seeing is someone who looks totally lost and could use a friend."

"Stacey, you're probably right, since you're almost always right, but here's the thing: I don't want you as a friend," Kenny said. "You should go home now and forget everything you just saw."

A glare of pure venom shot from Stacey's eyes. "Why don't you just go to Hell?" she said, and stormed off towards the subway station.

"I'm already halfway there," Kenny muttered under his breath.

17 十七

Kenny kicked his smelly sneakers off and padded into the living room.

"School just called," Charles said, looking up from his desk. "Said you were absent."

"What did you tell them?" Kenny replied, reaching for the cookie jar.

Charles pushed back his chair and wandered over. "I said that you'd woken up with a temperature and I was keeping you at home. You could at least have sent me a text."

Kenny took a large bite out of a chocolate chip cookie. "Dad, are you disappointed in me?"

Charles smiled and shook his head. "No, son. I know you well enough by now." He leaned over and sniffed Kenny's hair. "How was the aquarium?"

"Let's just say it's put me off sushi for a while. What are they saying on the news?"

"Two terrorist incidents in two days has everyone on edge."

Kenny dusted the crumbs off his hands. "What's for supper?"

"How about *okonomiyaki*?"

"OK."

"You'll need to set three plates, though."

"Who's coming over?"

"You left the balcony doors unlocked, didn't you?"

"Oh, no."

"He's in your room."

Kenny yanked open his bedroom door, expecting the worst. He wasn't wrong.

Drawers were pulled open, clothes tipped out, books scattered and, in the middle of the mess, was Poyo, lying back on Kenny's futon, legs crossed and leafing through a copy of *Sports Illustrated*.

Kenny stormed in and snatched the magazine away. "You great, fat, useless lump!" he said. "I'm down there fighting these creatures and you're just lounging around, going through my stuff!"

Poyo spread his arms and shrugged.

"Why didn't you help me out?" Kenny demanded.

Poyo reached a paw around, wriggled and extracted a bamboo whistle.

"Eww. Do I want to know where you've been hiding that?" Kenny said.

The *tanuki* grinned and shook his head.

BZZZT! Kenny checked his smartwatch. The message read: WILL COLLECT YOU TOMORROW AT 09:00 SHARP FOR TRAVEL TO OKAYAMA. BE READY. SATO.

"Great," Kenny muttered. "All right, you," he said to Poyo, "I'm going for a shower. When I get back, you and me are going to have some words. Until then, clean this mess up."

Poyo sat up on his haunches, saluted with a furry paw and then toppled backward.

It took Kenny twenty minutes of scrubbing before he finally got the smell of aquarium water off his skin. He looked in the mirror, checking for pimples, and noted the bluish finger marks on his throat. He was still covered in cuts, scrapes and bruises, but he felt a lot better now that he was clean.

Back in his room, Poyo had tidied everything away.

"So you can do it when you want to," Kenny said, pulling on a pair of sweatpants and a hoodie. The smell of frying food wafted in from the kitchen and his stomach rumbled. He sat down on a beanbag and gestured for Poyo to sit opposite him.

"I've been thinking," Kenny said. "About how to save Kiyomi. You know she's sick, right?"

Poyo flopped down with a whimper and covered his head with his paws.

"Well, I know how to make her better, but I want to know what you think, OK?"

The *tanuki* sat up again.

"Part of her soul is in Yomi – Hell, if you like. And this Susan guy is in charge. So, what if we go the direct route, use Kusanagi to open a sort of doorway and drop in for a chat? That sound like a plan?"

Poyo swung his puffy head from side to side, emphatically signaling no.

"Too dangerous? Do you have any better ideas?"

The furry creature nodded and waddled over to a notebook, taking a marker pen in his chubby fist. Kenny waited for Poyo to finish his labored scribbling. When he was done, he thrust the page towards Kenny.

"What's this? A banana and a manta ray?"

Poyo slapped a paw over his face.

"Oh, wait, I get it. The Japanese mainland. Four islands, and you've marked this one. That's by the inland sea, halfway between Kyoto and Usa. What's there?"

Poyo took the pad and drew two horizontal parallel lines with vertical legs and a sketch of a demon beside a house.

Kenny studied the picture. "A *torii* gate. This is a shrine, to Susie, is that what you're saying? He's in the *honden*?"

Poyo nodded, hopping from foot to foot.

"So if we can talk to him there, we can try and save Kiyomi?"

Poyo held up a paw for a high five.

*

After supper, Kenny sat down at the computer, went online and began writing train times and directions in a notebook.

"How can that be checkmate?" Charles said, his finger hovering over the chessboard. "Oh, I see it now. A disguised fork. Very good. You win."

Poyo grinned and helped himself to some more chips.

Charles stretched and checked his phone for messages. "Ah! Kenny, you remember that silver *oni* you asked me about?" he said. "I put a query out across the faculty and Professor Yoshihara's just come back to me."

Kenny set his pen down.

"He's not sure," Charles said, reading the message, "but he thinks there's a silver *oni* mentioned in an obscure 762 AD telling of the *Taketori Monogatari*."

"What? That's nearly . . . thirteen hundred years ago."

"Yes. Do you know the story?"

"No."

"It's fascinating. It's both an analog to the Western tale of *Thumbelina* and an early work of science fiction." Charles slipped into lecture mode. "I'm going from memory here, but it's about an old bamboo cutter who finds a glowing stalk. He cuts it open and inside is a baby girl, no larger than his thumb. He and his wife are childless, so he takes the baby home and they raise her as their own. Over time, she grows into a beautiful woman of normal size."

Charles went to the fridge, continuing his seminar.

"Word of her extraordinary beauty spreads far and wide, and five princes wish to marry her. Since she doesn't want to wed any of them, she sets them each an impossible task, knowing they will fail. When none of them proves up to the mark, she's left to live in peace with her ageing parents."

He took out a jug of iced tea and poured himself a glass.

"The story's third act sees the girl weeping at the sight of the full moon. It turns out that she's the daughter of the Moon God, sent to Earth for safety during a rebellion. With the war over, her father is sending a royal entourage to bring her home."

"So, why is she crying?" Kenny asked.

"She's lived twenty years on Earth with her adoptive parents and this is the only life she knows." Charles took a sip of tea before continuing. "There's a subplot with the Emperor falling in love with her, but I'll skip that. On the next full moon, a bridge appears, from the moon to Earth, and an army of silver warriors comes to escort the princess home to Tsuki-no-Miyako, the moon's capital. She drinks a magical potion and dons a white feather robe, which erases all memory of her life on Earth. She is taken up into the heavens, leaving her heartbroken parents behind. The end."

"Wow, that's really uplifting. Not," Kenny said. "So where does the *oni* fit in?"

"Yoshihara-*sensei* thinks he recalls mention of a silver

oni among the Moon God's loyal troops, but it could be a misreading of the *kanji*. Is that any help?"

Kenny rubbed his eyes and closed his notebook. "Not really, but thanks anyway."

Charles rinsed his empty glass in the sink. "I see you've packed a bag for tomorrow. I know you can't give me details, but how dangerous is it likely to be?"

"On a scale of one to ten? Come on, Dad. It doesn't work that way. Besides, I'll have Sato with me, so I'll be fine."

"Really? Sato-*san*'s made all the arrangements, which is why you've been checking *Shinkansen* departure times?"

"Look, Dad –"

"No, don't 'look, Dad' me," Charles said, drying his hands on a dish towel. "If I'm going to trust you to go off on your own, then you're going to have to trust me too."

"Dad, you can't stop me going . . ."

Charles hurled the towel onto the counter. "This isn't about that! This is about you being my son and me having a right to know where you are, in case –"

"I'm going to Matsue."

"Shimane Prefecture? Why?"

"I have to talk to someone there."

"Who?"

"I'd rather not say."

"And when will you be back?"

"Should be same day; it's a simple trip. I have to

do this, Dad, to save Kiyomi. If I don't, then she'll be as gone as Mum, and it'll be my fault."

Charles came over and wrapped his arms around Kenny's shoulders. "OK. Just make sure you call me."

Kenny nodded against his father's chest. "Dad, this might not even work, but I have to try. If I don't . . . she'd be better off dead."

18 十八

Across the moat from the Imperial Palace, on the east side of Hibiya Park, towered Central Government Office Building Number 6, the headquarters of the Public Security Intelligence Agency, otherwise known as the Japanese Secret Service.

Sato rapped on the door of a basement laboratory and hurried in. The team of white-coated technicians all snapped to attention. Sato motioned for them to stand clear of the stainless steel tables around which they were gathered and the pallid body of a huge white crocodile loomed into view.

"Suzuki-*san*," Sato said. "Report, please."

A small, balding, bespectacled man bowed, the bright lights reflecting off his head. "This way, please."

The crocodile lay on its back, its stark white underbelly scored by a deep cut from throat to tail.

Suzuki indicated side tables laden with overflowing metal bowls containing bright red viscera and entrails. "As you can see, we have removed, measured and weighed the primary organs," Suzuki said. "Everything is normal, apart from the size. Truly, this was a magnificent specimen."

"Normal, you say?" Sato turned back to the corpse, a sour expression on his face. "I see nothing normal about a twenty-five-foot-long, giant saltwater crocodile in a Tokyo sewer." He held out both hands, palms down, a few inches above the smooth scales. With slow and deliberate steps, Sato circled the carcass, keeping his hands in position. He moved down the body to the tail and back up again. When he reached the head, he paused, frowned and began tracing complicated patterns in the air.

One of the technicians looking on sniggered. Suzuki silenced him with a glare.

Sato brought his face so close to the gaping hole in the creature's head that his nose touched the cold, dead flesh. "Forceps," he said, holding out a hand.

Suzuki hurried over with the implement. "There was so little brain tissue left . . ." he said, wondering what he had missed.

Taking the long-nose tweezers, Sato reached in under the jaw and into the cranial cavity. He closed the grip and tugged gently.

Suzuki gasped as Sato retrieved a flat, metal disk, with microscopic wires attached. "What is that?" he asked.

"Part of a neural interface," Sato said, half to himself. "One of Akamatsu's earlier experiments, no doubt. Kiyomi was right. It was a trap."

*

Kenny had set his alarm for 6:00 a.m. He woke up, crawled out of his futon and got dressed quickly.

"You're up early," his father observed when Kenny tiptoed into the kitchen. "You must be really keen to avoid Sato-*san*."

Kenny went to a cupboard, took out a box of cereal and poured out two bowls of muesli. He set one down on the floor, poured milk into the other and sat at the counter, spoon in hand.

Charles finished his coffee and toast, ruffled Kenny's hair and set off for work. "Remember to call," he said, pulling on his shoes. "I've left you some money in an envelope by the toaster. Be careful, OK?"

"Sure, Dad," Kenny said between crunches.

"I mean it." The door closed and Poyo waddled in to sniff at the cereal set out for him. He made a retching sound and pushed the bowl away.

"Just because Kiyomi's too soft to put you on a diet doesn't mean I won't," Kenny warned.

TAP-TAP came a knock on the front door. Kenny and Poyo exchanged wary looks.

"Who is it?" Kenny called.

"Domino's Pizza," said a girl's voice.

Kenny looked through the peephole in the door. "Stacey? Go away."

"Sorry. Should I have said Pizza Hut, instead?"

"I don't care if you said Santa Claus. Get lost."

"Let me in, or I'll sing the national anthem right here in this corridor. I'm sure your neighbors would love that."

Kenny opened the door, glared at Stacey and stabbed a finger in the direction of the living room.

Stacey went inside. "This is a nice place you have. Do you live here with your – wow, that is one fat, ugly *tanuki*. Are you allowed to keep that in here? Is it even hygienic?"

Kenny scowled. "Stacey, this is Poyo. Poyo, Stacey. Don't look at me like that, she's a classmate."

Poyo stuck out a paw in greeting, which Stacey ignored.

"Is that your pet?" she went on. "No, wait, he's your sidekick, right? Robin to your Batman."

"What are you doing here? I thought you were mad at me, like everyone else."

Stacey waved a hand, as if shooing a fly. "That was yesterday. I've had some time to think about what happened and it's amazing that I'm not suffering some kind of post-traumatic stress episode."

"I'm really not interested," Kenny said, putting his empty bowl in the sink.

"I had a dream last night saying that I should help you."

"Really?"

"No. Would it matter? I brought you breakfast," Stacey said, pulling a Mister Donut bag out of her pack. "Call it a peace offering."

"I just ate."

Poyo whimpered and reared up on his hind legs, snatching at the bag. Stacey whisked it away, out of his reach.

"Come on, there's even a *Hello Kitty* one in there, with a pink bow," she said. "No? OK. Listen, all my life I've heard stories about *yokai* and, until yesterday, I didn't think any of that was real. Then you come along and they're crawling out of the woodwork. Do you have any idea how amazing that is?"

Kenny stared for a moment. "You're out of your mind."

"Are you kidding? Imagine what would happen if someone found the actual Loch Ness Monster. It'd be worldwide media carnage."

Kenny glanced at his watch. "I have to go."

"To school? Cool, I'll walk with you." Stacey set the doughnut bag on the counter.

"No," said Kenny. "Not to school." He ducked into his room and grabbed his backpack.

"Ooh. You're cutting class again." Stacey made a quick decision. "OK. So where are we heading?"

"There is no 'we.' You are going to school and I'm going . . . somewhere else."

"But wait. I can help you. Yesterday, for instance, I –"
"No."

"You don't even speak Japanese. How are you going to –?"

"No."

"I'll tell everyone . . . about you."

Kenny took a deep breath and counted to ten. "No, Stacey," he said in a quiet, resigned voice. "No, you won't, because if any of those things out there think they can use you to get at me, they will find you, and they will kill you, and it will be slower and more hideous than anything you can imagine."

"I don't believe you."

"You saw those things yesterday. They're nothing compared to what's out there."

Poyo crept silently backward, rounded the corner of the kitchenette and stretched up a paw. His arm slowly elongated, stretching like toffee.

"Stacey, do you want to help me. Really help me?" Kenny asked, resting a hand on her shoulder.

Stacey nodded. "If I can."

"Then go to school and run interference for me. If anyone asks, tell them I'm ill. Say I've got tonsillitis. Tell them anything, just cover for me. Can you do that? Please?"

Stacey tightened her lips. "On one condition: that when you come back to class you tell me what this is all about."

"Deal."

Poyo's little hand closed stealthily on the paper bag of doughnuts and he lifted it off the counter.

Four hours later, Kenny switched off his iPod and took out the earbuds. He straightened up and yawned. Multi-colored fields and hills shot past the *Shinkansen* window.

He had traveled to Shin-Osaka and then transferred to the Sanyo bullet train, which was taking him to Okayama. From there, a local Yakumo express would go to Matsue and a cab would complete the journey to the Kumano Taisha, the main shrine of the dreaded Susano-wo.

Kenny zipped open his pack and took out a copy of *The Japan Times*, the English language newspaper he'd bought in Osaka. The front page was dominated by the upcoming launch of the solar reflector, but he flipped quickly through until he found the Tokyo aquarium story.

The official version was that a minor earth tremor had weakened the seal between two acrylic panels to the extent that it had suddenly given way. Authorities were keen to stress that it was an accident and that no foul play was suspected.

Kenny smirked. Sato was doing a good job of keeping the media at bay. He opened a package of peanut butter M&M's.

At the sound of the wrapper tearing, a furry nose poked out from under the seat and Poyo squeezed himself into the adjacent chair.

"I was thinking," Kenny whispered. "We're changing at Okayama. Isn't that where I was supposed to be going with Sato?"

Poyo flipped a piece of candy into the air and caught it in his mouth, smacking his lips noisily.

"Do you think he might be at the station, at the same time? What if he sees us?"

The *tanuki* scratched one ear with his foot and shrugged.

"OK, when we arrive, you go and scout to make sure it's clear. If he isn't wearing his shades, he can't see you. Got it?"

As it was, they passed through Okayama without incident and Kenny arrived at Matsue Station mid-afternoon. He stopped at the Tourist Information desk, and was soon in a taxi, winding its way through the mountain roads. The air was hot and sticky, with low cloud hanging over the hills. The taxi stopped beside a convenience store with four vending machines outside and a crooked sign.

"Is this it?" Kenny asked, looking around at the few houses that comprised the village. "Uh, *taisha-wa, doko desu ka*?" he tried.

The driver pointed a white-gloved hand across the street, where a thick stone pillar with carved lettering stood beside a concrete *torii* gate, about fifteen feet high.

Kenny crossed the road, with Poyo at his feet, and saw a tree-lined gravel path leading away from the *torii*. Two statues rested on plinths on either side. Each was pitted with age, scarred by lichen and moss, and resembled an angry cat. The front paws were lowered, with bared fangs in a wide mouth, while the hind legs were straight, and a fat bushy tail curved up and over the back. Poyo shrank back from the vile creatures.

"Man, you're such a coward," Kenny scolded. "They're just statues. They can't . . ."

The stone figures both turned to glower at Kenny.

"Our massster is expecting you, Kuromori-*sssan*," the nearest one hissed.

Kenny swallowed hard. Maybe this wasn't such a great idea after all.

19　十九

Splotches of gray-green moss mottled the gravel path, which led east towards the shrine, giving it a diseased appearance. Twisted, skeletal pines lined the way, standing like spindly sentries, their branches arching and intertwining overhead to block out the autumn sunlight.

Kenny shuddered in the chill shadows, trying to ignore the damp smell of decaying mulch rising from underfoot.

The path ended and, to the left, a vermillion-hued footbridge spanned a shallow river, flanked on each bank by towering *torii* gates. Beyond, gray stone steps led into the thickly wooded grounds of the shrine.

Dragging his feet, Kenny made his way to the base of the stairs. He stopped at the *temizuya*, the purification area, and rinsed his hands and mouth.

At the top of the stairs, two more *komainu* statues glowered at him, watching his every step. An enormous rope hung across a roofed gateway leading to the inner courtyard. Kenny stared upward; the rope was made of straw and each intertwined coil was three feet thick.

"Stay close," Kenny warned Poyo, who was straggling behind.

The *honden* was a wooden building with a sloping slate roof, plain apart from some gold ornamentation on the front, where a roofed porch covered the offering box and supported another gigantic length of rope. It was nowhere near as grand as the other halls Kenny had seen in Kyoto.

He approached, bowed twice, clapped twice and bowed again.

Nothing happened.

Poyo scratched his ear with a hind leg. Wind rustled through the leaves, as if telling Kenny to shush. A fat crow eyed him with an unblinking gaze.

"Should I do it again?" Kenny whispered to Poyo. "More reverence? Do I need to make an offering?"

Poyo's ears twitched, his nose wrinkled and he jumped for Kenny's leg, wrapping his front paws around the boy's calf.

"Ew, what are you doing?" Kenny yelped. "Get off my leg, you –"

A scraping, shuffling, shambling sound drew closer, making Kenny's arms prickle with goose bumps.

"*Chotto matte*," a hoarse voice wheezed.

Kenny spun around to see who was approaching and recoiled from the sight of an emaciated figure.

What once had been a Japanese man was now little more than a rotting shell. Its skin was purple with blue blotches. One eye dangled from its socket and the other was pure white apart from a tiny black pupil. Patches of scalp supported islands of long white hair and its teeth were as long and yellow as its claws. The thing limped closer, leaning on a staff for support, and Kenny saw that one foot was broken off and dragging behind, held by a ribbon of leathery skin. A pink loop of intestine drooped from under its ragged shirt and flapped with every jarring step.

"*Kinasai*," the creature said, curling a finger.

For a moment, Kenny regretted not taking Stacey up on her offer to come along and translate, but the meaning was clear.

The thing hobbled away, lurching on its ankle stump, and Kenny followed it around to the rear of the *honden*. It stopped by a pair of black lacquered doors, decorated with a gold-leaf inlay depicting an eight-headed dragon. The creature rapped once on the door with the base of its staff and tottered away. Silently, the doors swung inward, revealing stone steps descending into darkness.

Kenny wiped his clammy palms on his jeans and knelt to ruffle Poyo's ears. "I don't suppose you want to come in with me?" he asked.

Poyo's head dropped to the floor and he covered his eyes with his paws, whining.

"I'll take that as a 'no.' Listen, if anything should happen . . . if I don't come back . . . tell Kiyomi that I . . ." Kenny rubbed his cheeks, to hide the pink flush.

"Just tell everyone that I tried, OK?"

Poyo whimpered and sat up. He stuck out a paw for Kenny to shake.

His heart pounding and his mouth dry, Kenny stood at the top step and peered down, trying to see how far the stairs went, but it was no use; the darkness swallowed everything like a hungry gullet.

Inari's warning sprang into Kenny's mind: "Susano-wo is cunning, unpredictable and insane. He is not to be trusted. Put aside any thoughts of bargaining with him for the girl. No good will come of it. Now do your sworn duty and go to Mount Chikurinji."

"Too late for that," Kenny muttered to himself. "I caused this mess, so . . ." With a last look back at Poyo, he began the long descent into shadow.

Kenny stopped counting steps after the first thousand.

In the palm of his hand burned a small flame, providing just enough light by which to navigate. The stairs seemed endless and the air was as dank and chill as a tomb.

Kenny reached out once to touch the walls, but couldn't find any. He had a horrible sense that the staircase was somehow floating in the gloom, not fixed to anything solid. If he was to slip and fall . . . He pushed the thought away; it was too awful to consider.

After twenty minutes, Kenny discerned the faint glow of lights from below. Grateful, he hurried down the remaining steps and found his feet on bare earth. Tiny creatures scuttled away and the soil churned underfoot as unseen things burrowed to safety.

Two rows of stone lanterns faced each other, like landing lights on a runway, marking out a path. Kenny made his way forward, aware of movement from beyond the puddles of light. Large things lurked in the shadows, tracking his every move.

At the end, two stone braziers stood on either side of a huge throne, carved from ivory. A dinosaur skull adorned each arm and an enormous rib cage fanned out to form the back of the chair.

"*Ryu no hone da!*" boomed a deafening voice from behind Kenny, making him jump. He dived to the floor and rolled to a crouch, hands up in a defensive stance.

Glaring down at him was a heavily-built giant of a Japanese man, easily twenty feet tall. Long black hair draped to his shoulders and a thick beard covered half of his face. He wore a white smock, red *hakama* breeches and heavy leather strap boots.

Susano-wo leaned over the huddled boy and sniffed the air with a snarl of disdain.

"A *gaijin*?" he said, the words pushing into Kenny's mind. "You wish to visit me here, in my home, and you do not even have the courtesy to learn my language?"

"*Gomen nasai*," Kenny said. "*Watashi no nihongo wa warui desu.*"

Susano-wo stared for a moment, then burst into laughter, which sounded like a series of short barks. "You are right to be sorry. Your Japanese is more than bad, it is atrocious. Offend my ears no more. We will commune directly." He marched past Kenny and sat on the enormous throne. "How do you like my chair?" he asked.

"Uh, it's very . . . bold," Kenny said, straightening up.

Susano-wo patted one of the huge dinosaur skulls which served as a hand rest. "Dragon bone," he said. "Killed each one myself. What is your name, boy?"

"Kenny, sir. Kuromori."

Susano-wo narrowed his eyes and stroked his luxuriant beard. "I have heard of you, Kuromori, chosen one of Inari." He spat the last few words. "I thought you would be older."

"That would be my grandfather you're thinking of."

The god tilted his head in thought. "Ah, yes, that would explain much. And you are continuing his work?"

"Not exactly . . ."

"Then why are you here, Kumatori?" Susano-wo exploded. "Inari has no business with me."

Kenny fought the urge to turn and run. "It's a personal matter," he said, ignoring the deliberate mispronunciation of his name and keeping his voice steady. "Nothing to do with Inari."

Susano-wo leaned closer. "Is that so? Nobody sent you?"

"No."

"Then who knows you are here?"

"No one."

"Interesting. So, if I was to kill you now and keep your soul, no one would know? You are either extremely brave or extremely foolish. Which is it?"

Kenny shrugged. "Is there a difference?"

A broad smile broke across Susano-wo's face. "How may I be of assistance?"

A cold bead of sweat trickled down Kenny's spine. "Someone I know . . . died a couple of months back."

Susano-wo shrugged. "These things happen. You wish to express regrets? Ask them where they've hidden a treasure? Apologize for being a bad son?"

"No, nothing like that," Kenny said. "This friend of mine, she didn't stay dead. We brought her back, but not all of her . . ."

A scowl darkened the gruff features. "You stole from me – took what was rightfully mine?" Susano-wo slammed a fist on the dragon skull.

"It wasn't her time," Kenny protested.

"And who are you to decide that?" The god settled back again. "Tell me, how did you commit this despicable act?"

"An *oni* gave his soul in exchange."

"Hah!" bellowed Susano-wo. "All *oni* belong to me. I am their King and they obey my every command."

"That's what happened," Kenny insisted.

"So you gave me what was already mine as recompense for stealing from me? That does not bode well, does it?"

"That's the problem. Some of her is still here. In Yomi, with you."

The smile widened, revealing crooked black teeth. "Is that so? And what is this girl to you?"

Kenny looked away from the god's unblinking gaze. "I told you, she's a friend."

"Kusanori, I have studied the hearts of men since they first beat in these lands. I do not need to probe your mind to know you lie. This girl, is she worthy?"

Kenny shuffled his feet, squirming. "I don't know. She's all right, I suppose."

Susano-wo rubbed his palms together. "Is she brave? Strong? Clever?"

"Yeah, all that too."

"And are you deserving of such a prize?" The black eyes glittered with malice.

"I don't know. What does it matter, if she's dead?"

"Indeed." Susano-wo leaned back. "Indeed. Tell me, Kumohori, what would you do to prove yourself worthy? To save the girl?"

Kenny closed his eyes. "I'd do anything."

"Excellent," said Susano-wo, an evil glint in his eye. "Then I have a proposal for you."

20 二十

Kenny looked up. "What do I have to do?"

Susano-wo sprang to his feet. He rested one knee on the ground and drew a circle in the dirt with his finger. From the center, a flickering pale-blue wisp rose. It coalesced into the ghostly form of a teenage girl.

"This is why you are here, why you have put yourself at my mercy?" Susano-wo asked, his voice rising.

"Yes," Kenny said, his eyes stinging with concentration as he stared into the faint image.

Kiyomi's spirit self turned at the sound of Kenny's voice, saw him and raised her hands to her mouth in surprise.

"Then know that while you may have cheated me once, you will not do so again!" A sword materialized in Susano-wo's hand and he sliced downward, cutting Kiyomi in two.

"No!" Kenny cried out.

Each half of Kiyomi's spirit collapsed inward, shrinking down, condensing into a tiny circlet. They fell to the ground with a glassy tinkle.

Susano-wo scooped up the objects, holding them out for Kenny to see. Each was a jade ring, one a creamy white color, the other a cranberry red. He slipped them onto his fingers and returned to his throne.

"Your grandfather rescued many sacred relics from the hands of foreign invaders and hid them away for safekeeping," Susano-wo rumbled. "But some have remained lost for centuries. I want you, Kuromori, to find two for me, and in return I will give you the two halves of the girl's soul; one ring for each treasure. Can you do that?"

Kenny set his jaw and nodded. "I can do that."

"We shall see. The first object is the Yata no Kagami, a mirror belonging to my sister Amaterasu. It has not been seen for hundreds of years."

"That figures. What's the other item?"

"You will need the mirror first, if you are to locate it. The one leads to the other."

"OK. Do you have any suggestions where I should start looking?"

Susano-wo leaned forward on his throne. "If I knew where the mirror was, I would have no need for you." He raised a finger in warning. "One last thing: no one must know what you are doing for me. No human, no god, no creature. This must remain our little secret. Do you understand?"

Kenny nodded. "I get it."

"Excellent. You may return to the light."

Kenny was about to leave when Susano-wo spoke

again: "Tell me, is the world as beautiful as I remember it or has man despoiled it?"

"It's still amazing," Kenny said, "especially at this time of year. The maples are red and the setting sun makes everything look like gold. I saw Mount Fuji last week and it was . . ." Kenny trailed off, seeing a single tear escape Susano-wo's eye and roll down his cheek, leaving a shining trail.

The god wiped it away. "Go now, and do not look back," he commanded.

Kenny ran before Susano-wo could change his mind.

"You want the good news or the bad news?" Kenny said to Poyo while they waited for the bus back to Matsue. Poyo drooled in reply.

"Serves me right for not asking a yes-no question," Kenny muttered. "OK, the good news is I know what we have to do to save Kiyomi."

Poyo nodded his furry head.

"The bad news is I haven't a clue where to start."

They boarded the Ichibata Bus and wound their way down the mountain road, with the sun dipping behind them. As soon as the city of Matsue came into view, Kenny's watch and phone both buzzed with messages. He checked his watch first.

Message one read: WHAT ARE YOU DOING? WHERE ARE YOU? YOU'RE SUPPOSED TO BE WITH UNCLE IN OKAYAMA. PAPA IS DOING HIS NUT. I

AM SO MAD AT YOU RIGHT NOW.

The second message said: MEET ME AT OKAYAMA STATION TONIGHT AT 18:00. LAST CHANCE. SATO.

"Like that's going to happen," Kenny said, switching the device back to watch mode. It was already five fifteen.

He flipped through his phone messages. Stacey had sent one, confirming that as far as his classmates were concerned, he was struck down with crippling diarrhea from eating bad sushi.

Charles had also sent one: CALL ME.

Kenny tapped in the number.

"Kenny," his father said, after two rings. "How are you doing?"

"I'm fine, Dad. You asked me to call."

"Yes. Yes, I did. You're in a lot of trouble, I think."

"But I thought you said it was OK –"

"In trouble with your grandfather, not me. You need to give him a call, preferably now."

"Did he say what it was about?"

"No, but he wants to know where you are. He chewed my ear off for letting you go 'gallivanting' on your own in a foreign country."

"Did you tell him anything?"

"I assured him that you were safe, that I knew where you were, and that you would call him. Will you do that for me?"

"OK, Dad."

"As soon as you hang up this call?"

168

Kenny sighed. "Yes, Dad. I said OK, didn't I?"

"Good boy. When will you be home?"

"Depends when I can catch a train. I'll call you as soon as I know."

"OK. Be careful, son."

"Thanks, Dad."

Kenny stared at the phone, not wanting to get into a fight with his grandfather, but at the same time, who better to ask if you wanted to find a lost Japanese artifact?

The bus was now clattering through the outskirts of Matsue and in a few minutes Kenny would be at the station. He made the call.

"Hello?" The elderly voice was as strong and clear as ever.

"Grandad, it's Kenny."

A long pause. "Where are you?"

"I can't tell you."

"I see. How close are you to Okayama?"

"Not close enough to meet Sato, if that's what you're asking."

"I don't care for your tone, young man."

"And I don't care for being your whipping boy, but you didn't give me a lot of choice."

"Millions of lives were at stake, Kenny."

"Grandad, I get it. I understand. We all do what we have to do, right? That's just what I'm doing right now."

"Inari needs you in Okayama. So does Sato. You made a promise."

"I made more than one promise. What happens if they conflict?"

"Then you make a choice and you live with the consequences."

"And that's what I'm doing."

Another long pause. "Is there anything I can do to help?"

Kenny's heart beat faster. "There is something. In your travels, while you were working over here, did you ever come across anything to do with the Yata no Kagami?"

Kenny thought he heard a gasp from the other end of the line, but he couldn't be sure.

"Kenneth Blackwood, you listen to me and you listen very carefully," Grandad said, a steely edge to his voice. "You are to have nothing to do with that object. It has been hidden for over a thousand years, and with good reason. I neither know where it is, nor do I care to. Whatever idea is in your head, I suggest you forget it, return to Tokyo and make as many apologies as you need to in order to regain the trust of those who have given up so much for you. Have I made myself clear?"

Kenny was about to mumble yes when a surge of annoyance flashed through him. All day long, he had been pushed and pulled around, trampled in the tussle between duty and conscience, and now, to be scolded like a child . . .

"Sorry, Grandad, it's a bad line. You're breaking up." Kenny ended the call.

21 二十一

After booking train tickets back to Tokyo, Kenny stopped at a noodle bar in the station concourse and ordered a steaming bowl of traditional buckwheat *soba* with a slice of deep-fried, battered eggplant on top. A Japanese game show squawked from a TV on the wall.

Poyo worked his way down the counter, finishing off the leftovers from abandoned bowls.

Kenny checked his watch; ten minutes until his train was due to leave, so just enough time to call his father.

"Dad, I'm leaving soon, so I'll be home around midnight."

"OK, let me know if you get stuck anywhere and I can come out and meet you."

"Will do." Kenny swiveled on the stool and his gaze came to rest on the television. A sweating Japanese man was struggling to answer a question and a telephone was handed to him. Kenny's eyes widened as an idea came to him.

"Hey, Dad, what's the Japanese folklore equivalent of 'phone-a-friend'?"

"I beg your pardon?"

"I mean, what would the gods do if they couldn't come up with the answer to something? Who would they ask?"

"Let me see . . . there are a number of Japanese gods of knowledge. There's an ancient story, recorded in the *Kojiki*, about the arrival of a boat bearing an unknown god. Who he was remained a mystery until the toad suggested asking Kuebiko, the Crumbling Prince, who does not walk but knows everything. He identified the newcomer as –"

"Dad, I'm in kind of a hurry here. This Kuebiko, does he have a main shrine anywhere?"

"Wait just one moment."

Kenny listened to the sound of fingers tapping a keyboard.

"Ah, there it is. In Sakurai, part of the Omiwa Shrine complex."

"Dad, you're a genius. Thanks a lot."

Kenny ended the call and sprinted for the Tourist Information desk, his shoes squeaking on the tiled floor.

Ten minutes later, the Yakumo limited express pulled out of Matsue Station. Poyo struggled to sit up, watching while Kenny unfolded a train map and began tracing a route with his finger.

"We stay on this train until we get to Okayama. From there, it's *Shinkansen* to Osaka, then local trains to Sakurai. That puts us in around eleven, so we're going to have to find somewhere to sleep."

It was now after six and Kenny felt a stab of guilt that he had failed to meet Sato, as promised. *Oh, well,* he thought, *I'm sure he'll manage.* He watched the countryside fly past his train window and, soothed by the food in his stomach and the gentle rocking of the train, he soon drifted into sleep.

Kenny sat up and yawned, stretching his arms.

Outside the window was blackness, dusted with stars; the train was soaring through space. Kenny pressed his face to the cool glass, squishing his nose against it, and stared at his own distorted reflection, wreathed by a halo of his breath.

The train slowed to a stop and the doors opened with a hiss. Kenny stepped out, alone, onto a dimly-lit, misty platform. An overhead clock struck noon and Kenny squinted up at the starry sky.

"Kenny! Help me," Kiyomi cried out.

Kenny whirled around and stumbled in the direction of her voice. A leather-clad figure knelt in the dark, her hands over her face.

"Kiyomi? I'm here," Kenny said, dropping beside her. "You're OK now."

"You call this OK?" she screamed, stabbing her outstretched fingers towards his throat. Her eyes blazed amber and two pointed horns grew from her forehead.

Kenny kicked out and scrabbled backward.

"You're too late!" Kiyomi shrieked. "You took too long, and now . . . now, I'm *this*!" She drew her *katana* and leveled it at Kenny's heart. "You made me into a monster and for that I'll kill you – unless you kill me first."

"No. Kiyomi, don't do this."

She lashed out with the sword. Kenny threw himself aside and summoned Kusanagi. Nothing happened. He tried again, but the sword would not appear.

Kiyomi moved in for the kill, raising her weapon for a death blow.

"*Matte*!" barked a deep voice and Kiyomi froze.

Kenny scrambled to his feet and found himself gazing up at Susano-wo.

"Where is my mirror?" the god demanded.

"I don't know," Kenny said.

"Try harder!" Susano-wo wrapped a huge fist around the boy and pitched him skyward, like a doll.

Kenny couldn't breathe as wisps of cloud rushed past his face and he hurtled helplessly towards a shining disk of light which hovered amid the stars.

At first, Kenny thought it was the full moon, but as he drew closer he saw a tiny dot at its center. The spot wavered, grew and took on the form of a fair-haired boy, growing ever larger as the distance closed. Kenny raised his hands to shield his face before he smashed into the giant mirror, shattering it into millions of glistening splinters. Stunned by the impact, he flailed his arms weakly and tumbled back towards the Earth, far below.

Kenny awoke with a start. He hadn't dreamed anything that vivid for weeks, and he suspected it meant something, but what?

He patted Poyo on the head. "Are you missing Kiyomi?"

The *tanuki* nodded, his pink tongue lolling.

"Me too. Remind me never to eat *soba* before bedtime."

The two travelers disembarked at Okayama Station and transferred to the Sanyo *Shinkansen* to Shin-Osaka.

Kenny found his seat and was pleasantly surprised to discover that he had the car to himself. He reclined his seat, pulled out the footrest and settled back for the journey.

Without warning, the lights went out, plunging the car into blackness. Kenny sat up again and felt the temperature begin to drop. Poyo whimpered and dived under the seat.

"Hello?" Kenny said, getting to his feet. He looked back to see that the next car down was fully illuminated; whatever was happening was in his car only.

A thump came from the far end. Kenny summoned Kusanagi and tiptoed towards the sound, his heart pounding. He stopped by a luggage compartment, its lid popped open.

Reaching up to close it, Kenny failed to see the monstrous shape which dropped silently from the ceiling and reared up behind him.

22

With a low growl, Poyo shot out of his hiding place and sank his sharp little teeth into a spindly leg. The creature bellowed and struck out, flinging the small *tanuki* across the car to slam into a window.

Kenny whirled at the sound and was faced by a nightmarish vision. The thing was some kind of enormous spider with a spotted abdomen, tiger-striped legs – each ending in a vicious hook – and a semi-human head. Two bulbous yellow eyes glared at him, above the paired maxillae and palps of an arachnid mouth. Bristly tufts of hair dotted its scalp and venom glistened on the fangs. It was so large, it filled the aisle.

It rushed at Kenny with a deafening screech. Unable to see in the dark, he swung the sword in a desperate arc. The spider-thing sidestepped with a nimbleness that belied its size and raked a talon across Kenny's chest.

A tearing sound reached his ears and Kenny prayed it was clothing, not flesh. Pain etched a sharp line along his front and his ribs burned as if on fire. He flailed with the sword again, lashing out in wide horizontal strokes, but the creature ducked low and kicked out, sending Kenny flying backward and sliding on his rear. It moved in for the kill.

Gasping and clutching his chest, Kenny dug the heels of his sneakers into the carpet and kicked backward, propelling himself towards the connecting door to the next car. The beast wasn't giving him any time to think and, in the weak light bleeding from the other car, he saw it bearing down, jaws clacking. His head bumped against the door and, to his left, he saw a red canister standing behind a pane of frosted glass.

The spider screeched again and thundered forward. Punching a fist through the glass, Kenny grabbed the fire extinguisher and squeezed the trigger levers, aiming the hose at the onrushing monster.

FSSSSSHHH! Carbon dioxide blasted into the creature's face in a white cloud and it reared up, firing a string of shining web into the mist. Kenny felt it hit the canister and a powerful tug ripped it from his hands.

"You want it? You can have it!" Kenny growled, slamming Kusanagi down on the nozzle of the departing extinguisher, slicing clean through it.

The pressurized contents shot through the hole, launching the metal container like a missile – straight into the jaws of the spider-thing. There was a sickening crunch, a squeal and the creature backpedaled, its feet slipping in its own gore.

Kenny dragged himself to his feet and advanced

on the retreating beast. Its mouthparts were staved in, crushed by the extinguisher which was now embedded in the pulped, dripping maxillae. It leapt into the air and twisted, hooking its legs into the ceiling and continued backing away.

"Oh, no you don't," Kenny shouted and ran after it, sweeping the sword high overhead as he passed beneath, slicing it from head to tail. The spider shuddered and its insides plopped out in a stinking, steaming, yellow tide.

Kenny twisted away, but the soupy guts still splattered him. "Ugh!" he groaned, dragging a revolting, sticky blob from his hair. His hoodie was shredded and soaked with his own blood.

The spider carcass disintegrated into dust which sifted downward like sand in an hourglass. Poyo rolled to his feet, shook himself and dived into Kenny's backpack.

"Are you OK?" Kenny asked him, leaning against a seat to catch his breath.

The *tanuki* looked up to nod before resuming his rummaging.

"Why is it that when these things crumble away, any muck they leave behind stays where it is?" Kenny mused, wiping mustardy gunk onto his jeans.

Poyo scampered over and presented a small plastic box to Kenny.

"The first aid kit? Thanks."

Kenny stumbled to the semicircular bathroom cubicle

at the end of the car. Sliding the door open, an immaculate WC faced him with a round sink to its left and a small window at the top. He filled the sink with hot water, pulled off his tattered shirt and inspected the wound. Shreds of T-shirt fiber were pressed into an ugly, livid tear which started under his right nipple and continued to just above his heart. It was about eight inches long and burned in the dry air. Every breath he took caused a sharp pain.

He wet some wadded-up paper towels and cleaned out the gash as best he could, gasping as he did so. He followed up by applying half a tube of antiseptic cream before wrapping a gauze strip around his middle. Finally, Kenny popped two painkillers from their packaging and swallowed them.

His head ached and his vision swam. He splashed cold water on his face and gripped the sides of the basin as a wave of nausea rose within him.

TAP-TAP-TAP. Kenny looked up in the direction of the sound. It came from the roof, but that was impossible. The bullet train was hurtling along at 175 miles per hour – faster than the winds of a Category 5 hurricane. Anything up there would be literally blown away.

Kenny waited, his eyes darting across the ceiling, but the noise had stopped. He must have imagined it. He stooped to pick up his bloodstained sweatshirt – and the window exploded in a hail of tempered glass. A spindly leg coiled around his chest, dragged him upward, through the opening, and hurled him out of the train, spinning into the night sky.

The shock of speeding air punched the wind out of Kenny's lungs and he saw the lights of the *Shinkansen* cars spiral crazily away into the distance. Glimpses of tea bushes in tidy rows alternated with the star-filled heavens as he whirled through the sky. A distant point of growing light allowed him something to focus on and, reaching into his *ki*, he summoned a blast of wind to steady his descent. That's when he realized the beacon was the headlight of a train on the opposite track – and it was coming straight at him.

Kenny's mind pushed against the railway tracks and the wind boosted him higher into the air. The second *Shinkansen* thundered below him and was gone in a flash.

"I've had enough of this," Kenny muttered to himself, and a surge of white-hot anger coursed through his veins. With an angry roar, he collected the rage, imagined it as fuel for a jet pack and channeled it out behind him. The wind bearing him aloft suddenly propelled him forward, as if he was caught in the shock wave from an explosion.

Kenny could hardly breathe and tears streamed from the corners of his eyes while he soared high above the tracks. He tried to spread his arms, like wings, to steer as best he could, but the slipstream plastered them to his sides. Houses, power lines, overhead gantries all flashed by, barely registering. Kenny was alarmed to feel the skin on his face begin to warm from the friction of the air and was about to slow down when he saw the snaking line of his train draw into view.

He adjusted the angle to coast downward and landed with a rolling thump on the *Shinkansen* roof. Careening to a stop, he threw out his arms and legs to gain purchase on the smooth, curving surface. He was about to try and stand when the wind caught him, slamming him towards the edge of the roof. Kusanagi shimmered into his hands and Kenny drove the sword down into the metal skin of the car. He slid fifteen feet, carving a long trail, before the blade held.

This time, Kenny concentrated on keeping a blast of wind pushing at his back, to counter the thrust of onrushing air, before he staggered to his feet.

A second spider-creature turned to confront him, even larger than the first. Kenny saw that it had fastened itself to the roof with long cables of webbing. It opened its palps and shrieked in rage at him, its voice hardly audible above the howl of the air.

Kenny set his feet in a fighting stance and raised the sword.

The spider twisted its abdomen and squirted globs of webbing from its spinnerets onto its claws. It then released its hold on the safety lines and scuttled towards Kenny, its gluey feet sticking to the roof.

Kenny could hardly open his eyes in the buffeting wind, but he made out the large shape looming closer. It lashed out with four hooked claws, striking in different directions at once: at Kenny's head, chest, waist and legs. He blocked the upper thrusts with the sword, but his feet were swept from under him. Once again, Kenny found himself bowling head over heels down the length of the car. The spider-creature skittered after him.

Kenny slammed Kusanagi down into the roof and hung on as it sliced another furrow into the metal surface, acting as a brake. An idea came to him and he quickly punched the blade down several more times before backing away from the monster. He was now at the end of the car with a sheer drop behind him. Sensing this, the creature clacked its mandibles and rushed at him.

Waiting until the last moment, Kenny leapt into the air, increased the force of the counter wind and flew over the beast's head, dropping into a crouch behind it. The spider skidded to a stop, spun around – and put its leg through the perforated section of roof. With a squeal of rage, it toppled forward, before steadying and pulling at the jagged metal anchoring its limb. Kenny charged, the sword held high, and brought the blade down, slicing the creature's head in two. The body shuddered, its legs went slack and it crumbled away, the dust whipped along by the rushing winds.

Kenny slumped back into his seat beside Poyo. The *tanuki* guiltily brushed away doughnut crumbs, removed the earbuds and handed the iPod back to its weary owner.

"Nah, it's OK," Kenny said. "What are you listening to anyway?" He looked at the screen. "'Highway to Hell'? Too right. Maybe I should've gone to Okayama with Sato, after all. This is the worst train ride ever."

His smartwatch buzzed, signaling a new message from Kiyomi. KENNY, IT'S TOO LATE. YOU NEED TO COME BACK – NOW.

"Too late is right," Kenny agreed. "Only there's no going back."

23 二十三

Sato shivered in the chill night air. He pulled his coat tighter and crept through tall wiry grass for a better vantage point from which to view the illuminated observatory. The domed structure housing the telescope looked like a Roman centurion's helmet with the tall crest of the shutter running along the top.

It had taken half a day for Sato to make the trip from Tokyo to the Okayama Astrophysical Observatory at the peak of Mount Chikurinji. Once there, he had revamped the site security measures with a fortified roadblock, before opting to wait outside in anticipation of unexpected visitors.

He huddled behind a rock and wondered, yet again, where Kenny could be. He had not known the boy for long, but he had seen enough to know that Kenny could be relied upon to do what was right, which made his absence all the more puzzling. What possible reason could Kenny have for disobeying a direct instruction – from a goddess, no less?

An odd, rhythmic, thumping noise carried on the

breeze. Sato stood up, straining his ears to track the sound – then flung himself to the dirt as the huge, juddering shape of a Boeing CH-47J Chinook helicopter roared out of the sky, blotting out the stars. Landing lights stabbed downward and doors opened in the side.

Sato clambered under a bush for cover, the downdraft from the twin rotor blades blasting him with dirt and leaves. He jabbed a customized pair of sunglasses onto his nose and a dozen *oni* blinked into view, dropping to the ground and heading straight for the dome. They were all wearing uniforms and carrying weapons.

The final *oni* to disembark was silver faced. "Four and Five, blow the doors. I want a quick in and an even quicker out. Move!" it barked, then stopped, sniffed the air and turned around to look directly at Sato's hiding place. "Hey, you! Human. There's twelve of us and one of you. You want to party?"

It leveled the largest handgun he had ever seen at Sato, who broke from cover, dived over the crest of the hill and rolled, tumbling down the mountainside.

Kenny woke early the next morning, checked out of his capsule hotel and had a traditional Japanese breakfast of *miso* soup, grilled salmon, rice, *natto* and pickles, all washed down with green tea.

He settled the bill, collected Poyo from the dumpster he had preferred to sleep in, and was on his way back to Shin-Osaka Station when a new message buzzed on his watch.

YOU'RE SUCH AN IDIOT. BUY A NEWSPAPER AND SEE WHAT YOU'VE DONE.

Scowling all the way to the newsstand, Kenny bought *The Japan News*. The main story was the planned launch, later that day, of the final piece of the solar shield. Halfway down the front page, however, was a photograph showing the smashed eggshell dome of an astronomical observatory, belching flames into the night sky.

It took two hours to reach Miwa Station in Sakurai, by which time Kenny had read the story so many times he knew it by heart. In a copycat incident to what had happened in Tokyo two days earlier, unknown terrorists had blown up the National Astronomical Observatory facility on Mount Chikurinji in Okayama Prefecture. The 72-inch telescope situated there, the largest in Japan, had been destroyed in the explosion. No group had taken responsibility for the attack, but the timing, coming so soon after the recent terror incidents in Tokyo, led the authorities to believe the events were connected, and probably carried out by the same unknown party.

Kenny's stomach twisted in knots. Inari had wanted him to prevent the destruction of the telescope and he had sworn to serve her. Instead, he was off on some wild goose chase after disobeying her clear warning not to bargain with Susano-wo. Maybe Inari was right, that his feelings for Kiyomi were clouding his judgment, making him no longer of any use to her.

No, Kenny thought, *it doesn't matter. Nothing changes*

the fact that Kiyomi's fate is now in my hands. This is my mess and I have to put it right.

Miwa Station was small, little more than a covered platform. Kenny and Poyo filed past the black taxis waiting outside, studied the map in front of the station, and made a right turn onto a narrow street lined with eateries and souvenir stalls.

At the next junction, they could see a huge *torii* gate towering in the distance, marking the way to the Omiwa Shrine. A grade crossing took them back over the railway tracks and they passed a number of food stands before reaching the shrine itself, set at the foot of Mount Miwa.

The tree-lined route led uphill, past rows of red lanterns standing like sentries. A short footbridge ended in stone steps and, once at the top, Kenny was faced with a number of branching paths leading to an array of separate, smaller shrines, each dedicated to a different deity.

"This is nuts," Kenny said to Poyo. "How do we know which one's for this Kuebiko dude?"

Poyo shrugged, then scampered off towards a young couple, walking arm in arm, and tugged at the man's trouser leg. He looked around and saw Kenny standing behind him.

Kenny grimaced in embarrassment and mumbled in his broken Japanese, "*Sumimasen*, uh, *Kuebiko jinja wa . . .?*"

The man grinned. "Is OK. I speak English. Kuebiko

Shrine? Is that way." He pointed north. "Go down this hill, turn left, then you see path on right. Path go up many stairs. Kuebiko Shrine at top."

Kenny bowed in gratitude and quickly followed the directions, with Poyo at his heels. The steps led up through a thick grove of bamboo, past lanterns and under more *torii* gates.

"Whoever this guy is, they sure know how to keep him hidden away from view," Kenny muttered, stopping to catch his breath.

The shrine building stood at the peak of the low mountain and was a simple, one-room affair consisting of a worship hall about twenty feet across, with a small adjoining information stand. Tall trees hemmed it in on the right while the ground fell away to the left, affording unhindered views over the surrounding area. Kenny paused and saw three cone-shaped mountains in the middle distance with a huge ridge on the horizon. A scraggly scarecrow had been left to stare out over the city.

"Wow, you can see everything from up here," Kenny said to Poyo, before approaching the *haiden*.

He bowed, clapped and bowed again. Behind a rope barrier, which dangled overhead, a large wooden owl stared from an open-fronted cage, across from three bottles of *sake*, the traditional rice wine.

"This isn't what I was expecting," Kenny grumbled. He went around the side of the building and saw rows of pear-shaped wooden plaques hanging on a frame, each the size of his palm. "Those are *ema*, right?" he said to Poyo. "Inari had fox-shaped ones. I wonder what these are." He turned over a prayer tablet and saw an owl printed on the back. "Kuebiko's an owl? Duh, God of Knowledge. That makes sense."

He returned to the *haiden* to take a closer look at the carved owl. It was about twelve inches in height and width, with a squat charcoal-colored head and a torso covered in creamy feathers. A narrow angular beak arrowed downward and the large eyes on each side made it look cross-eyed.

Kenny paid his respects once more, bowing and clapping, but the owl continued to stare into space.

"Come on, help me out here," Kenny complained. "Is it because I didn't wash my hands? There isn't anywhere up here to do that."

"*Psst!* Hey, kid. Why are you talking to a lump of wood?"

Kenny whipped his head around, looking for the owner of the voice. Apart from Poyo, he was on his own.

"Hello? Who said that?" He glared back at the owl.

"What? So now you think the wooden statue is a ventriloquist? That must make you the dummy."

Kenny inched away from the trees, honing in on the voice, one step at a time.

"That's better. You're getting warmer."

"Who are you?" Kenny asked.

"Oh, come now. You travel all this way, demand my

attention and you don't even know who I am?"

Kenny reached the view point and gazed out over the mountainside, past trees, over the gray roofs of houses, and out towards the giant *torii* gate in town. Movement above his head caught his eye; a crow hopped along a branch.

"You're a crow?"

"How could I be a stupid crow if I'm not even an owl? That's just moronic."

Kenny kicked at a stone in frustration. It flew off his toe and thunked against the scarecrow.

"Ow! First you ignore me, then you call me a crow and now you attack me? You have a strange way of asking for help!"

Kenny skidded down the slope and came to a halt in front of the raggedy figure. "You're a scarecrow?"

The figure was roughly life-sized and constructed around two sturdy poles, lashed together to form a T. Two outstretched arms ended in hands made of twigs. A tatty *hanten* housecoat hung over a shirt stuffed with straw, and baggy breeches ended in tied-off stumps. A conical thatched hat sat on a saggy, rice bag head.

"I prefer to think of myself as more of an observer," Kuebiko sniffed.

"I see now why you're called the Crumbling Prince," said Kenny.

"How dare you!" said the scarecrow. "Just because I've been here a while doesn't mean you can go around poking fun at me. You'll be old one day and then you'll see."

"Are you really Kuebiko, the God of Knowledge?" Kenny said.

"Are you really the boy who defeated Hachiman in his own home?"

"I'll take that as a 'yes.' My name is –"

"I know."

"I'm here to –"

"I know."

"I've come all the way from –"

"I know."

"Then you'll also know that I didn't mean to offend you and that I'm here because I respect your vast wisdom."

"Hmm. Flattery is good, but that's not all of it. You need my help or your girlfriend turns into –"

"She's not my girlfriend."

"Hello? God of Knowledge. Nice try."

Kenny unclenched his fists and sat down on the cool grass. "How much do you know . . . about what's happening? About why I'm here?" he asked.

"You mean your secret deal with you-know-who?"

Kenny's shoulders slumped. "So you won't help me?"

"I didn't say that, now did I?" The button eyes glittered.

"How do you know all this anyway?"

"I know all things that humans know; everything they see and everything they do. You'd be surprised at what I've learned, just from observation, standing out here every second of every minute of every hour –"

"I get it."

"– of every day of every week –"

"OK, I can do the rest."

"– of every month of every year of every century of every millennium. I. See. Everything."

"I suppose being able to read minds helps too."

"Don't be so gauche," Kuebiko sniffed.

"I don't even know what that means."

Kuebiko tilted his head and studied Kenny closely. "Inari chose her champion well. So you wish to know the location of Yata no Kagami, the Eight Hand Mirror of Amaterasu?"

"Yes."

Branches crackled, bushes erupted and a furry ball bounced down the slope to stop by Kenny's feet. Poyo unfurled his limbs and sat up.

"You took your time," Kenny growled at him. Poyo shrugged and scratched his behind.

"Ahem," Kuebiko said, fixing Kenny with a piercing glare.

"Sorry, go on. The mirror is . . .?"

"I can't tell you."

"What?"

"Sorry, forbidden knowledge and all that."

Poyo circled a finger around his fuzzy temple.

"You mean you don't know," Kenny said. "You're just trying to cover it up."

"Aha! Reverse psychology. Very good. I can see your thoughts, boy."

Poyo lumbered to his feet, sniffed the base of the post supporting the scarecrow and raised his hind leg.

"Wait! What's he doing?" Kuebiko gasped in horror. "No! He wouldn't."

"I thought you knew everything," Kenny said.

The scarecrow thrashed wildly about. "Stop! Maybe we can do a deal."

"Poyo, wait," Kenny said. "Let's hear him out."

Poyo lowered his leg.

"Ugh. *Tanuki* urine stinks for ages." A shudder ran through the scrawny body. "You try concentrating with that stench wafting up your nose."

"Tell me more about this deal," Kenny said, his eyes narrow with suspicion.

24 二十四

"It's very simple," Kuebiko said. "So simple that even you can understand it."

"Go on," Kenny said, with a pinched smile.

"We play a game called Quid Pro Quo. You tell me something I don't know, and in return I shall tell you something you don't know. Does that sound fair?"

"What's fair about you reading my mind? That's ridiculous, not to mention impossible."

Kuebiko raised and lowered his shoulders in what Kenny took to be a shrug.

"How about we play a card game, instead?" Kenny suggested, delving into his backpack for his *MANDROID* trading cards.

"Uh, no," Kuebiko said. "I can't play cards without any hands, or did that escape your notice? Besides, you cheat."

"No, I don't. I've never cheated at –"

"I saw you."

"Then you'll know that I wasn't the dealer that day."

"Are we playing my game or not?"

Kenny shoved the cards back into his bag. "How many tries do I get?"

"I'll give you three goes to tell me something I don't know. For each new fact you give me, I will answer one question. Yes?"

Poyo shook his head. Kenny knelt to stroke his fur and whispered, "We have to find the mirror to save Kiyomi. What other choice do I have?"

"You *gaijin* never cease to amaze me," Kuebiko said. "Here you are, engaged in conversation with a supreme being, the keeper of all knowledge, yet you waste your time talking to a dumb animal."

Poyo shot him a dirty look and laid his chin on his paws.

"All right," Kenny said. "Let me see. Something only I would know . . . What color –"

"Blue," Kuebiko blurted.

"You didn't even let me finish asking the question!" Kenny said, spreading his arms in irritation. "That doesn't count."

"Sorry," Kuebiko said. "Couldn't help myself. This is so exciting. It's my favorite game."

"Yeah, and I bet you never lose," Kenny grumbled. "Some deal."

"Whenever you're ready," the scarecrow said.

Kenny dredged his mind for the most obscure piece of trivia he could remember. "How many vert –"

"Seven."

"You're supposed to let me finish! Jeez. How smart are you if you don't even know the rules to your own game?"

Kuebiko grimaced. "Sorry. I won't do it again."

"You'd better not, or it's a forfeit, OK?"

The ragged head nodded.

"Right . . . what's the biggest living thing on Earth?"

"Oh, that's easy," Kuebiko said. "It's a single member of *Armillaria ostoyae*, commonly known as honey fungus. Growing under the Malheur National Forest in eastern Oregon, it covers five point five square miles, weighs over six hundred tons and is an estimated two thousand four hundred years old. You thought I was going to say 'blue whale,' didn't you?"

Kenny's lip curled in anger. "You see everything on Earth, right? How about space? On what planet did scientists find frozen water in November 2012?"

Kuebiko smiled. "On Mercury. Yes, even though daytime temperatures reach over 750 degrees Fahrenheit – hot enough to melt lead and boil mercury – the planet is tidally locked to the sun, meaning it doesn't rotate, just like the Moon. Since the dark side is in permanent shadow and there's no atmosphere, it can get as cold as minus 280 degrees Fahrenheit. Comets, which are mostly frozen chunks of ice, crashed into the north pole and left ice buried deep in the impact craters. Amazing, isn't it?"

Kenny stared at the scrawny figure. "How do you know all this?"

Kuebiko gave a smug smile. "I told you. All things known to men are known to me. You have one more try."

Kenny put his hands over his face to blot out all distractions so he could fully concentrate. A small, furry hand tugged at his jeans.

"Not now, Poyo. I'm trying to think."

The pulling at his leg grew more insistent. Kenny looked down and saw that Poyo was holding something out to him.

"No, not now. What are . . .?" Kenny's eyes widened and he snatched the paper bag from Poyo's clutches.

"What are you doing?" Kuebiko asked, his pitch rising.

Kenny held up the Mister Donut bag. "All right, smarty pants. Tell me what's in here."

The scarecrow's mouth fell open. "You can't ask me that."

"Why not?"

"Because you don't know yourself."

"What's that got to do with it? You said I have to tell you something you don't know. Well, how do I know you don't know? You could be bluffing. This way I get to check if you know or not, first."

"That's absurd. You're suggesting I would . . . lie?"

"Let's just say it's a possibility."

"That's reprehensible. I've never been so insulted in all my life."

"You should get out more. Now, come on. Tell me

what's in this bag." Kenny waggled it, producing a dull tapping noise from inside.

Kuebiko glared, first at Poyo, then at Kenny. The *tanuki* blew him a kiss.

"Whenever you're ready," Kenny said.

Kuebiko cleared his throat. "Judging by the portly nature of your not-so-little companion, it's clear that he's not shy when it comes to calorific consumption. The bag is obviously from a fast-food franchise specializing in sugary wheat-based snacks so I can deduce that it once contained doughnuts, although with a *tanuki* it could hold anything now, given their propensity for going through trash cans."

Poyo scratched his bottom again.

"Are you going to tell me or not?" Kenny said. "We could be here for weeks, the way you're stalling."

"I am not stalling. I am concentrating my intellect on the matter in hand, using reductive logic to –"

"See? You're doing it again. Stalling."

"This is intolerable! It's a doughnut bag. Your fat friend is obviously fond of them. Your classmate Stacey Turner bought four doughnuts – one honey twist, one strawberry ring, one French banana whip and one *Hello Kitty* orange cream – with the intention of ingratiating herself with you in order to –"

"Do you give up?"

Kuebiko's mouth opened and closed several times before he said, "It's a stale piece of leftover doughnut he saved for you."

Kenny rattled the bag and his heart sank. Poyo crouched on the ground and covered his head.

"Hah! I was right," Kuebiko crowed.

Kenny set his jaw. "Is that your final answer?"

"You know it is. Now open the bag, child."

Kenny unrolled the top of the bag, tipped it and out plopped a pink chocolate bow which nestled on the grass.

"Noooo!" Kuebiko screamed, his straw arms rustling with outrage.

Kenny's knees buckled in relief and he slumped beside Poyo. "You mean you ate four doughnuts and all you left me was the *Hello Kitty* bow? Good boy!" He patted the *tanuki* on the head.

"Nobody must ever know about this!" Kuebiko spat. "You hear me?"

"Tell you what," Kenny said, "you keep my secret and I'll keep yours. Now, where can I find that mirror?"

Kuebiko sagged on the frame, head on chest, as if all of his stuffing had been removed.

"Hello? We had a deal," Kenny insisted.

The scarecrow didn't move. Poyo waddled over and raised his hind leg.

"All right, all right!" Kuebiko said, jerking upright again. "I'll tell you what I know, but if anyone asks, you did not get this from me. Understand?"

Kenny nodded. "Understood. What's the big deal with this mirror anyway?"

Kuebiko's black eyes glittered from under his brow. "Is that your one question?"

"No, forget it. Just tell me where it is."

"On Mount Kurama. In the hands of Sojobo. Amaterasu herself entrusted it to his care."

"Mount Kurama? Where's that? Who's this Sojobo dude? Is he another god?"

Kuebiko looked up at the clear sky and whistled tunelessly.

"It's like that, is it?" Kenny said, sampling a piece of the strawberry chocolate bow. "Talk about a sore loser." He made a face. "Yuck. No wonder you left it," he said to Poyo.

Taking out his phone, he called his father. "Hi, Dad."

"Kenny, you should have been home last night. What on earth is going on over there?"

"Huh?"

"In Okayama. The observatory attack. Are you OK?"

"Don't worry, that was nothing to do with me. I'm miles away."

"Really? You're still in Matsue?"

"No, Osaka. Dad, where's Mount Kurama?"

"It's northwest of Kyoto. Why?"

"I need to make another detour out that way."

"Kenny, this is ridiculous. When are you coming home?"

"I don't know. How far is it from Osaka to Kyoto?"

"About twenty-five miles."

"It's midday now, so I should be home tonight."

"Just call me when you know." Charles hung up.

Kenny felt Kuebiko's eyes boring into the back of his head. "He's worried about you," the scarecrow said.

"It doesn't take the God of Knowledge to work that out," Kenny said, gathering his things.

"He's right to be. The mountains are very dangerous." The button eyes flashed with malice.

"Really?"

"Oh, yes. It's the last refuge for many wild *yokai*. The cities of man have spread and pushed them into smaller areas. They don't like to be disturbed."

"I'll try to be quiet."

"One more thing, Kuromori." A wide grin split across Kuebiko's face. "A word of caution: don't rely on that sword too much. It won't be there when you need it most."

25 二十五

Kiyomi lingered outside the door to Kenny's apartment. She listened at the door, heard nothing and quickly picked the lock.

"Hello? Professor Blackwood?" she called from the *genkan*. "Anyone home?" She slipped off her boots and padded into the hallway. Kenny's room was on her left.

She entered the room and began going through cupboards and drawers, searching for any clue as to Kenny's whereabouts. Kiyomi was so absorbed in the task that she failed to hear the front door open.

She upended Kenny's wastepaper basket and was about to straighten out a crumpled ball of paper when a faint breeze drifted into the room. She whirled around and saw a startled girl staring at her, a can of pepper spray in her hand.

"What are *you* doing here?" Kiyomi and Stacey demanded at the same time.

"I asked you first," Stacey said.

"Did not," Kiyomi shot back. "Who are you?"

"I'm Stacey, Kenny's girlfriend," Stacey replied,

enjoying the momentary shock on Kiyomi's face.

"You wish."

Stacey's eyes narrowed. "Didn't he tell you about us?"

"It must have slipped his mind," Kiyomi said through clenched teeth.

"What are you doing here anyway?" Stacey glanced around the room at the disturbed belongings. "Are you stealing something?"

"What, in broad daylight, without any gloves? How stupid are you?" Kiyomi smoothed out the crumpled paper and recognized Poyo's handiwork.

Stacey peered over. "That's a very badly drawn map of Japan – oh, no way. You're trying to find him."

Kiyomi looked up in surprise. "Do you know where Kenny is?"

"No, but I saw him leave yesterday morning. Has he run away?"

"Stacey . . . Kenny's in a lot of trouble and maybe even danger. Is there any –?"

"Ahem." The sound of someone clearing his throat made the girls jump. They looked around to see Charles Blackwood standing in the doorway. "Have I missed something or did I forget to lock the door this morning?"

Stacey turned bright red while Kiyomi stood up, the map in her hand. "Professor Blackwood? I have to find Ken-*chan*."

"And that gives you the right to break into my home?"

"I'm sorry. I wouldn't normally do this, but it's very important."

"You don't know where he is?"

"No. He's off the grid. He's ignoring my texts."

Charles sighed and half smiled at Kiyomi. "He likes you, you know. He likes you a lot." Kiyomi nodded, her cheeks pink, and glanced across at Stacey. "He's gone to find you some help, something about a cure."

Kiyomi scowled. "Did he say where?"

"The last time we talked, he said something about Mount Kurama."

Kiyomi gasped. "Kurama? Oh, crap. He really is in trouble." She grabbed her phone and speed-dialed while Charles and Stacey exchanged puzzled looks. "Papa?" she said into the phone. "Is Genkuro-*sensei* still there? He is? Good. We have to go to Kyoto. Now!"

The journey from Miwa had involved four different train lines and the orange sun was low in the sky by the time Kenny and Poyo stepped off the cable railway at Kurama Temple, huddled on the lush green slopes of Mount Kurama, northwest of Kyoto. A red-and-white *tahoto* pagoda towered above the station.

The sheer path up the holy mountain wound through forested slopes, and the fragrant scents of pine, cypress and cedar carried on the fresh, cool breeze. Japanese pilgrims and tourists trudged up the slope, pausing to rest and enjoy the mountain views. Poyo stopped so many times that Kenny finally offered him a piggyback, which he gratefully accepted.

A steep stone stairway lined with red lanterns led up to a huge covered gate. This opened onto a courtyard and the main hall, a low gray-roofed building with square red pillars supporting the gable, and large white paper globe lanterns swaying gently.

"This is different," Kenny said, lowering Poyo to the ground and stretching his aching back. He was standing at the center of a paved area, formed into a geometric pattern. A triangle sat in a hexagon, itself enclosed by three concentric stone circles. A square surrounded the whole design with a triangle in each corner.

Kenny approached the main hall, searching for a *torii* gate or an offering chest, but he couldn't see either. A monk walked past wearing a pleated black outer robe over a white kimono which brushed his ankles.

On either side, a guardian statue crouched on top of a plinth and watched Kenny circle in bewilderment. He stopped at the base of one and looked up into a mouthful of snarling fangs.

"Whoa!" Kenny jumped back.

"Oh, so you *can* see us," the stone tiger said, its tail twitching back and forth. "I told you, Koji. He has the Gift."

The other tiger statue gave an exaggerated yawn. "Yeah, yeah. So what?"

"What do you mean, 'so what?' He's a *gaijin*. Look!"

Koji peered over and his blank eyes widened. "Uh-oh. That's not good. You remember the last time –"

"How can I forget? Quick, let's ignore him."

Both statues froze in place.

Kenny glared at them. "Come on, guys. I know you can talk, and you know I know, so how about you just help me and I go on my way?"

No response.

"Listen, I've had a pretty rough few days and I'm running low on patience," Kenny warned. "Can you just tell me where to find Sojobo and –?"

"SHHHHHH!" hissed Koji. "I can't believe you said that out loud."

"What? Sojobo?"

"AAAGH! You did it again. Moko, you talk to him."

"Why me?" the other tiger said. "You spoke to him first."

"No, I didn't. You did when he first wandered up here."

"Guys, give me a break! I don't care who talks to me, as long as I get answers," Kenny interjected. "You." He pointed at Koji, who shrank back. "I'm looking for –"

"I heard his name. You don't have to repeat it."

"OK. You know who he is, so can you please now tell me where he is?"

Koji shook his head slowly. "I'm not sure that's such a good idea. He doesn't get many visitors these days and he kind of values his privacy."

Kenny fixed the statue with an icy look. "Ask me if I care."

The tiger's lower lip jutted out and he sighed. "I'm not sure what you're expecting, kid, but this is a Buddhist temple, which is probably why you're confused. No one stays in these buildings. The gentleman you seek lives higher up this mountain. Take the trail up, past the museum. Keep going on up and, if you're still alive, then I'm sure Mr. S, or one his boys, will eventually find you. Then you'll wish they hadn't."

"I'm not afraid," Kenny said.

"You should be."

The path up the mountain changed from stone steps to packed earth, zigging and zagging around huge trees which stood like the legs of giant creatures, with gnarled claws grasping the dirt. The thick roots of ancient cedars wove and twisted across the track like knots of writhing worms.

Kenny stopped for one last look at the multicolored mountains marking the horizon. The vibrant reds, yellows, oranges and browns of the autumnal trees reminded Kenny of sponge painting with poster paint from his preschool days.

"Poyo, you had enough?" he asked the panting *tanuki*.

Lying on his back, Poyo nodded.

"You don't have to come any farther if you don't want to. It's not a problem."

Poyo lifted his head to gaze back down the path and then into the thick woods off the trail. His head swiveled back and forth, like he was watching a tennis match, before he rolled to his feet and marched off into the foliage. "Thanks, buddy," Kenny said, plunging after him.

The forest floor was carpeted with pine needles and fallen branches. Sunlight sparkled through gaps in the trees and clumps of bright-green ferns waved their fronds. Kenny had no idea where he was going, only up, towards the summit.

A stream gurgled, out of sight, and a pygmy woodpecker broke from cover, startled by the two visitors.

"This isn't so bad, is it?" Kenny whispered to Poyo. The *tanuki* craned his neck by way of reply. Kenny felt it too: the distinct, hair-prickling sensation of being watched.

Kenny checked the time. It was now past five in the afternoon and the sun would be setting soon. Mentally, he chastised himself for not packing food and water, but he had not expected a prolonged hike in the woods. At any rate, hunger wasn't a problem; the priority was shelter since the overnight temperature would drop to single digits.

"We need to find somewhere to crash before it gets too dark to see," Kenny told Poyo.

A branch snapped overhead. Kenny's eyes shot up in the direction of the sound and he saw two squirrels chasing each other through the branches. Another sound carried on the breeze: a high, keening wail.

"Poyo, is that a child crying? Out here?"

Poyo shook his head.

"Are you sure? Maybe he got lost, separated from his family?"

Again, Poyo signaled an emphatic no.

"What is it then? If it is a child, we can't just leave him out here overnight. Come on, let's take a closer look."

Kenny pounded through the undergrowth, with Poyo waddling to keep up. The sound of crying grew louder, coming from behind a low ridge. Kenny hurdled a fallen tree and scrambled down a slope to a narrow brook.

Standing in the water was a small child, about four years old. His face was muddy, streaked with lines of tears and snot. He was wearing a blue *Doraemon* raincoat and had only one sneaker. He saw Kenny and froze, eyes wide and chest heaving.

"Easy, there," Kenny said, holding out a hand. "I won't hurt you. You're safe now."

Poyo jumped out behind the little boy and snarled. With a shriek, the child bolted into Kenny's arms, burying his tearstained face into Kenny's own filthy sweatshirt.

"There, there. It's OK," Kenny said, giving Poyo a dirty look. "The nasty *tanuki* isn't going to eat you, is he?"

Poyo scowled and lapped water from the creek.

"What's your name?" Kenny asked the boy. "Uh, *watashi-wa* Ken *desu. Anata wa*?"

"Hiroshi," the boy squeaked.

"All right, Hiroshi. How did you get up here? Where's

your family? Who did you come with?"

The boy stared up with wide uncomprehending eyes and shook his head. "*Wakaranai.*"

"Great. Let's get you home. Come with me." Kenny took the boy's hand and began to hike back up the slope, but the child didn't move. "What's the matter?"

Hiroshi pointed at his shoeless foot. His sock was bloodied and the papery skin of a burst blister flapped from a tear.

"Ouch. No wonder you're crying."

Before Kenny could set down his pack and search for the first aid kit, Hiroshi held both arms up, his eyes wide and pleading.

"OK, if I can carry Poyo, then I'm sure I can carry you." Kenny reached to pick up the child.

In that instant, Hiroshi flung his arms around Kenny's neck and jumped to wrap his legs around his rescuer's waist.

"Urgh!" Kenny grunted, trying to retain his balance.

"See if you can carry me now," Hiroshi's voice hissed in Kenny's mind – and his weight doubled, then doubled again.

Kenny's knees buckled and he fell backward into the soft mud, crushed by the ever-increasing weight of the child. Kenny felt his rib cage compress and the air was squeezed from his lungs. It was when the mud began to squish up past his ears that he knew he was really in trouble.

26 二十六

Kenny's heart felt like it was about to explode. The wound across his chest tore open; his pulse hammered in his ears and spots danced before his eyes. It was like an elephant standing on his sternum and pressing steadily down, driving him ever deeper into the soft ground.

From the corner of his eye, Kenny saw a flash of brown fur and heard a low growl, followed by a meaty chomp.

"*Aiii! Ketsu ga itai!*" yelped Hiroshi, and the weight on Kenny's chest eased for a moment.

With his shoulders no longer pinned, Kenny brought his arms up and slapped his cupped palms hard against Hiroshi's ears. The boy's head flew back and he screamed in pain, releasing Kenny to clutch his ringing ears. He stumbled to his feet, which wasn't easy with Poyo hanging from his backside, and pranced in a circle, trying to dislodge the snarling *tanuki*.

Kenny's chest ached and he strained to sit up, but couldn't; the suction of the mud was too great.

Poyo clamped his jaws down harder and the boy shrieked louder. He started to spin on the spot, gathering speed until he was rotating so fast that the startled *tanuki* was lifted into the air. *RRR-IPP!* The seat of Hiroshi's trousers tore loose, Poyo flew into a thicket of ferns and the monstrous child ran howling into the woods.

Poyo lumbered over to the half-buried Kenny and raised his arms in triumph.

"Yes. Very good," Kenny groaned. "When you're done celebrating, would you mind helping me up?"

Poyo spat out a piece of bloodied fabric and waited.

"OK, I'm sorry," Kenny said. "I should have listened to you. Happy now?"

Poyo grinned and started digging.

Ten minutes later, a cold, wet Kenny was picking his way through the darkening trees. "Keep an eye out for shelter," he reminded Poyo, who was leading the way. "We're running out of light and I don't fancy camping in the open."

Leaves rustled from above and Kenny scanned the shadows. Again, he had the strong impression of being watched. Poyo stopped and sniffed the air. His ears twitched and he pointed off to the left, before creeping into the bushes and was gone.

"What is it?" Kenny said, his voice low. "Something coming?" He crept carefully after the *tanuki*, along a narrow rabbit track through the undergrowth. A high-pitched chirping noise reached his ears, barely audible above the rustle of leaves. "What's that? Bats? Birds?"

Poyo put a stubby finger to his lips and edged towards the sound. Drawing closer, Kenny recognized the unmistakable cadences of voices in conversation. He ducked under a low branch and whispered, "Who would be out here at this –?"

THWACK!

Kenny pitched forward, his head ringing, and crashed into a bush. It felt like he had just been walloped with a baseball bat. Gingerly, he touched a hand to his aching skull and saw blood staining his fingertips. With a grunt, he rolled onto his back to see what had hit him – and bolted upright.

Hanging from the branch above the trail was a disembodied horse's leg. The upper part was skewered by a branch, but the knee, shin, fetlock and hoof dangled freely.

"You've got to be kidding me," Kenny said, wiping his bloodied hand on some grass.

As if in answer, the horse leg kicked out again.

"Whoa!" Kenny scrambled out of reach and grabbed hold of a tree trunk to steady himself as he stood up again. His head pounded and he felt slightly dizzy.

"Poyo, I know I've said this before," he groaned, "but you have some seriously weird monsters in this place."

He pushed away from the tree and stumbled along the track in the direction from which the voices had come. They were silent now.

Kenny rounded the trunk of a large red cedar, looking

down to step over a twisted root. When he had avoided the ankle-twisting hollow, he raised his head – and a dark shape lurched at him with a piercing cry.

"*MRRR-huh-huh-huh-huh!*"

Kenny dropped and rolled, covering his head with his hands. The thing swooped above him and its teeth snapped shut. It swung back and forth in the tree, its mad eyes bulging and its jaws dripping foam.

Kenny rose on one knee and stared at the bizarre sight: a horse's head dangled from a bough, tied by its long mane. Its fiery yellow eyes rolled and it bared its pointed teeth at him.

"That is wrong on so many levels," Kenny said. "First a leg. Now a head. What next? Its butt?"

A squeaky giggle came from behind him. Kenny slowly turned, but saw only forest.

Poyo sniffed at the roots of an odd-looking tree. Its trunk bulged outward, like a vase, and branches radiated like the spokes of an umbrella. The bark had a glossy sheen and its dark-green leaves were long and thin. A number of fist-sized pinkish fruit hung from it like Christmas tree baubles.

Thrusting his paw into the long grass at the base of the trunk, Poyo gathered up one of the fruits which had fallen. He licked his lips and opened his mouth.

"No! Not Miyo!" a tiny voice cried.

"Poyo, wait," Kenny cautioned. He moved closer to the tree and reached up to examine a fruit.

"Careful. I bruise easily."

Kenny gently rotated the fragrant object and jumped back in alarm. A pair of eyes blinked back at him above a squished nose and a small mouth. The fruit had a distinctly human face; in fact, the whole thing looked like a bald man's head.

"He can see us," said one fruit.

"Of course he can see us," snapped another.

Kenny sat down, hard, and looked up at the fruit, all jabbering away again.

"It's a boy" – "A *gaijin*, to" – "How can he see us?" – "I can't see him from here" – "Does he look hungry?" – "*He* doesn't, but you should see the fat *tanuki* with him."

"Can you guys shut up a minute?" Kenny said, cutting across the chatter. "Thank you. What's with the horse back there?"

"The head? That's *sagari*," answered the nearest fruit. "A horse died by that tree years ago and its ghost chose to stay there."

"And the leg?"

"Oh, it's just hanging around."

A chorus of giggles went up from the fruit.

"You've been here a while then?" Kenny pressed.

"Hundreds of years," the nearest fruit said. "Oh, the things we've seen. The tales we could tell. Did you know that Yoshitsune himself once came wandering through these woods? This is before he teamed up with –"

"I'm sure it's a lovely story, but it's getting kind of

215

dark and I'm stuck out here," Kenny said, keeping an eye on the lavender sky.

"That's a nasty bruise you've got there," a fruit remarked.

"Thanks for noticing. Do you know anywhere safe and dry I can sleep for the night?"

"Why are you here?" another fruit asked. "We don't see many people these days."

"I'm looking for someone," Kenny said. "Can we stay on one subject? Wait, maybe you can help. His name is –"

"Sojobo," a female voice said. "He won't see you."

A slender Japanese girl stepped out from behind a tree. She was about Kenny's age and wore an emerald-colored tunic which rippled like leaves as she moved. Her hair and skin were tinged with green.

"And you are?"

"Katsura," she said.

"You live here?"

She smiled. "Of course. Where else would I live?"

"You know Sojobo?"

"I know who he is."

"And?"

"He is guardian of this mountain. Every tree that grows here is under his protection. You should be careful."

"All I need is somewhere warm and dry to crash for the night."

Katsura stretched out a finger. "Up there. You see that

large rock? There's a cave beside it."

"Thanks," Kenny said, making a mental note of the location. He whirled around. "Hey, where'd she go?"

Poyo waddled up to a sprawling tree and tapped on the trunk.

"She's in there? A tree spirit? Oh sure, why not? It's that kind of day."

Minutes later, Kenny finished the climb up the slope and stopped to catch his breath, leaning against a boulder. The fruit had given him a cheerful send-off and now, with the light fading, he was relieved to see a cave set into the side of the mountain. A brook trickled past and moss bearded the mouth of the grotto.

Poyo sniffed at the ground and scratched with his front paws, excavating a shallow trough into which he slumped. Kenny crawled into the cave mouth, grateful to rest his weary legs, and pulled off his shoes.

The *tanuki* whined and put a paw over his nose.

"My feet don't smell that bad, you cheeky lump," Kenny said. He patted the spongy ground, which was damp from the stream outside. "Dinner would be nice," he said, delving into his backpack. "What do you say to half a cereal bar?"

Poyo scowled and turned his back on the offer.

"Suit yourself. More for me." Kenny leaned back, fighting off a wave of drowsiness. It had been quite a day.

He leaned against his backpack and closed his eyes

for a few seconds. "Man, what I wouldn't give for a nice juicy burger right now. Kiyomi, wherever you are, you owe me for this. Just don't eat yours raw."

When Kenny opened his eyes he sensed that something was different. Something had changed, he was sure of it, but what? And then realization dawned, like an icy hand on his heart, as he gazed at the jagged white stalactites and stalagmites which were extruding from the mouth of the cave. Those weren't rock formations – they were teeth!

Kenny sprang to his feet, just as the floor lifted, and the entrance to the cave slammed shut.

27 二十七

Kusanagi was in Kenny's hand before he hit the floor. A dull grinding from the side walls indicated molars emerging to crush him to a pulp. Saliva rained from the roof in sticky curtains. He only had seconds.

Kenny focused his *ki* and a glowing sphere of light the size of a tennis ball pulsed into existence. The ground surged again, sloping towards the crushing teeth. His feet slipping, Kenny stabbed his *katana* down into the meaty tongue. A low roar shook the cave and the roof rose twice as high. It then plummeted down again with full force.

Lying flat on his stomach, Kenny whipped the sword out and rolled over, bringing the point upward, the handle jammed against the floor.

SPLUNCH! The ceiling crashed down and the tempered steel disappeared into the rock. Another bellow rolled through the cave and the roof stopped its descent, inches from Kenny's face. It lifted again and Kenny seized his chance, withdrawing the blade, and dived headlong towards the entrance.

Interlocking white fangs formed a wall, sealing the

front, and the saliva rain pooled knee-deep. Kenny drove his sword deep into the groove where two teeth met and dragged the cutting edge across in a wide sweep. He then drew back his arm and launched a haymaker punch, leaning in with his full weight.

A crackling, splintering, popping sound filled Kenny's ears and three huge incisors shot outward. His momentum carried him through the gap to land on the grass beyond in a heap, shaking and gasping for breath.

Poyo bounded up to him, leaping over the fallen teeth. He licked Kenny's face, tasted the cave mouth's secretions and gagged.

"I know," Kenny said. "Just when you think this day can't get any worse, right? This place is *yokai* central." He sat up, soaked to the skin with stinking drool. The sky was indigo now, sparkling with a frosting of stars. The trees all around were silhouettes of twisted black pillars. "We're still stuck for somewhere to –"

GNRRRR. Stone scraped against stone, like a concrete block being pushed across a road. Poyo yelped and grabbed Kenny's shoulders, hauling at him. Movement accompanied the grinding sound; two long shadows stretched out on either side of the large boulder, which lay half buried by the cave mouth.

"You can't be serious," Kenny said, watching the two rocky arms flex, streaming dust and dirt from the cracks. The ends flattened into spade-like paddles and chiseled into the ground. Across the rounded front of the boulder, a horizontal crack widened and split open, revealing a huge, single yellow eye. It fixed its angry red iris on Kenny and heaved its arms, thrusting backward against the soil.

Poyo dived into the foliage and scampered downhill.

"Oh, crap!" Kenny leapt to his feet, hurtling forward on the sloping ground. He overbalanced, tripped, rolled and somehow landed upright again. Ignoring the twigs and pine needles sticking into his palms, knees, back and shoulders, he crashed through the undergrowth, skidding and slip-sliding down.

From behind, he could hear saplings snapping as the huge stone barreled after him, flattening everything in its path. Kenny dashed at full pelt, while the sounds of destruction at his heels grew louder; the thing was gaining on him. He changed direction, running at an angle. The boulder responded by digging a brawny arm into the ground and altered course to follow.

Charging down a mountain in near darkness was a terrible idea, Kenny decided; the footing was treacherous, with tree roots and rabbit holes ready to trip you at every step, and low branches threatening to brain you. A twinkling light flickered through the trees ahead. Crashing through a bush, Kenny recognized it as the stream, and where there was water . . .

With a final surge of strength, he vaulted a rotting log and splashed into the marshy grass where the brook widened. His shoes were swallowed by the mucky ooze, but he didn't care, wading out into the deepest part where the muddy water was knee-deep.

"This had better work," he muttered, steeling himself.

The rumbling boulder smashed through a tree, reducing it to splinters, and bounced towards Kenny. It rolled through the mud, spraying up huge plumes of muck on either side. Kenny watched the dark shape loom closer. The eye opened in triumph and then grew wide as the body began to slow, losing momentum.

"HRRNH?" it grunted, paddling its oar-like arms.

It continued to rotate while its speed decreased to a crawl, but it didn't stop. Kenny's mouth opened as it inched inexorably towards him. He pulled at his feet, trying to get them up from the ooze, but they were stuck fast. And, to make things worse, he was also sinking.

Kenny took a deep breath, centered his *ki* and imagined a fiercely blazing fire. Flames licked his fingers and he pointed at the base of the advancing rock. He focused again and two incendiary blasts leapt from his hands. The mud around the boulder hissed and steamed as moisture boiled away, to leave it as hard and dry as cement. The large stone ground to a halt only inches away. It swayed, wobbled and rolled backward, where it started to sink into the sucking, gurgling mud.

Kenny let out a sigh of relief and doubled over, his hands on his knees. A cold, tickling sensation around his fingers made him look down to see that the murk was rising up his legs. Panic clutched at his chest.

"Poyo! Poyo!" he called. "Where are you, boy? This stuff's like quicksand."

The hush of wind through trees and the squelch of mud was the only reply.

"Great," Kenny grumbled. He stopped struggling, knowing that it would only hasten his sinking; the mud was up to his waist now and held him firmly in its grip.

While Kenny racked his brain for ideas, a small bubble crested and popped in the mud, preceded by another, like links in a chain. Kenny watched the string of bubbles beeline towards him. He held his breath and dared not move, fearing it was a crocodile or worse.

The sludgy surface trembled in front of him, before convulsing and coalescing to form a nub. It split into three and wound slowly upward, like a strange tree branch. Syrupy ripples radiated from a second limb emerging from the mud, and the round lump of a head formed between them. Its bald dome rose up, revealing a single eye and a wide mouth, dribbling ooze.

Kenny groaned.

"*Tanbo o kaese*," the thing wailed, stretching its three-fingered hands out towards Kenny. "*Tanbo o kaese!*"

"Sorry, I can't help you," Kenny said, shrinking back from the mud man. "Try the temple down the hill. Or the nice cave."

The creature shook its fists and waded towards the boy, moving through the mire with ease.

"Look, can you just give me a hand out of here and

we'll call it quits?" Kenny said.

"*Tanbo o kaese!*" the mud creature bawled, and clamped a swampy hand over Kenny's face.

"Bleurgh!" he spluttered, his mouth and nostrils filling with sludge.

Once more, Kenny concentrated on fire, this time picturing a raging inferno, imagining skin-blistering temperatures and shimmering air. He brought his arms in front of his chest, side by side, with fists turned inward and released a white-hot blast of heat in a searing wave.

"*Tanbo o* – urk!" the mud thing said, stopping in mid-cry.

Kenny opened his eyes. The hand over his face was rough and powdery, tattooed with hairline cracks. He jerked his head back and spat the muck from his mouth.

Before him, the mud creature was as still and sturdy as a terracotta statue, baked solid along with half of the marsh. Glowing flecks of orange ash were all that remained of the reeds, floating on the air like fireflies.

Looking down, Kenny noted the good news that he was no longer sinking; the bad news was that he was now half buried in mud as hard as rock. He placed his palms flat against the earth and heaved upward with all his might, but it was no good.

Darkness closed in all around and the damp chill of autumn made Kenny shiver. He knew he couldn't spend the night stuck on the mountainside.

And then it came to him: the answer was so simple

and so obvious that he had missed it before now.

Kusanagi materialized into his hands. Kenny upended the blade and drove the *katana* into the ground. With great care, he inscribed a circle, keeping the hilt close to his waist until he had completed the loop. He then set the sword down, pressed his hands to the earth and pushed for all he was worth. His arms ached but, inch by inch, his legs lifted, encased in a solid block of earth. He raised them as high as he could, leaned back and then used the pommel of the sword to hammer at the clay, freeing his trapped limbs.

Exhausted, he collapsed, lying flat on his back amid the debris. He stared up at the stars while breathing deeply to slow his racing pulse. A shooting star streaked across the heavens and, for a horrible moment, Kenny remembered his nightmare from the previous evening. He was thinking about making a wish when a beam of light skimmed across the ground.

"Hello? *Dare ga imasu ka?*" a woman's voice called out from the hillside.

Kenny levered himself up on one elbow. "Who's there?" he replied.

The flashlight backtracked and fell on his face, blinding him momentarily.

"Oh, thank goodness I found you!" the woman said, the relief clear in her voice.

Kenny heard boots pounding closer and the light bobbed and dipped. A slim Japanese woman held out a hand. She wore the mustard-yellow shirt and olive-colored trousers of a park ranger.

"We had a report of a visitor going off the path," she said. "I'm Emi Yamada, of the National Parks service."

"Kenny Blackwood," Kenny said, taking her hand and rising to his feet.

"What happened?" Emi said, sweeping her flashlight over the scorched earth.

Kenny watched the beam pass over the mud man and relaxed when Emi failed to react.

"I must have set fire to a gas pocket," he said, thinking fast. "I was lost and lit a match."

Emi frowned. "You're very lucky not to have burns." She directed the light towards the three-foot-deep hole Kenny had cut and knelt beside it. "This is strange," she said, touching the side. "It's so smooth. Some kind of borehole or core sample. Do you know anything about this?"

Kenny held out his hands. "Uh-uh. Not me. No way."

Emi stood up. "OK. I'll radio this in later. Right now, I need to get you somewhere warm. You're probably hungry too."

"Starving," Kenny said.

"There's a Ranger Station not far from here. How about we get some food and then I can escort you back to the temple?"

"Sure," Kenny said, grateful for some company.

They headed back into the trees, Emi picking her way

expertly through the terrain.

After a few hundred yards, something large rustled in the foliage above, making Kenny look up.

"What's the matter?" Emi said, following his gaze. She aimed the flashlight beam into the tree and a pair of small black eyes blinked in the light, above a yellow beak. "*Fukuro*," she said. "A big one."

"Huh?" Kenny managed.

"*Strix uralensis* is the Latin name. Ural owl in English." Emi laughed. "He won't hurt you."

Kenny said nothing, but he was sure of two things: one, the thing he had heard was a lot bigger than an owl; and, two, it was watching him.

28 二十八

"How did you stray so far off the path?" Emi asked Kenny, as they tramped through the woods.

"Uh, I sort of fell," Kenny replied. "I went skidding down and by the time I stopped, I didn't know where I was."

"Like Alice, down the rabbit hole?"

"You could say that."

Emi nodded to herself. "That explains it."

"Explains what?"

"Well, you're looking pretty beaten up. How long you been out here?"

Kenny checked his watch. "About three hours."

Emi raised an eyebrow. "That looks like more than three hours' dirt on you. You're on your own?"

"Yeah."

"Hmm. May I ask why? I mean, you don't speak Japanese, you're not dressed for a hike. You seem lost, in many ways."

Kenny reddened. "What are you, my school counselor?"

"Don't be rude," Emi gently chided. "I'm helping you, remember? How long have you been in Japan?"

Kenny's mouth twisted while he contemplated how much to disclose. "About two months now; since mid-July."

"Do you like it here?"

"It's pretty amazing. It's funny, I've moved a lot, so I don't feel like I belong anywhere, but this, this feels right."

"And who are you staying with? Is it a homestay?"

"No, my dad lives out here. I stay with him."

"And he treats you well? You don't fight?"

"No, we get along fine." Kenny wondered where this line of questioning was going.

"So, it must be a girl, then." Emi laughed at Kenny's shocked expression. "There's usually only one reason people stray into lonely woods, and that's to end it all. Aokigahara is the most popular spot, but we get a few up here too."

"It's nothing like that," Kenny said firmly. "I just took a wrong turn, that's all." Emi started walking again. "So, tell me about this girl. Is she special?"

Kenny blushed. "Oh, yes. Very special. She's smart, and gutsy, and so full of life . . . Well, she is usually . . ."

Emi tilted her chin. "Why not now?"

"She's ill. It's pretty bad."

"Oh, I'm so sorry to hear that. Is she getting better?"

"I hope so." Kenny decided to change the subject. "How about you? Why did you become a ranger?"

Emi sidestepped a rock, hidden by ferns. "That's easy. I love it up here. It's so peaceful. I'd live here forever, if I could. No one ever bothers me."

"Really?" Kenny said. "Day or night, nothing . . . weird ever happens?"

"No. I know these woods like I know myself."

The trees thinned and Emi led the way across a clearing, at the far end of which stood a battered wooden shack.

"Here we are," she said.

"This is a Ranger Station?" Kenny said, unable to keep the skepticism from his voice.

"Yes. At least, it was. Then we had budget cuts. It needs some repair, but it still keeps the rain off." Emi unlocked the door and went inside, the rusty hinges groaning in protest. She struck a match and lit several candles.

Kenny followed her in and was reminded of a large garden shed, smelling of mold and old wood. In the middle of the room stood a rickety table, with mismatched chairs. A sideboard, stacked with chipped crockery, leaned drunkenly against the wall. Cans of food were arranged under a filthy, cobwebbed window, and a cooking pot sat on a camping stove. A tattered *shoji* screen door closed off the room.

Emi went to the stove and stirred the pot. "I've got some stew here, if you want something hot; otherwise, you're welcome to the dried stuff." She opened a cupboard to reveal packets of snacks.

"You're well prepared," Kenny said, inspecting a bag of dried squid.

"It's all camping stuff," Emi explained. "Hikers often leave their extra food here. You should eat something. Anything you want."

Kenny decided to avoid the tuna and mayonnaise Doritos and chose a packet of plum-flavored chips instead, which he took to the table. Emi busied herself warming the stew.

"There's a barrel of rainwater in the back, if you want to clean yourself up," she said.

"Thanks. Maybe later," Kenny said, munching chips.

Emi brought her steaming bowl to the table and sat across from Kenny. "It's getting late," she said. "Maybe it's better if we wait until morning to head back." She placed her hand over his. "I can make you a bed in the corner."

Kenny coughed on a chip that went down the wrong way and stood up. "Uh, I wouldn't want to be any trouble to you."

"It's no trouble at all," Emi said, smiling up at him. "You'll be safe here."

"Safe? From what? You said there's nothing dangerous here that you'd seen."

"That's right. Is everything –?"

A distant voice cut across her, lingering in the air.

"What was that?" Kenny said, cocking his head to listen.

"I didn't hear any –"

"It was a girl's voice. I think it was calling my name.

Listen, there it is again." He went for the door.

"Wait," Emi said. "It's night out there and you don't know your way. I'll go and see if someone else is lost." She grabbed her flashlight.

"I'll go with you," Kenny said.

"No. You stay here. I'll be faster on my own. Don't touch anything and stay in this room, OK?"

"Wait a sec," Kenny said. "Earlier, you said someone had reported me missing. Who was that?"

"I have to go," Emi said, disappearing out of the door. "Lock this behind me and stay here." The sound of her running feet faded quickly away.

Kenny peered into the night, but it was as if the darkness had swallowed her whole.

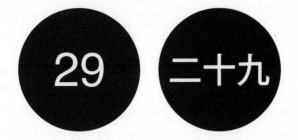

Kenny waited in the doorway for a full two minutes, but there was nothing, not even a flicker of light from the woods.

"Poyo!" he called. "Poyo! If you can hear me, head downhill, follow the stream and find the Ranger Station!"

He turned back into the room and began rifling through cupboards and drawers. There had to be a spare flashlight somewhere.

He had heard Kiyomi's voice calling him, he was sure of it – unless some weird creature was impersonating her. But that wouldn't explain how it knew his name – and if she was wandering through these *yokai*-infested woods on her own . . .

In addition to the dried and canned food, drawer after drawer opened to reveal neatly organized collections of odd items: one held wristwatches; another had mobile phones; a third contained lighters and boxes of matches.

Kenny froze, poised to open a sealed cardboard box he had spied tucked under a stool. The hairs on the back of his neck were prickling and the unmistakable sense of being watched had returned. He whipped his head around, but the room was empty.

Taking a dirty dish towel from the stove, he wet it and scrubbed the grime off a corner of the windowpane, polishing it until it squeaked. Then he returned to the box, set it beneath the window and tore open the tape. Bundles of wallets, passports, credit cards, driver's licenses and other documents lay inside.

Kenny thumbed through a random selection and frowned. Something was wrong here. He glanced up at the clean corner of the window – and jumped at the reflection. Dozens of eyes were scrutinizing his every move. He spun around again and everything was as before. Rising to his feet, he picked up the nearest candle and carried it across the room to the *shoji* screen door.

"I know you're there," Kenny said. "I saw you, so let's cut to the chase. Show yourself."

Nothing happened.

"OK, you had your chance." He brought the candle flame closer to one of the *washi* paper squares in the door, making it glow brighter in reflection. "Three seconds and then I set fire to this place. One . . . two . . ."

Hundreds of eyes instantly appeared, blinking in each panel of the door. They all turned to glare at Kenny.

"I've heard of walls having ears, but not eyes," Kenny said, sliding the door open, candle in hand.

A mound of backpacks lay piled in the doorway. Stepping over them, Kenny swept the candle in a circle. All around him, a selection of camping equipment rested on the floor in tidy heaps. There were sleeping bags, stoves, tents, gas canisters, toilet paper rolls, groundsheets, cameras, maps. A low table stood in the center of the room and something metallic glinted from it.

The soft circle of candlelight crept forward and slid over the wooden surface of the table, illuminating an array of butcher's tools, all laid out: cleavers, saws, hooks, shears, choppers, plus specialized knives for skinning, boning, filleting, carving and slicing.

Kenny's blood felt like ice water in his veins. The tools all bore nicks from heavy use and the gouges in the tabletop affirmed its use as a chopping block. Kenny didn't want to know what the brown stains were that covered the floor.

Tiptoeing around the table, Kenny's mud-caked sneaker thunked against something solid. He stooped for a closer look and shrank from the sight of a human thigh bone. It had come loose from a rack of bones propped against the wall next to a small pyramid of skulls. Kenny backed away. He had seen enough.

"I told you not to touch anything!" Emi shrieked from behind him.

Kenny was so startled, he dropped the candle. It plopped onto a blanket and the flame caught hold.

Emi was a fearsome silhouette, blocking the doorway. She was twice as large as she had been before, with eyes glowing yellow, a gaping mouth and short pointed horns.

"Why didn't you listen?" she lamented. "It could have been so good, just you and me together."

The fire spread, working its way to the rolled up tents.

"And then what?" Kenny said, backing up towards the rear wall. "Put me on the menu, like these poor souls? No thanks." His heels touched the wall.

Emi stalked closer, her long pointed tongue licking the air. "There is no escape for you." She flexed her claws and reached for a cleaver.

"We'll see about that," Kenny said, summoning Kusanagi. He spun on his heel and swiped at the wall, slashing across and downward.

"NOOO!" Emi howled, diving towards him, at the same moment that a camping gas canister exploded.

Kenny shoulder-charged the makeshift door he had fashioned and pelted out into the pitch-dark forest. Behind him raced the flaming figure of the mountain hag, her hair ablaze.

"You can't escape," she taunted, waving the cleaver. "I know these woods and I can see in the dark." She turned in a slow circle, her gaze sweeping the clearing.

Kenny waited for her back to turn and burst from cover, only to catch his toe in the loop of a tree root and slam into the ground. Scrambling to his feet, he then plowed through a bush, snagged his hoodie and was thrown against a tree trunk.

"I can hear you," sang the creature, patting out the flames in her hair. "Ready or not, here I come."

Kenny groaned and bumbled his way through the woods. It was no good. He could hear the hag closing in fast. He crashed through a patch of ferns and into another clearing. Grateful for the momentary absence of obstacles, he stumbled forward – until a vine caught him under the throat, and tightened.

"Huurkh!" Kenny gasped, clawing at the sinewy limb as it lifted him into the air. His feet kicked out and his head pounded. A second grasping creeper snaked around his waist.

"Yes, yes! Hold him," commanded the hag, her voice growing louder.

Kenny couldn't breathe; he knew that in seconds he would lose consciousness. Straining to concentrate, he tried to summon his sword. He felt the weight of Kusanagi settle into his grip and lashed out at the twisting tendril overhead. The tree squealed and warm sap gushed from the wound. It flung Kenny away and he landed on his ankle, a sharp pain shooting up his leg.

"Owww!" he groaned through clenched teeth, rolling to a stop. He spat to clear the taste of blood from his mouth, then realized it wasn't his. *The tree was bleeding.*

"I see him!" cried the hag triumphantly. "He's all mine."

Kenny thrust the sword into the ground and levered himself upright. He was as good as blind in the dark, unable to stand or fight. This was not a good way to end things.

The hag's footsteps faltered. "No!" she wailed. "No, he's mine. You can't have him."

Kenny's ears were filled with the sound of furiously beating wings. He felt the rush of wind at his back before talons locked on his shoulders, his stomach heaved and he felt himself being yanked high into the air.

"It's not fair. I found him first!" the hag cried, her voice fading away to nothing.

Kenny saw the black swathe of forest dwindle beneath him and moonlight filled the sky. In seconds, he was looking down on a silver sea of swirling clouds before whatever was holding him released its grip and he fell, spinning towards the ground far below.

30　三十

Kenny had gained plenty of practice over the past few days in tapping his *ki* to control the wind. The neural pathways, the mental images, the spirit channels, all of these had become second nature, like learning to balance on a bicycle or to kick legs and churn arms when swimming.

He glided on the breeze, allowing the air currents to bear him far away from the mountain hag and her burning shack. Seeing a clear slope below, he shaped the wind to set him down. Once on firm ground, Kenny rolled down his sock to check his sprained ankle. The skin around the joint was swollen and puffy. Ice would be good right now, but he was once again stuck on the side of the mountain.

The flapping of wings from behind made him turn around. The creature facing him was some kind of fusion of bird and man. Each foot had three toes ending in eagle claws; long powerful legs joined a narrow torso below a massive chest; muscular arms extended, with talons in place of fingers; and human eyes blinked above a hooked beak. Its gray plumage was streaked with emerald and scarlet.

It rose to its full height and Kenny thought for a moment that a cloak of feathers hung across its back – until the edges flexed, fanning open like the wings of an angel, except there was nothing angelic about it.

Kenny hobbled to his feet, sword in hand. "I was going to thank you for helping me back there," he began, "but then you went and dropped me, and now you're looking surprised that I'm not dead, so I guess that wasn't an accident, right?"

The bird creature cocked its head, watching the sword tip waver in front of it.

"Afraid of the sword, huh? You should be," Kenny said. "Hey, wait, maybe you can help me. I'm looking for –"

The creature moved so fast, it seemed to disappear. One moment it was in front of Kenny, eyeing the sword; the next its right fist launched in his stomach, its left hand chopped down on his sword grip and it spun to deliver a roundhouse kick to the side of his head.

Kenny crashed to the ground, his head ringing. He had been disarmed and flattened in the time it took to blink. His eyes rolled back and he gratefully blacked out.

The dull chime of a gong filtered through the wall of sleep. Faint chanting also drifted into Kenny's ears and he cracked one eye open. He was lying on a futon in a darkened room. A simple lamp, no more than a wick in a dish of oil, burned on the floor, radiating a puddle of soft light. His tattered clothes had been removed and he was wearing a baggy pair of *jinbei* pajamas.

Kenny sat up, expecting his body to hurt all over – it certainly ought to, given the past couple of days – but he was pleasantly surprised at the absence of pain. He touched his temple, where the kick had knocked him out, but other than some tenderness, there was no bruise. His ankle had been bound with a strip of cloth and a salve had been applied, judging from the medicinal odor. His chest wound had been similarly treated.

"You're awake. Good. Make yourself presentable." The hoarse voice belonged to a robed figure sitting *seiza*-style across from Kenny, its face hidden by a hood. It rose and left through a door.

Kenny saw that a wooden bucket of ice-cold water had been left for him, along with a washcloth. Stripping down, he cleaned himself up as best he could, and put on a pair of baggy breeches and a wide-sleeved shirt that were laid out beside the futon.

The hooded figure reappeared in the doorway. "Come."

Kenny followed, stepping into a short passageway that led to a narrow wooden staircase spiraling upward. They hurried down corridor after corridor, all of them wooden, with intricate carvings of lotus flowers embellishing the walls and oriental dragons entwined around pillars. The sweet smell of incense permeated the air.

The guide stopped before a pair of huge doors, each twenty feet tall, lacquered a deep red and adorned with complex geometric patterns in gold leaf. The figure pushed back its hood and Kenny was surprised to see a human face glowering at him. The man was Japanese with flowing black hair and piercing close-set eyes above a long hooked nose.

He clapped his hands once and the doors swung silently inward. The man ushered Kenny into the largest hall he had ever seen. The walls and ceiling stretched for hundreds of feet in every direction. Candles and braziers burned like constellations in the immense void. A thick blue haze of incense swirled in the eddies created by the sweep of the doors.

Kenny's escort led the way down the central aisle to the very front of the room. As Kenny hustled to keep up, he was horrified to see that hundreds of pairs of eyes were gauging his every step: kneeling on each side, in perfect rows, were throngs of bird-creatures, like the one that had carried him here.

Advancing through the crowd, Kenny noticed a gradual change as he went; the creatures became more human the closer they sat to the front. They started as little more than giant birds at the back, but wings and claws gave way to human arms and legs. The beaks too changed from hawkish bills to prominent, fleshy noses. Bright plumage blended to become colorful complexions. By the time he reached the first rows, the creatures assembled could have passed as fully human, although oddly featured.

The attendant stopped before a low stage with a *tatami* mat covering. He bowed so low that his hair brushed the floor.

"Kneel," he ordered Kenny.

Kenny did as instructed. Cool air whipped around his neck, as if suddenly displaced.

"You may look up now, child," a deep voice rumbled.

Raising his eyes, Kenny saw an ancient, ruddy-faced man sitting on the stage, atop a plump cushion; neither had been there before. Despite his advanced age, there was nothing frail-looking about this individual. He was over six feet tall, with a barrel chest and tree trunk arms. A long nose emerged from a flowing white beard and kindly yellow eyes sparkled amid a nest of deep laughter lines. On his head, a tiny, round black hat perched on a white mane, and in his hand was a fan made from seven perfect white feathers. Everything about the man exuded power, authority and control.

Kenny swallowed hard.

"We will conduct proceedings in the boy's native tongue, as befits the gravity of his trial," the bearded man announced.

"Trial?" Kenny repeated. "For what? I haven't done any –"

"Silence!" commanded the usher. "Your turn to speak will come."

"Bring forth the first witness," the judge said.

A stocky young man with a blue-tinged pallor stepped up from the front row and bowed.

"State your name, please, for the record," the judge said.

"Zengubu, my lord," the witness replied.

"State only what you saw."

"Yes, my lord," Zengubu said. He paced for a few seconds, hands clasped behind his back. "I was stationed, as usual, at the gates of the Kurama-dera. I saw this *gaijin* child enter with a *tanuki*, but thought nothing of it until I saw him speak with the tiger guardians, Moko and Koji. He was asking after you, my lord."

The judge leaned back. "Was he now? Hmm. An assassin perhaps?"

"The boy then deliberately left the path and began making his way up the holy mountain," continued Zengubu.

"An act of great bravery or great foolishness," the judge noted. "How did he fare?"

"By now, my lord, I was suspicious, so I followed the child. First, he was tricked by the *konaki-jiji*, but the *tanuki* helped him to escape. Then he found the *jinmenju* and again asked after you, but Katsura the *kodama* sent him to the *ayashii-ketsu* to shelter."

The judge chuckled. "Ah, Katsura is a clever one."

"Yes, my lord, she is," Zengubu agreed. "I watched the mouth close on the boy and thought the matter ended . . ."

"But?" said the old man.

"But the child punched out three teeth and

244

climbed free."

"Did he now?" A look of faint amusement played over the judge's face.

"And then he outran the *tsuchikurobi*, baked *dorotabo* and went with the *yama-uba* to her hut."

"All this and still he lives?" The judge studied Kenny closely, as if seeing him properly for the first time.

"That is so, my lord. The boy is not without some skill in *mado*, but he is untrained. Nonetheless, he is clever and resourceful."

The judge scratched his chin. "Did he kill anything?"

"No, my lord," Zengubu answered.

"Then no crime has been committed," the old man said, straightening up. "Why has he been brought here? Who has done this?"

"It is I, master," said Kenny's guide.

"Kokibo, explain yourself," the judge demanded.

"I was on patrol, my lord," Kokibo said, "when I noticed fire on the mountain. I watched the accused flee from the *yama-uba* and then . . . then he cut down the *jubokko*."

A collective gasp of horror came from the crowd of onlookers.

The judge glared at Kenny. "Is this true, boy? You may answer."

"Like, duh," Kenny said, throwing out his hands. "That freaky vampire tree was trying to kill me. It was self-defense. Ask him." He thrust out a thumb in Kokibo's direction.

"This is true," Kokibo said. "But it changes nothing. He cut down the *jubokko*, even though he had been warned by Katsura not to harm any living tree on this mountain. He cannot plead ignorance; he was told."

The ageing master closed his eyes, as if in prayer, and said, "What are we to do with him?" The eyes snapped open. "You have no weapon, child. How did you strike down the *jubokko*?"

"With this," Kenny said, summoning his sword.

Another gasp rippled through the restive crowd.

The judge leaned forward, his forehead creased with furrows. "I . . . seem to know this sword . . . Does it have a name?"

"Kusanagi," Kenny said.

The sense of disquiet and consternation in the room was palpable by now.

"For what purpose were you seeking me?" the old man said, his eyes narrow.

"I need your help, master Sojobo," Kenny said.

Anger blazed in the yellow eyes. "Yet you come to me, bearing a stolen weapon, and use it to slay one of my subjects? How do you plead?"

"I didn't steal it," Kenny protested. "I won it in combat. Ask the sword, if you don't believe me."

"There is no need," Sojobo said. "The boy pleads guilty as charged. The sentence is death."

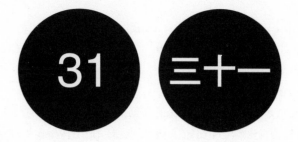

The entire assembly of bird-men rose as one. Kokibo and Zengubu took up position on either side of Kenny.

"I am sorry, child," Sojobo said. "You are brave but foolish. You should learn to heed the warnings given to you."

"Yeah? Well, so should you," Kenny snarled, rounding on the old man. He leveled the sword at him, pressing the tip against Sojobo's nose. "I'm not going without a fight, so who else is going to die today? I promise, I'll take you with me."

It was only the merest flick of the fan in Sojobo's hand, but to Kenny it felt like a freight train had flattened him. The hurricane-force blast of wind slammed him head over heels and he skidded down the aisle, the sword spinning away. Zengubu and Kokibo were at his side, each seizing an arm, before he had stopped sliding.

"Brave but foolish," Kokibo hissed into Kenny's ear, dragging him back to the front.

Sojobo stood up, towering over Kenny. "Fear not, child. The end will be swift."

"Master," Kokibo said, bowing his head, "may I perform the deed?"

"Since you apprehended him, you may do so, although your eagerness to take life reflects poorly on you. Take him outside and execute him," Sojobo said, turning away.

"No!" Kenny cried, struggling against the iron grip.

"Not so fast, you drunken old buffoon!" a high, clear voice rang out.

Kenny's heart leapt at the sound of Genkuro's voice. He twisted but was unable to see past Kokibo's chest.

"What? You mangy, flea-bitten cur!" Sojobo roared, his eyes fixed on a point behind Kenny. "I thought I told you never to darken my door again."

"Or what, you bloated windbag? You might break a sweat getting to your feet?"

Sojobo stepped down from the *tatami*. He lifted his head and sniffed the air with his impressive nose.

"What is the meaning of this?" he demanded, extending a finger. "What is this creature and why do you bring it here, knowing its presence defiles the sanctity of this place? Explain yourself, *kitsune*."

"Hey, Santa Claus! 'It' has a name, if you don't mind."

Kiyomi! Butterflies swirled through Kenny's chest on hearing her voice and hope surged anew.

"Let her pass," Genkuro said in a low, calm voice.

"No, she is unclean," Sojobo insisted.

"Let her pass or answer to me." This time, there was no mistaking the hardened edge in Genkuro's voice.

Sojobo bristled, glaring down at the old man. "You dare threaten me, under my own roof?" He held out a hand and a follower slapped a long spear into his open palm.

Genkuro beckoned him closer, leaned forward and dropped his voice to a confidential whisper. "I will not fight you at this time and in this place, oh great Sojobo. It would serve no purpose for me to defeat you in front of your loyal subjects."

"Hah!" Sojobo roared. "Why, you worm-riddled pup! I should break you in two and feed you to the *ko-tengu* for your insolence."

"*Sensei*, no!" Kenny said. "I'll fight him."

"Stay out of this, Kuromori," Genkuro ordered, drawing a symbol in the air. "Sojobo won't be harming anyone with that weapon."

Sojobo gaped at the spear in his hands which drooped, as limp and useless as overcooked spaghetti. "Enough of this nonsense!" he declared, pulling it straight again. He handed the spear back to its bearer and looked closely at Kenny. "What did you say the boy's name is?"

"Kuromori," answered Genkuro.

Sojobo stroked the end of his long nose. "And he has the sword . . . So, the prophecy is true? He is the one?"

"It would appear so," Genkuro said, interlacing his fingers.

"Well, well . . ." Sojobo gestured for Zengubu and Kokibo to release Kenny, before pacing in a circle around the boy, never once removing his eyes from him. He returned to Genkuro and said, "Forgive me, old fox, but your mistress . . . is she out of her mind? *This* boy? This . . . miserable scrap of man flesh?"

"Do not underestimate him just because he is a *gaijin*," Genkuro said. "It sets him apart in many ways."

Sojobo returned to his *tatami*, hands clasped behind his back, and nodded in Kiyomi's direction, at the back of the room. "And that . . . thing?"

A low growl escaped Genkuro's lips. "Speak kindly. The girl is as much an unwilling participant in these events as the boy."

Sojobo settled onto his cushion. "Very well. She may proceed."

The guards blocking Kiyomi from entering the room shouldered their spears and she strode quickly along the aisle to the front, with Poyo waddling by her feet. Sojobo motioned for the crowd to sit again.

Kiyomi ran up to Kenny and whispered in his ear. "You are in so much trouble right now, you idiot."

Kenny grinned at her. "And? What's new about that? I am so glad to see you. You're looking . . . really good." He blushed.

"Yeah? Well, you look like someone ran you over with a truck then reversed over you for good measure."

Poyo hugged Kenny's bare leg.

"You have yet to explain why you are here," Sojobo said to Genkuro.

"I need the boy," Genkuro said. "Something has happened. Something . . . catastrophic."

Sojobo's huge white furry caterpillar eyebrows rose slightly. "It is not like you to be so dramatic, Genkuro," he said. "What is this disaster you speak of?"

"Throw open your doors and see for yourself," Genkuro said. "Anything less and you will not believe me."

The crinkles around Sojobo's yellow eyes deepened. "Do not try my patience, old fox."

"Just go outside and see with your own eyes."

"Bring them," Sojobo said, and he was gone.

Zengubu placed one hand on Kiyomi's shoulder and the other on Genkuro. He blinked and all three vanished.

"Now you." Kokibo grabbed Kenny's collar – and every color exploded at once. At the same time, he felt like he was being turned inside out and back again.

Cold night air hit his face and Kenny dropped to his knees. If there had been anything in his stomach, he knew he would be staring at it right now. Kokibo wrenched him to his feet and Kenny saw the purple contours of Mount Kurama falling away beneath him.

"Wh–?" he gibbered.

"Shhh," Kiyomi said, rubbing his back. "Teleporting is always rough the first time."

They were on a walkway, running along the inside of a high fortress wall, enclosing the *tengu* garrison.

"What is it you wish me to see?" Sojobo said, looking up at the mantle of stars.

"Sojobo," Genkuro said in a soft voice, "which way is east?"

The *tengu* king scowled and pointed at the mauve horizon. "Why that way, of course. Soon it will be dawn."

"Ah, yes, the hour before sunrise," Genkuro said. "And when is that?"

"Around the sixth hour, by human counting. We measure time in prayer."

"Indeed," Genkuro said. "Kuromori-*san*, please be so kind as to show Sojobo-*sama* your watch."

"Uh, OK." Puzzled, Kenny held out his wrist. The time read: 9:57.

"Whoa," Kenny said. "If it's ten in the morning, then why's it still dark?"

"Because," said Genkuro, "the sun didn't rise."

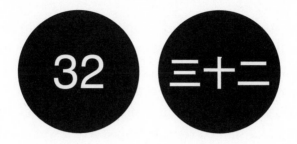

"What manner of *kitsune* trickery is this?" demanded Sojobo.

"This is not my doing," Genkuro said. "This is the work of someone far more cunning and powerful."

"But where is the sun?" Sojobo repeated, searching the sky.

"We both know you will not believe anything I tell you – we have far too much history between us for that – so why not ask a more . . . trustworthy source?" Genkuro said.

"That I will," Sojobo said, and vanished.

Kokibo placed his hand on Kenny's back. "Come," he said.

"Oh, no," Kenny groaned. "Not aga–"

Kenny wrapped his arms around a pillar and clambered to his feet. Kiyomi moved to steady him.

"Urgh. How does anyone ever get used to that?" he complained.

They were now in a large chamber with a high ceiling. Wooden columns supported the gable roof and hanging lamps cast soft red hues. The only furnishing was an altar at the back of the room, around which Genkuro and the *tengu* crowded.

Kenny crept closer for a peek. Upon the altar was a wooden structure with miniature steps, balconies, pillars, doors and a slanted roof. It looked like a scale model of a *honden*.

Sojobo bowed before the altar and approached the small building, chanting under his breath. He knelt and reached forward to open the double doors. Genkuro and Zengubu both dropped to their knees. Kiyomi grabbed Kenny's hand and motioned for him to kneel too.

The wooden doors swung open and Kenny was half expecting mist or blinding light to spill out. But the only thing inside was a dull bronze disk, about the size of a trash can lid.

"The Yata no Kagami!" Kiyomi gasped, pressing her hands to her mouth.

"Huh?" Kenny said. "That? That's the sacred mirror? It looks more like a shield."

"How do you know about it?" Kiyomi whispered.

"Uh, something my grandad talked about. What's the big deal with it anyway?"

"You don't know the story?"

Kokibo and Zengubu took up the chant, joining their voices with that of Sojobo.

"OK, very quickly," Kiyomi said. "Way back when, Susano-wo, the Storm God and all-around rogue, committed an outrage so great that Amaterasu, the Sun Goddess, shut herself away in a cave and refused to come out, meaning the world was in total darkness."

"That sounds horribly familiar," Kenny muttered.

"The gods all got together and decided something had to be done, so they threw a party. Amaterasu heard the music and laughter and wondered what was going on – after all, she'd left the world in permanent night – so she opened the cave door a crack and wanted to know why everyone was so happy."

Genkuro scowled and placed a finger over his lips.

"Sorry," Kiyomi said, and continued in hushed tones. "Anyway, the gods had hung a mirror outside the cave and told Amaterasu that they'd found a new and better god to replace her with. She looked in the mirror and, sure enough, saw a new Sun Goddess. Wanting to find out more about this newcomer, she opened the cave door and that's when the other gods grabbed her and pulled her out, to save the day."

"And she kept the mirror?"

"Yes. It's rumored to hold some of her essence. It's very powerful."

"Why? What can it do?"

"I have no idea. I didn't even know it was here."

The chant ended and the still air was silent. Rising as one, the three *tengu* slowly backed away from the altar. Sojobo's hands remained outstretched, as if he was pleading.

Without a sound, the metal plate glided out of its cabinet, remaining upright. It spun through half a turn, and Kenny realized that he had been looking at the back of it. The front was so brightly polished, it shone like silver.

Sojobo cupped his hands and a bright ball of light appeared in them. Molding the light, he reshaped it into a bright beam. He pointed the gleaming shaft at the mirror, which glowed with a blinding intensity.

Kenny shielded his eyes with his palm.

"Look at the wall, dummy," Kiyomi whispered.

Kenny squinted and saw a bright circle on the wall: the mirror's own reflection. Shadows emerged within the glimmering shape, as insubstantial as charcoal smudges on a chalk canvas, and swirled to form a woman's face.

"State your desire," she said.

Sojobo bowed before the image and said, "I wish to know why the sun has not risen this morning."

"The sun has risen," the mirror replied. "Only you cannot see it." The face faded away. In its place, the circle darkened to a soot black, with a slate-gray spot in the center.

"The sun?" Kokibo spluttered. "It has been . . . blacked out?"

"My lord," Zengubu said. "That is not possible. It must be an eclipse."

"Not for this long," Sojobo said. "There must be a shield, a barrier of some kind."

"Oh, no," Kenny said. "The space mirror . . . the solar reflector thingy . . . But, how? What could possibly have gone wrong?" He stepped towards the reflection. "Show me the space station," he said.

"Silence, boy!" Sojobo commanded, glaring at Kenny with nostrils flared. "You have no part in this."

Genkuro stepped between the boy and the *tengu*, placing a steadying hand on Sojobo's arm. "Remember what I told you. Do not underestimate this young one."

The *tengu* king scowled, then relented. "Show him."

Pinpricks of light punctured the black circle. A curved sail of silvery foil drifted past and into the distance, from where it resembled a lustrous parasol. The angle changed, revealing the blue marble Earth below. A black circle of shadow moved with the slowly revolving planet.

"A geosynchronous orbit," Kiyomi said. "It's locked in parallel with the Earth."

"And the shadow's right over Japan," Kenny noted. "I thought the shield was only supposed to deflect one percent of the light, not all of it. There's no way this is an accident."

"You're saying someone caused this?" Zengubu ventured.

"But who would do such a thing?" demanded Sojobo. "Without sunlight, crops will fail, temperatures will drop, weather patterns will change. It will be a disaster for the world."

"Everything will die," Kokibo said in a flat voice.

"Who would be so insane as to do such a thing?"

Sojobo shook his head. "This . . . cannot be." He closed his hands, extinguishing the light. The mirror went dark and returned to its resting place inside the miniature shrine. "If I hadn't seen it with my own eyes . . ."

"A mirror shows only the truth," Genkuro said.

Sojobo slammed his fist into his palm. "What are we to do, old fox? For every hour we do nothing, plants go without food and animals remain in their burrows."

"A mirror in the sky . . ." Genkuro said. "Who would have thought of such a thing?"

"Humans!" Kokibo spat. "Who else?"

"Precisely," Genkuro said. "And who, then, would be best placed to undo this madness?"

"Why, humans, of course," said Sojobo.

"And that is why I need the boy," Genkuro said. "Can you take us back to Tokyo?"

"This boy?" Sojobo said, scowling at Kenny. "This Kuromori? He can stop this thing?"

Kenny straightened up and stared back in defiance. "Sir, I'll do my best."

Zengubu bowed before Sojobo. "My lord, I have seen it for myself; this boy is no ordinary mortal."

"What can he do?" Sojobo asked Genkuro.

"He has some limited control over the five elements of earth, water, fire, metal and air."

Sojobo waited. "Is that it?"

"I had two days with him, not two hundred years,"

258

Genkuro grumbled.

"And yet he is in possession of the sword . . ." Sojobo mused, stroking his beard. "Very well. We have nothing to lose. Genkuro, you had better be right."

The old *sensei* shrugged. "If I'm wrong, it won't matter."

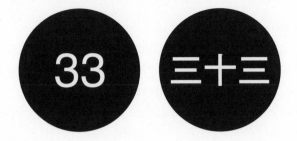

Oyama balanced the tray of sandwiches on one hand, slid open the door and eased his bulk into the main room, as carefully as a truck driver maneuvering into a parking space.

Harashima and Sato were red-faced, shouting at each other, fingers waving in front of noses. It was like old times, the manservant thought to himself. Neither paid any attention to him. He set the platter on a chair, moved the five trays already on the table to clear a space and positioned the fresh snacks.

"It's too dangerous," Harashima said to his brother. "I won't allow it."

"Do you have any better idea?" Sato fired back. "Because as of now, it's the only option we have."

"It's a terrible option! There are too many variables, too many things that could go wrong. There must be another way."

Oyama tiptoed to the door, slid it open and screamed like a little girl. Two tall, lean, fierce-looking men with odd complexions and extremely long noses were crowded into the hallway.

"Boo," Kiyomi said, grinning at Oyama's startled face. She brushed past him, followed by Genkuro, Poyo and Kenny, whose hand was clamped over his mouth. "Hi, Papa," she called out, silencing the discussion. "We found him and we've got guests."

Genkuro bowed and ushered in the *tengu*. "Please may I introduce Kokibo-*sama* and Zengubu-*sama*, two *tengu* in the service of the great Sojobo."

The *tengu* nodded in greeting. Harashima recovered his composure and hurried forward to bow deeply.

"We shall leave you now," Kokibo said.

"Please, stay a little longer," Sato said. "Time is short and your assistance may still be required."

"Your instructions were to help in any way," Genkuro said. "Stay and you can give a fuller report to your noble king."

Zengubu nodded and stationed himself by the wall.

"Ken-*kun*, it is good to see you again," Harashima said, beaming at Kenny. "I feared the worst."

"Yeah, well, me too," Kenny admitted, scooping up several sandwiches. "It did get a bit hairy at times."

"Where have you been?" Sato snapped at him. "This is your doing."

"Oh, not again," Kenny said, taking a bite and making a face at the filling. "How can a messed-up satellite be my fault?"

"Show him," Genkuro said.

Harashima picked up the remote control and lit up the bank of television screens. A 3-D wire-frame diagram flashed up, showing a model of the *Hoshi no Kagami* space platform. It resembled a huge umbrella, with spokes radiating from a central column.

Sato pointed to the lowest section of the central assembly, the "handle" of the parasol. "This part here is the control module, which was delivered into space last night. It docked successfully with the solar shield and the system went live. It was during the testing stage that a malfunction occurred. Extra backup panels were deployed and the positional thrusters fired all their fuel, taking up a new orbit."

"That's why it blacked out the whole of Japan," Kiyomi added.

"This is when all the pieces fell into place," Harashima said. "Once we identified it was a software problem, it narrowed down the suspects."

"The Aosugi Corporation, to be precise," Sato said.

"Hidetoshi Aosugi is someone we've been tracking for a long time," Harashima said. "Another one with known extremist views. He's bankrolled a lot of politicians in return for major public construction projects."

"His company is a major sponsor and contributor to the *Hoshi no Kagami* program," Sato said. "They developed the software, propulsion system and shield design. I always wondered why they their bid was so low."

262

"Let me guess," Kenny said, inspecting a sandwich stuffed with fried noodles. "They hired that plane four days ago."

"Through a subsidiary, yes," Sato replied. "They only bought the company a week before, hence the paperwork wasn't all filed and it was difficult to trace ownership."

"But what would the Aosugi Corporation want with a stupid telescope?" Kenny said.

Harashima and Sato exchanged glances.

"As soon as the shield malfunctioned, attempts were made to manually override the software," Harashima explained. "When these failed, a self-destruct command was sent."

"And that also failed, right?" Kenny said.

Sato nodded. "So we called in a favor from the US Navy. They helped us to modify two ship-based missiles so they could be used as antisatellite weapons."

Kenny frowned. "That still doesn't explain why –"

"It's easier if we show you," Sato said, motioning for Harashima to change the television picture. A bulky gray warship appeared on-screen, taking up the whole wall.

"This is the guided missile destroyer Kirishima," Sato said. "If you watch, you'll see the two missiles being launched . . ."

Kenny flinched as two blinding columns of white flame belched from missile silos on the bow of the ship. Twin warheads rocketed up from the blaze and soared into the night sky, trailing columns of vapor. The camera angle changed to track the missiles charging through the atmosphere. They both then exploded into fireballs and disappeared.

"What just happened?" Kenny said, eyes fixed on the screen. "Where did they go?"

"That's what the Self-Defense Force was asking until someone checked footage of the space station," Sato said. "Watch carefully."

The image cut to show the space mirror orbiting the Earth. Two fiery dots crawled into the bottom of the picture, growing brighter and larger. The floating platform tilted and a shudder went through the metal structure, rippling the sodium-foil canopy. Two tiny rings flared beneath the control module and a dazzling beam of raw energy pulsed downward, detonating the incoming missiles.

"That's not possible," Kenny said, forgetting his disgust at the strawberry and whipped cream sandwich pinched in his fingers.

"It gets better," Kiyomi said. "Zoom in, Pops."

Harashima adjusted the picture, zeroing in on the area below the control module. At first, Kenny saw only the blackness of space, but after Harashima adjusted the contrast he made out two crystalline disks, suspended below.

"Now you know why they wanted the telescope," Sato said. "Or, more specifically, why they wanted the giant lenses inside."

"What are you saying?" Kenny faltered. "That . . . that's like a giant magnifying glass effect in the sky?"

Sato nodded. "It's not a new idea. The Nazis were developing a similar weapon during World War Two. In fact, Hermann Oberth put forward the concept in 1929. *Sonnengewehr*, they called it – that's 'Sun Gun' in English. The mirror collects solar radiation and the lenses concentrate it into a beam."

"And now someone's gone and done it for real?" Kenny glanced back at the image on screen.

"Yes. The Americans launched another antisatellite missile, but it too was shot down."

"By who? Is that thing automated or is someone up there pulling the trigger?"

"Good question," Sato said. "The control module does have a habitable section, but no astronauts were sent up."

"As far as you know." Kenny sighed. "So now that thing's up there with no way to stop it? Is that what you're saying?"

Harashima turned off the satellite footage. "Well . . . there is one idea." He glared at Sato.

"It is, as you say, a long shot," Sato said. "Nothing has been decided. I am waiting on my superiors to come back to me with the appropriate authorization."

Kenny's eyes narrowed. "Authorization? To do what?"

"We have one chance," Sato said. "As you saw, any hostile approach gets destroyed by the Sun Gun. However, one final routine launch was planned . . . of an Automated Transfer Vehicle to deliver propellant, air, water and spare parts to the control module. I have requested that modifications be made to the payload, so it can support two passengers: me and you."

Kenny dropped his sandwich. "Whoa. You want me . . .? But sir, I don't know the first thing about space travel. Doesn't it take years to train an astronaut?"

"Desperate times call for desperate measures," Sato said. "This is not my preferred solution either, but someone has to go up there to stop this thing. I've seen what you can do when you put your mind to it. Plus, I suspect there is more to this than meets the eye."

"Uncle's talking about *oni*," Kiyomi said. "If there's any kind of *yokai* threat up there . . ."

"So, what's your plan?" Kenny asked. "We blast into space, hope we don't get shot down by an orbital laser –"

"More of a heat weapon," Kiyomi corrected.

"Whatever," Kenny growled. "We dock with the space mirror, and then?"

"We either override the controls manually to correct the course, or we destroy it," Sato said.

Kenny sighed. "And if we do nothing, Japan dies."

"It's already started," Harashima said quietly. "There's been mass panic, a run on banks, riots in some areas, stampedes at the airport, looting in supermarkets . . ."

"Can't you just load this delivery ship with explosives and blow the thing up, you know, like a Trojan horse?" Kenny tried.

"It's too risky," Sato said. "We'd need to destroy the mirror completely, otherwise the debris could make things worse."

Kenny fought down the nausea and dread welling inside. "All right, count me in," he said. "If you can do this, then so can I."

"There is one other thing you should know," Sato said, his face grim. "The supply vessel was not designed for reentry. I've asked the Space Agency to add shielding and parachutes, but they are not confident it will hold. They estimate only a thirty-six percent chance of a successful return."

"Well, let's cross that bridge when we get to it," Kenny said. "If we're still alive by then."

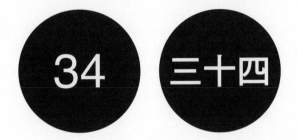

Kiyomi picked up a tray of curling sandwiches and headed for the door. "Ken-*chan*, can you give me a hand with these?" she said.

Kenny scowled in annoyance. "No thanks, I'm not –"

She rolled her eyes. "Just come with me to the kitchen."

"Ohhh, I get it." Kenny balanced two trays and followed Kiyomi out of the room.

Kiyomi dumped the sandwiches in the sink and yanked opened the fridge door. Pushing her face inside, she sniffed and honed in on a paper-wrapped package. She unrolled the soggy butcher paper, grabbed a knife and sliced some hearty chunks from the large rib-eye steak, spearing them with the knife point and jamming them into her mouth.

"I'm going with you," she said to Kenny, still chewing.

"Are you crazy?" he said, setting his trays on the counter.

"What? You think I'm going to sit on my butt here while you and my uncle . . .? You're going to need my help. And we're a good team."

Kenny looked away; the sight of blood on Kiyomi's lips made him queasy.

"Besides," she continued, "if Uncle is right and there are *yokai* involved, then who better than me at your side? He can't even see them without his special shades."

"But what about . . . your condition? I can't think of anything more stressful than being strapped into a tin can with a ton of explosive up your backside."

"I'll be fine," Kiyomi said. "I haven't had . . . an episode for three days now."

"That's because you've been shut away, keeping calm," Kenny said.

Kiyomi finished off the steak and rinsed her hands. "Just tell me one thing," she said, dropping to her haunches and rooting around inside a cupboard. "Joking aside, who would you rather have covering your back? Me or my uncle?" She stood up, clutching a black duffel bag.

Kenny kept his eyes rooted to the floor and absently rubbed the bruises on his neck. "Truthfully? Right now, I'd take your uncle."

Kiyomi smiled and patted his cheek. "You always were a terrible liar."

"Ahem." Genkuro cleared his throat from the doorway. "Your presence is required."

Back in the main room, Sato tucked his phone back into his pocket.

"Kuromori-*san*," he said, "we are authorized to proceed."

269

"I'm going with you," Kiyomi blurted. "To say good-bye."

"Out of the question," Sato snapped.

"Say it here," Harashima said.

"It's OK," Kenny said. "I want her to come along, to see us off. Call it a last request . . ."

Genkuro looked from Sato to Harashima. "What harm can it do?"

"All right," Sato said grudgingly. He looked up at the *tengu* who were watching silently. "Zengubu-*sama* and Kokibo-*sama*, may I ask you to perform for us a last service?"

"Of course. What is it you require?" Kokibo asked.

"Can you please take three of us to the Tanegashima Uchu Senta? It'll save us two hours."

"The what?" Kenny whispered to Kiyomi.

"The Tanegashima Space Center. It's off the southern tip of Japan, about six hundred miles away," she answered.

"I know where it is," Kokibo said. "We can take you."

"Kuromori-*san* . . . Kenny . . ." Harashima began. "I have watched you for a long time, seen you grow from a boy to . . . almost a man. I know your grandfather is very proud of you, as am I." He sighed. "I - I did not expect us to be saying good-bye this soon."

Kenny's mouth was a razor-thin line. "It's OK, Mr. H."

"You're like the son I never had." Harashima bowed and dashed out of the room.

The *tengu* exchanged glances. Poyo scratched his ear.

"That was awkward," Kiyomi said.

Genkuro bowed before Kenny. "You are not ready for this, Kuromori-*san*. I doubt even your grandfather would have been, despite all I taught him. But you have proven me wrong many times already. I hope you will do so again."

"Thank you, *sensei*," Kenny said with a slight dip of his head. "I'll try."

"If I have any advice to give you, it is to always have a clear mind. Seek the light and it will find you."

Sato cleared his throat. "We must go. Time is against us."

"Come," Kokibo said, reaching out a hand.

"*BW-AWWKH!*" Kenny's stomach still hadn't adjusted to teleportation and he regretted filling up on sandwiches.

Sato thanked the *tengu*, who vanished with a faint pop of imploding air.

Kenny raised his head. They were on a concrete apron, surrounded by gleaming white buildings. Powerful lights illuminated the whole area and vehicles hurried in all directions, stirring the warm, humid air.

"Look behind you," Kiyomi said, pointing.

Kenny twisted his head and craned upward, tracing the majestic lines of a slim H-IIA rocket. The main body was painted orange, apart from the top quarter and booster rockets, which were white.

"We're . . . going up . . . in that?" Kenny stammered,

his stomach doing somersaults again.

A small electric cart whirred towards them and stopped. Kenny squinted past the headlights and saw two people climb out. One was a portly Japanese man in a business suit; the other, a woman wearing a white lab coat. Sato stepped forward to make introductions.

"You're not making the best first impression," Kiyomi tutted at Kenny, who was wearing his *tengu*-supplied clothing, now flecked with sandwich remains from his teleportation sickness.

"I think I have more important things to worry about," Kenny muttered.

"Oh, yeah. I forgot – you hate flying."

The suited man held out his hand for Kenny to shake, then thought better of it and bowed instead. "Takashi Ogose," he said. "Assistant Director of this facility. Very pleased to meet you."

Bowing, the woman said, "Ibuki Nomura. Welcome to the Yoshinobu Launch Complex. I've been assigned to help prepare you for this mission." A flicker of concern crossed her brow. "You're younger than I expected."

"Yeah," Kenny agreed. "But not too young to die, eh?" He forced a weak smile.

Kiyomi's sharp elbow caught him in the ribs. "Be nice," she hissed in his ear. "These people are trying to help."

They rode in silence towards a towering white slab of a building, standing at the western edge of a huge runway.

At the opposite end, two orange-and-white painted lattice towers flanked the H-IIA rocket moving into position on a launchpad overlooking the Pacific Ocean.

A shooting star streaked across the night sky.

"Quick, make a wish," Kiyomi whispered.

"That's easy," Kenny said. "I wish not to become a shooting star myself."

The cart pulled up outside the huge edifice and a team of technicians in white coveralls ran out to meet it.

"This is the Vehicle Assembly Building," Ibuki explained. "Normally, we'd prepare you over at the Block House, but we don't have time, so we're going to have to wing it, as you say."

Technicians poked and prodded Kenny as he followed Ibuki into the building.

"What's the mission status?" Sato asked.

"The weather is holding, although there's rain coming in, which wasn't forecast," Ogose said.

"That's because of the solar deflection," Ibuki added. "The sun's heat, plus Earth's rotation, drive air current and pressure. Already, it's a mess."

"How long have we got?" Sato said, extending his arm so it could be measured.

"The Mobile Launch Platform is in position on Launchpad One. Propellant loading operations have commenced and we're about to run flight slew testing on the attitude-control system," Ogose reported.

"Which means?"

"We're good to go. Terminal countdown operations will commence as soon as the slew test is complete. You'll have sixty minutes, providing the rain stays away."

Kenny and Sato were taken into a makeshift medical bay and hooked up to an array of sensors.

"Why were you sick earlier?" Ibuki asked Kenny. "Is there any preexisting medical condition I should know about?"

"Not really," Kenny said, unsure how to explain teleportation by *tengu*. "It's just travel sickness."

"I'm going to give you a shot of promethazine," Ibuki said, reaching for a hypodermic needle. "This will help alleviate motion sickness when in space."

After she had administered the injection, Ibuki read off Kenny's printout and scowled. "Your heart rate is elevated," she noted. "So is your respiration and blood pressure."

"That's because I'm trying not to poop myself," Kenny said. "I'm just a kid in the wrong place at the wrong time."

Ibuki turned to Sato. "The boy does have a point. He has no training, no psychological evaluation. Are you absolutely sure about this? Major Hoshide is ready and willing to accompany you, if needed."

Sato scowled. "Dr. Nomura, you don't need me to remind you that this mission has been authorized by the Prime Minister himself, and signed off by the Joint Chiefs of Staff. I understand that my methods may seem . . .

unusual to you, but please do not question me again or I will have you removed from this launch site."

Ibuki reddened, but then leaned closer. "And may I remind you, Sato-*san*, that, as a physician, I have a duty of care to my patients. If I decide that either you or the boy is unfit to travel, then no one goes anywhere. This is my facility and in here you do as I say. If you don't like it, leave now." She tore off a strip of paper and marched out.

"Ouch. That's you told," Kenny said, his eyes crinkling in a smile.

"She totally owned you!" Kiyomi said. "I like her."

After the battery of medical tests was complete, Ibuki returned. She raised an eyebrow at Sato.

"You're still here?" she said. "Countdown has commenced. We're X minus fifty-eight, so you'd better get suited up. This way, please."

They followed her into another room where more technicians were ready with two sets of undergarments. An engineer wheeled in a rack with two space suits hanging from it.

"Normally, these space suits would be custom-made to fit you exactly," Ibuki explained, "but we've had to adapt them as best we can."

"Time for you to say your good byes," Sato said to Kiyomi.

"Can't I wait until you're all dressed and going out to

the pad?" she said. "Please?"

"No. This is now a men's locker room. No place for a girl."

"Fine." Kiyomi put down her black duffel bag and held out her hands. "You first, *ojisan*. You can give me a hug, not a bow, this time."

Sato leaned forward stiffly.

"You're my favorite uncle, and I'm going to miss you so much," Kiyomi said, reaching inside Sato's jacket as she embraced him. "Oops."

CLACK! A black object bounced off the tiled floor.

"I'll get it, I'll get it!" Kiyomi said, stepping back. *CRUNCH!* She stooped to pick up Sato's mangled sunglasses. "Oops."

"Kiyomi-*chan*, what have you done? *What have you done?*" Sato looked as if he might explode.

Kiyomi stuck out her bottom lip. "Hmm, I'd say I accidentally broke your shades, which means you won't be able to see any you-know-what up there. Which also means you're not really much help to Ken-*chan* on this mission, are you?"

"Do you realize what you've done?" Sato howled.

"Yes, *ojisan*, I do!" Kiyomi shot back. "I have a limited time left before . . . And there's no way I'm just going to sit here and wait for it to happen. It's better if I go this way, at my own choosing."

"Kuromori-*san*," Sato pleaded, "tell Kiyomi-*chan* that she's not doing this. That you won't allow it."

"Sir," Kenny said, choosing his words with care, "if Kiyomi won't listen to you, there's no way she'll listen to me."

Kiyomi smiled in triumph and nodded to Ibuki. "Measure me up."

35 三十五

It was a long wait for Kenny to be fitted into his space suit: a liquid cooling and ventilation bodysuit encased in a two-part shell assembly. Once his gloves had been locked in position, he was escorted to a holding area where Kiyomi stood waiting, similarly dressed, her duffel bag at her feet.

"I feel like a Teletubby in this," Kenny said. "How do I look?"

"Like a dork, as usual," Kiyomi said. "I can't believe they're making us wear diapers."

"You signed up for this," Kenny reminded her. "Anyway, it's a Maximum Absorbency Garment, not a diaper."

Sato strode over to join them. "I see you're ready." He flashed a dirty look at Kiyomi. "Remember, the mission priority is to disable the weapon. If you do that, then a missile will do the rest. Otherwise, I want nothing fancy; just enter the control module, insert the override chip and correct the course."

"And if that doesn't work we destroy the whole thing," Kiyomi said.

"All you need to do is set its course for reentry. The sodium foil will vaporize in the atmosphere; the rest will burn up."

"Got it," Kenny said. "Seems simple enough."

Ibuki arrived with a clipboard. "X minus thirty minutes. I need to get you two out to the launchpad."

"I need one small favor," Kiyomi said, taking Ibuki to one side. "Can you fit my bag in the hold? I weigh less than my uncle so I know you have to recalculate the weight and everything. It isn't much."

Ibuki lifted the bag, assessing its weight. "I'll see what I can do."

The bus stopped at the base of one of the towers flanking the H-IIA rocket. Kenny and Kiyomi disembarked and climbed into a cage elevator. Ibuki closed the sliding grille and the elevator ascended smoothly.

At the top, a narrow walkway led to the supply vessel. Ibuki guided Kiyomi first, through the small hatch in the nose cone, and returned for Kenny. She held out her hand and, as Kenny reached to clasp it, he saw a flat object lying in her palm.

"I made a promise to Sato-*san* that you would call someone before . . ." Ibuki said.

"I'm not in a talking mood right now," Kenny said. "Can you send a text for me, to my dad?"

Ibuki nodded and led him to the capsule.

Inside, amid the plastic crates and tanks, all strapped

down, two stainless steel chairs had been welded into position, backs braced against the floor and facing the ceiling. Technicians helped Kenny clamber into his seat and settle in beside Kiyomi. Nylon webbing was tightened around his chest, shoulders, waist and legs. Ibuki positioned his helmet and carefully rotated it until it locked into place.

"Comm links are open on all channels," she said. "You'll be able to hear us and we can hear you. Everything on this flight is fully automated, including docking. All you have to do is float out when the door opens, straight into the control module. Float back when you're done and the craft will disengage and commence reentry."

"And if something goes wrong?" Kenny asked, his stomach doing flip-flops.

"Worst case?" Ibuki said. "You won't know about it. But we have provided two MMUs as standard issue, even though you're never going to use them."

"MMU?" Kiyomi asked.

Ibuki pointed to two large white backpacks strapped to the wall. "Manned Maneuvering Unit. That's what astronauts use if they need to go outside. Do you have any last questions?"

"Yeah. Is there a bathroom in here?" Kenny quipped.

Ibuki smiled and tapped Kenny's faceplate. "One tip for you: try not to throw up inside your suit."

She climbed out of the hatch and the metal door slammed shut, the echo reverberating through the hold.

"Well, this is it, I guess," Kenny said, trying to crane around and look at Kiyomi. "How are you feeling?"

"Me?" Kiyomi said. "Absolutely terrified. You?"

"I'm so scared I can hardly breathe. I think I'm going to need a bigger diaper."

"All right," a voice said in their helmets. "This is the Launch Director speaking. I need all Flight Directors to give me a Go/No Go for launch . . . Retro?"

"Go flight," a voice replied.

"Booster?"

"Go flight."

"Payload?"

"Go flight."

"Trajectory?"

"Go flight."

"FIDO?"

"Go flight."

"CAPCOM?"

"Go flight."

"Confirmed, ATV-12, we are ready to go. This is Takesaki Control Center. We are X minus one minute. Capsule, be advised we are in a smooth count."

"Capsule? That would be us," Kenny said.

"Ken-*chan*, I've been wondering about something," Kiyomi said. "What were you doing on Mount Kurama?"

"Huh? You're asking me that now?"

"When else am I going to get a chance?"

Kenny thought about lying for a moment, before

deciding against it. "I was looking for Sojobo."

"That was stupid. Why?"

"To help you, of course."

"Ohh."

"Anyway, how did you guys find me?"

"I had Poyo put a tracker in your backpack. That's why he was so keen to help you pack. Once we knew you were on Kurama, the rest was easy."

"X minus thirty-one seconds," the Launch Director said, his voice transmitting into their helmets. "You are go for auto-sequence start. Commence APU pre-start."

"Clear to launch," another voice said.

"X minus twenty seconds."

Kenny tried to twist his head around again to look at Kiyomi, but the straps held him in position. Reaching out to offer his hand was no good either.

"Ten, nine, eight, seven . . . Ignition sequence started . . ."

The cabin shuddered, as if in the grip of an earthquake. A low roar grew steadily louder, like an onrushing avalanche.

"Four, three, two, one . . . We have main engine start. We have booster ignition. And liftoff!"

Kenny's teeth clattered in spite of his clenched jaw. He felt like he was strapped to a jackhammer.

Outside on the launchpad, blinding white light flooded the runway. Clouds of vapor billowed outward and the H-IIA rocket knifed into the black sky.

Sato watched it soar, a gleaming arrow of hope, until it was swallowed up by the darkness once more and lost from view.

36 三十六

Kenny's ears were filled with the thundering blast of the chemical explosion taking place fifty yards below him. As every bone rattled in his body, and the accelerative force crushed him into his seat, he tried not to imagine the fiery detonation beneath.

A jumble of ground crew voices overlapped inside his helmet: "Tower is clear . . . Starting roll maneuver . . . Approaching maximum speed."

But there was something else: a higher-pitched sound. Kiyomi was screaming.

"RAAAAAAARGH! Let me out of this thing! I'll kill you for this!" she shrieked in rage. "Release me, you depraved human scum!"

Kenny twisted his neck as far as the strap allowed and, from the corner of his eye, he saw Kiyomi thrashing wildly against her restraints. The stress of launch had awakened her inner *oni*. Her fists were shaking and her back was arched like an angry cat. Spit sprayed the inside of her helmet.

"We have SRB separation," the calm voice said in Kenny's ear.

"I'll separate your head from your shoulders!" Kiyomi shrieked. "AIEEEEEE!"

"Running on single engine."

The rumble died away as the Earth's atmosphere thinned to nothing.

"Kiyomi!" Kenny said. "Listen to me. It's Kenny. You know, your favorite dweeb."

"Silence, mortal!" Kiyomi barked. "Your wretched words have no meaning to me. Release me and I will feast on your heart!"

"Listen to me, Kiyomi. Focus on my voice. I know you're still in there. Remember the good things, like . . . like fireflies, and your motorbike, and . . . and Poyo. Come on! Focus!"

"Quiet! Your words are . . ."

"Main engine cut out on schedule. Stats are good," the technician intoned.

"Kiyomi! Fight it. Take control again."

"I . . . I'll . . . Kenny?" Kiyomi said, faltering. "You made the soccer team . . ."

"Yes, that's right. You laughed at my gear."

"And . . . you caught me, when I fell . . ."

"Yes. At the aquarium . . ."

"Telemetry is up and running. Prepare for first and second stage separation," said the voice from Mission

Control. "On my count, three, two . . ."

"Kenny! Oh. What just happened?"

"Uh, nothing. You blacked out for a few seconds. You know, from the g-force."

"What, and you didn't? Nice try, vomit boy."

"Astronauts, you are now free to move around the capsule," said the technician.

"About time," Kenny said, and he unbuckled the safety harness holding him down. As soon as the last clip opened, he floated up from his chair. "Oh, wow. This is weird."

Kiyomi drifted up alongside him. "Whoof. My stomach doesn't know which way is down. And my nose is all stuffed up."

"We have a visual on *Hoshi no Kagami*," the ground crew said.

Kenny grabbed hold of a strap and used it to maneuver himself to the tiny round window in the access hatch.

The huge pale-blue orb of the Earth floated majestically below. The seas were a glassy blue, dappled by clouds as white and lumpy as cream cheese.

"Look, down there," Kiyomi whispered, tapping the glass.

As the capsule bulleted towards the horizon, a black circle crawled into view, sitting like a cancer on the face of the world.

"There's the shadow," Kenny said.

"It's like a black hole over Japan," Kiyomi muttered.

"Who would be so insane to do such a thing?"

"ATV-12, please confirm visual on the space mirror," requested the ground technician.

"Where is it?" Kenny twisted his body so that his boots scraped the ceiling while he strained to see out of the tiny porthole. Tracking up from the black shadow, he made out a tiny crescent of light drawing into view, like a miniature new moon.

"Yeah, we can see it," Kiyomi called out.

"Initiating retro burn," the voice said. "Prepare for first phase of docking procedure."

Kenny continued to watch the space mirror grow larger. It was truly a miracle of modern engineering. As the angle changed, he saw that the underside was cast in blackest night but the upper was bathed in the full brilliance of the sun. The central spokes radiated out as if from a giant wheel and, at the center, was the control module.

"Attention, ATV-12. Be aware that the solar shield is adjusting course," the Mission Control voice said. "It is tracking your incoming trajectory."

"Which means it's taking aim," Kenny said. "Crap." He bent his knees and pushed off the ceiling, crashing headfirst into his chair. "Buckle up," he said to Kiyomi, wrestling into position.

"Because that'll really help if it opens fire. I'm staying here." Kiyomi clung to the window and stared out at the approaching space station.

"We have target lock," the technician said. "Weapon system is powering up."

"I thought this was a scheduled mission," Kenny said, fumbling with the straps. "Why would they shoot down fuel and air?"

"Am resending all flight ID protocols, including proximity, access and handshake codes. Hold tight, ATV-12."

"That's easy for you to say," Kenny grumbled.

"We're passing under the lenses now," Kiyomi said, tensing up. "I can't look." She ducked her head.

Kenny held his breath, listening to his heartbeat thumping in his ears.

"ATV-12, you are clear. Target lock deactivated. Proceed to final docking approach."

Kenny slumped in his chair. He would have been bathed in sweat were it not for the cooling and ventilation bodysuit he was wearing.

"This is pretty incredible stuff," Kiyomi said, her eyes wide in wonder at the superstructure gliding past the window. "You should check this out."

"No thanks," Kenny said. "I'm going to wait right here."

"Switching to telegoniometer and videometer for final approach and docking. Stand by, ATV-12," the technician said.

"I can see the hatch," Kiyomi said. "It's coming up real fast."

"Speed now three feet per second . . ." the technician said. "Nice and slow . . . Sixty feet . . . Thirty feet . . . Looking good on radar . . . Fifteen feet . . ."

KA-LUNKK!

The hull shook and mechanical clamps latched into place.

"Locks are engaged and we have soft dock. She's all yours, ATV-12. Initiating propellant transfer now; fuel pumps primed. Good luck."

Kiyomi drifted down beside Kenny. "How are you feeling, Ken-*chan*?"

Kenny undid his seat straps. "Like I'd rather be anywhere else right now."

"I just can't believe we're up here. It's so quiet . . . and so beautiful."

Kenny reached out and grabbed Kiyomi's hand, pulling her closer. "This is so stupid."

"How do you mean?"

"Well, I can't even give you a kiss for luck, if I wanted to, not with this stupid helmet on. We're like two goldfish in different bowls."

"Aww, that's sweet." Kiyomi gently knocked her helmet against Kenny's. "Tell you what, you can owe me."

"Huh? How?"

"You can survive in space for maybe fifteen seconds without a helmet, before you black out."

"Really? I thought your blood boils and you explode like a balloon."

"Nah, you've been watching too much *Star Trek*. Your body's a pressurized bag of warm liquid. We'll be good for fifteen seconds before . . . you know."

"If we make it that far."

"That's what I like about you; you're always so positive." Kiyomi mimed kissing the thumb of her glove and pasted it onto his face shield. "That's for luck." She kicked against the floor and coasted towards the access hatch, pulling Kenny along. "OK. You ready?"

"No."

"Good." Kiyomi cranked the air lock handle and the hatch swung open. "Let's go and see which lunatic is behind all this."

37 三十七

Charles Blackwood stood on the balcony, holding the phone, and stared up at the blackened sky. The glow of fires lit the city far below and the sounds of chaos drifted upward.

He stepped back inside the apartment and dialed the number yet again. This time, the connection went through.

"*Moshi moshi?*" a man's voice answered.

"Harashima! Where is my son?" Charles demanded. "And what on earth have you got him doing now?"

Harashima sighed. "He's not on Earth. He's in space. He's trying to fix the *Hoshi no Kagami*. The shield malfunction was not an accident."

"What? You've got to be kidding."

"Do I sound like I'm joking?"

"You sent a child into space? What were you thinking?"

"There was no other choice." Harashima's voice was flat, drained of emotion. "My daughter is with him."

Charles hooked his toe around the swivel chair, slid it over and sat down. "Tell me everything." He reached for a pad and scribbled notes while Harashima spoke. "There's only a one in three chance you can get them down safely? That's not acceptable."

"What else can we do?" Harashima countered. "The International Space Station is too far away. The Space Shuttle program has ended."

"And that's it? You're giving up?"

"Charles-*sensei*, they are twenty-two miles straight up. There is no other way to bring them down."

"Other than praying that a jerry-rigged tin can holds together? There has to be another way. There has to be."

"You sound like your son."

Charles ended the call and looked over his notes. Scooting over to his desk, he logged on to the computer and found the names of his colleagues in the Astrophysics Department.

"Let me see . . ." he muttered to himself, a sheen of sweat moistening his brow. "We need some way to transport . . . oh." Charles picked up the phone again and dialed.

"Dad," he said, "it's Charles. Do you still have the Prime Minister's number? I need you to call in a favor."

The hatch from ATV-12 opened into a short connecting tunnel, at the end of which was the control module's docking compartment.

"Now what?" Kenny said. "Do we knock on the door and say, 'Trick or treat?'"

"I don't think so," Kiyomi said. "Technically, we're not meant to be here."

"Neither is whoever's behind that door."

"*If* there's anyone there. The whole thing could be automated."

"Let's hope so. It'll make life a lot easier."

Kenny held on to the edges of the hatch and pushed off, floating down the tunnel to the outer door of the air lock. Bracing himself, he pulled down on a red lever and the door opened silently. Kenny beckoned Kiyomi and she drifted over to join him. They entered the compartment and Kenny sealed the door. He pulled a second handle and the inner door opened.

Banks of electronic equipment covered every surface, with screens, monitors, consoles, keypads, cables, dials, gauges, wires, tubes and racks all crammed into the space. But what caught Kenny's eye was the last thing he had expected to see in such a high-tech environment. It stood, positioned to the front of the inner air lock door.

"A *torii* gate?" Kenny said, half to himself. "Someone's made a shrine in space? Dedicated to who?"

"To me, of course," purred a voice as cold as space itself.

Kiyomi ducked low, shielding herself with the half-open air lock door. Kenny stared as all the shadows in the room seemed to slither and converge on a single point, where they mingled and combined to form the dark outline of a man.

The figure was very tall and lean, with flowing white hair, skin so pale as to be almost transparent and deep shadowed eyes, which glowed crimson. He wore a black hooded cloak that seemed to suck in all surrounding light, although flecks of silver sparkled from deep within.

"So you are Kuromori?" the figure said, steepling his sinewy fingers. "I have heard much about you. Is it all true?"

"The good stuff is. You can forget the rest," Kenny said, motioning for Kiyomi to hang back.

"You have proved yourself a worthy adversary. Here you are, in spite of my many attempts to have you removed."

Kenny pushed himself away from the door. "Thank you. I do my best, Mr. . . . uh, who are you?"

The figure chuckled, a low, grating sound like glass crushed underfoot. "You do not know me? I am disappointed. Let me help you." He moved towards a computer terminal. "My own beloved sister banished me from her sight and ordered me never to set eyes on her again. I, who was once as bright as the sun itself, was condemned to dwell in eternal shadow."

Kenny carefully set his back against the nearest wall, bracing himself.

"Except that now Amaterasu's face is hidden once again, shrouded just as it was when she sulked in her infernal cave, mine is the only remaining light in the sky. Now all the world is subject to me and is my rightful dominion once more. I will be worshipped as the sole celestial light." The crimson eyes had become hate-filled slits. "I am Tsukuyomi no Mikoto, God of the Moon, and you are nothing before me."

He waved his bony hand and the air lock door clanged shut.

"You alone will have the privilege of bearing witness to my triumph." He slammed his fist down, hammering a button on the console. With a thunk, the clamps disengaged and the air lock tunnel began to retract. No longer tethered to the control module, the transfer vehicle started to drift away.

A ripple of panic washed over Kiyomi like ice water. Fear bubbled up and brought with it a fierce, consuming rage. She slammed her fist against the outer hatch.

Her first thought was to attack the door, to batter it into submission. But then she caught herself; that was the reaction of the *oni* inside her. She was in serious trouble and the only way out was to stay calm, to focus, to think . . .

Quickly, Kiyomi analyzed the situation. She was trapped in the air lock. The connecting tunnel was gone and ATV-12 was floating away. If she stayed where she was, she'd be a sitting duck, effectively neutralized and of no use to anyone. What would Kenny do? The answer came to her in a flash.

She jumped up and yanked the red release lever.

The outer door uncoupled and Kiyomi kicked it open, sending herself flying headfirst against the inner hatch. Like a swimmer making a kick turn, she upended herself, braced her feet on the metal door and kicked with all her strength. Arms outstretched, Kiyomi sailed through the hatch and into space.

ATV-12 rolled lazily away, as if in slow motion. Kiyomi watched it grow larger as she soared towards it, then her eyes widened in horror. She was going to overshoot the capsule and miss it completely.

"No, no, no, no, no, no, no, no!"

The smooth white surface cruised below, tantalizingly out of reach. Kiyomi's fingers scrabbled in frantic search of a handhold, but it was no good. She was shooting past, into nothingness.

Against the sparkling expanse of space, a solid black rectangle reared up, erasing a swathe of stars. Kiyomi grabbed for it, but her fingertips only brushed the glassy exterior.

"No!" Kiyomi kicked out again and the tips of her boots hooked under the solar panel array. She gasped, feeling the solid contact, and her movement stopped. She jerked her foot upward, to bring her arms down to where they could grasp the wide glass slats. Hand over hand, Kiyomi guided herself down the solar array to the support pole, and from there around the body of the craft to the open hatch.

Maneuvering herself inside, Kiyomi went to the

payload storage racks and opened a compartment. She pulled out her black duffel bag, unzipped it and grabbed several belts from inside, strapping them on over her space suit with practiced ease. Once done, she hit the transmit button on her wrist control and whispered, "Ken-*chan*. I'm in the capsule."

She then kicked over to the opposite wall, took down one of the white backpacks and removed the MMU.

The unit was a squat, rectangular box, with a semicircle cut out, and twenty-four nozzles fixed around it in different positions. Two handles were folded on top. Kiyomi scanned the printed diagram and flipped up the handgrips to form two hooks. These she slung over her shoulders, so the main unit fitted snugly under her bulky life-support-system backpack, with the curve around her waist, and she locked it in place. Finally, she fixed the control box to the front of her space suit. She was ready.

Tsukuyomi spread his arms in a grandiose manner, encompassing everything around him.

"Magnificent, is it not? For thousands of years, I bided my time, waiting for an opportunity to escape the shadows. And now, thanks to mankind, I will have my revenge."

"I don't get it," Kenny said, one eye on the air lock. "How are you going to have any followers if everything dies?"

"Foolish mortal," Tsukuyomi said. "I have followers,

thousands already. Who do you think built this shrine for me? Know that darkness is the natural order of things; light is but a temporary relief, yet light always fails. When humans are huddled in the dark, fearful of what lurks without, do you truly believe they will not flock to me for protection?"

"Well, since you put it like that . . ." Kenny reached into the storage pouch on his space suit and closed his hand on the override chip.

"All that remains is the final stamp of my authority, the warning to any who may dream of opposing me . . ."

Tsukuyomi tapped instructions into a keyboard and a large flat screen monitor blinked into life, displaying a map of Japan. A red, blinking crosshair symbol hovered over the center. It panned to the southwest, stopping at the edge of a wide bay.

"The Ise Jingu," the Moon God sneered. "Most sacred of sites dedicated to my sister Amaterasu, and her resting place on this Earth. How ironic that I, Tsukuyomi, will turn her own power against her and burn every trace of her existence from the planet."

"Whoa. Seriously?" Kenny thumbed the "transmit" button on his glove. "You're going to fire that Sun Gun and kill thousands of people on the ground?"

Tsukuyomi smiled. "It will be glorious. Imagine huddling in the icy darkness, praying for a light from the heavens . . . and then your prayers are answered. Sunlight, as pure and as powerful as the sun itself, pours

298

downward, incinerating everything for miles around. And the best part is that humans will learn to hate and fear the light forever afterward."

Inside the ATV-12 capsule, Kiyomi was about to launch herself towards the exit hatch when Kenny's voice filled her helmet. *"You're going to fire that Sun Gun and kill thousands of people on the ground?"*

"You are totally insane," he said to Tsukuyomi. "Don't do this. You can't just force people to worship you through fear."

"I know of no other way," the Moon God replied. "And you cannot stop me."

"Maybe no, maybe yes. I can certainly try."

Tsukuyomi arched an eyebrow. "Really? Then stop me doing this." The pale finger stabbed a red button.

"No!" Kenny cried.

The targeting picture changed abruptly to show the ATV-12 spacecraft gliding below the solar lenses. A tremor shuddered through the space station, the shield flared and a pulse of energy blasted downward.

The capsule exploded, fragmenting like a silent firework display and Kenny imagined he heard Kiyomi scream.

38 三十八

"NOOOOO!!"

Kenny kicked against the wall and flew at Tsukuyomi, Kusanagi in hand. Flashing past, he lashed out with the sword. The blade ripped through the starry cloak and sliced the Moon God in half.

Kenny careened off the far wall and bounced to the floor. He rolled to stare up at the unharmed Tsukuyomi.

"When you have lived in the shadows as long as I have, the shadows become part of you," the god said, his flesh swirling and settling to close the wound. "You, on the other hand, have lived but a short time and are all too human."

"Why did you do it?" Kenny raged. "Why did you blow up the transport vehicle?"

"It had served its purpose," Tsukuyomi said. "We needed the extra fuel for the final positioning of this vessel; otherwise, Ise would be out of range. Now, however, we are adjusting course for the final strike. It is merely a matter of minutes." His glowing eyes flared with excitement and again he steepled his stringy fingers.

"Who's 'we'? All I see is you, and you're going to pay for what you just did." Kenny pushed himself back to his feet and gripped the sword, ready for battle.

"Do you really think I would operate all this myself?" Tsukuyomi smirked. "This is 'we.' Please meet my loyal workforce."

He waved a hand, and every metal surface seemed to bubble and erupt, as if coming to a boil. Dozens of fist-sized silver blobs floated up in the weightlessness, like mercury in a lava lamp.

Kenny hesitated, watching the nearest one float towards him. It quivered and five wires thrust out on each side. The strands thickened to form spikes which then crimped into joints.

"*Kingumo*, I call them," Tsukuyomi said, like a proud father. "I bred them to interface with human technology."

"It's . . . a metal spider?" Kenny said, still staring in horrified fascination.

"The claws and fangs are needle sharp," the Moon God said, "which means they have only to puncture your costume and you will die in minutes."

"Oh, crap," Kenny muttered, backing away from the deadly swarm. The cluster of spiders hung like a sparkling cloud before rushing towards him.

Kiyomi whacked into one of the graphene struts that supported the mirror's foil canopy, and clung on. Below her, a mass of debris spread in every direction, as the wreckage of the transport capsule billowed into the upper atmosphere.

That was way too close, she thought, reminding herself to breathe deeply and to stay calm. A head-up display inside her helmet projected text onto the faceplate. Her oxygen level was already down to twenty-eight percent.

Kenny's warning had prompted her to hit the controls of the MMU, firing the nitrogen-jet thrusters on the backpack unit to go darting through the hatch and into space. Her intention had been to reach the lenses of the Sun Gun, to try and disrupt the firing mechanism, but, unfamiliar with the MMU controls, she had overshot – seconds before the weapon fired and destroyed the transport craft, and their only way back to Earth.

Hanging on to the structure, Kiyomi calculated that she must be about a third of the way out from the center. The vast expanse of the solar shield stretched out like a hundred football fields.

She had just seen, close up, the enormous power harnessed by the space station, power that was only minutes away from being directed earthward. Ise was a city of over a hundred thousand people and, even though it was known as "The Holy City," it would need more than the protection of the gods right now.

Kiyomi turned herself around, aimed in the direction of the solar lenses and pushed the joystick control. Compressed nitrogen shot out of the jet pack nozzles, thrusting her forward, on course for the energy-weapon array mounted below the control module.

Seconds ticked by. *Come on!* Kiyomi thought. *This is way too slow. I ought to rip out its circuits and smash . . . no, no, no . . . Breathe . . . Stay calm . . . Keep a clear head.*

As she drew closer, she began to understand the mechanism a little better. The huge deflector shield was curved inward, like a satellite dish. When tilted at the correct angle, it directed the collected sunlight onto a single receiver plate. This in turn funneled the energy down through the telescope lenses, concentrating and intensifying the beam. If she could somehow disable any of those elements, the device would no longer work.

Kiyomi landed with a bump on the solar-collector plate. The mounting was a lattice framework of graphene rods. If she could just . . .

"Well, well, well. Look who's here," crackled a voice in Kiyomi's headset.

She spun around to face a hulking figure in a black space suit.

"Did you miss me, Toots?" the silver *oni* said, grabbing hold of Kiyomi. "Ooh, looks like you forgot the first rule of spacewalking: always use an anchor line, in case you drift loose."

He pulled her in close, raised his elbow to shoulder height and flung out his arm, pitching Kiyomi away, spinning towards the depths of space. "Because, in a vacuum, there's nothing to slow you down."

Silver's grinning face shrank to a dot as Kiyomi flailed her arms and soared past the edge of the shield.

Kenny swiped and slashed, flailing at the oncoming spiders. They were small targets to begin with, but with his movements hampered by the bulky space suit and no way to plant his feet, the weightlessness threw his balance off. He was missing more of the creatures than he was hitting. Kusanagi leapt and bucked in his hands, but for every creature he sliced in half, another two jumped in to take its place.

"A brave effort, Kuromori, but bound to fail," Tsukuyomi said. "There are too many and it only needs one to breach your suit."

Kenny swatted two *kingumo* with the flat of his sword and took another down with a reverse sweep.

"And then your precious air will escape and your lungs will explode," Tsukuyomi said. "What's left of you will suffocate and freeze."

A spider landed on Kenny's faceplate and drove its spiky legs in, etching tiny lines on the glass. Kenny jerked his head back, flicked it away with the sword and toppled backward. The swarm closed in and a wave of spiders scuttled over his suit, lancing their needlelike limbs into every fold of cloth. A hiss of escaping air filled Kenny's ears and the oxygen count on his helmet display started to drop.

How can I fight these things when I can't even

stand up? Kenny screamed mentally.

In that split second, a fragment of memory flickered behind his eyes – a lake, a warm evening, water sparkling below – and the answer came to him.

I stopped gravity once. I don't know how, but I did – and if I can stop it, then maybe I can create it too.

The *kingumo* continued to scurry over Kenny, their jaws and claws searching out weak points in the suit.

Kenny pictured the metal of the ceiling. In his mind's eye, he imagined the atoms squeezing and linking together, increasing their mass. He added more and more atoms, multiplying the density . . .

Kiyomi's words replayed in his mind: "I trust you."

Something clicked inside. Light flared in his mind and he felt the telltale surge of power within.

As one, the *kingumo* flew upward and smashed into the ceiling.

"No!" Tsukuyomi cried in disbelief. "That is not possible. No mortal can –"

"Will you shut up?" Kenny growled, righting himself. He swept his hand to the left.

BAM-BAM! WHAP-SNAP! CRUNCH! The spider swarm thudded into the wall.

"And one for luck," Kenny said, palming to the right.

The mangled cluster of broken spider bits rattled into the opposite wall and stayed there, embedded in the metal and circuitry like a million splinters.

"Now it's just me and you," Kenny said, adopting

a combat position, Kusanagi at the ready. "And I owe you."

Tsukuyomi smiled and reached into his cloak, drawing out a long black staff with a vicious-looking crescent blade at each end. He leveled the staff, one sickle edge aimed at Kenny's throat. "I can't die, remember? While you most certainly can – and will."

Kenny glared at the Moon God with narrowed eyes. "Ask me if I care."

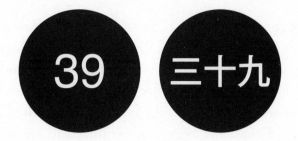

39 三十九

Kiyomi cartwheeled past acres of sodium foil, fingers fumbling and slipping as she struggled to reach the belts she had clipped on over her space suit. Her movements were as restricted as if she was wearing twenty sweaters.

The edge of the shield slid closer and Kiyomi knew that she was moments away from being lost forever. She had tried slowing her course with the MMU jet pack, but it was too weak to counter the *oni*'s strength.

Come on . . . Come on . . . she told herself. *Nearly there . . . Oh, thank you!*

Her right hand closed on a straight rod while the other gripped a small curved object. In a flash, she had snapped on the carabiner and launched the first item back in the direction of the shield.

The silver-edged perimeter sailed past and Kiyomi twisted her head to escape the dazzling glare of the mirror's solar-facing side. In the opposite direction, the *kaginawa* grappling hook punched through the foil canopy and kept going, with lengths of black nylon line unspooling from the reel at her waist. The cord snapped taut as it reached its limit and jerked the hook backward. Kiyomi seized the line in both hands and focused her will.

The four-pronged grapple shredded the sodium foil as if it was tissue, filling the nearby space with twirling tatters of sparkling ribbon. It continued to rip through the lustrous material until it snagged a rib of superstrong graphene – and held firm.

Kiyomi yanked as hard as she could on the line and propelled herself back in the direction she had come.

The silver *oni* was cleaning a focal lens on the solar weapon and humming to himself when a small movement caught his eye: a tiny dot in the reflector lens was sliding over and growing larger. He leaned closer for a better look and the next second, the lens fractured and exploded into thousands of tiny, spinning, glittering fragments.

"What the –?" The *oni* twisted around and his fanged mouth fell open in disbelief. Kiyomi flew towards him, her *katana* in one hand and an automatic pistol in the other. She fired again, each shot blasting silently from the barrel in a spherical puff.

Silver pushed himself clear as the bullets zipped past, tearing through the solar collector. Kiyomi ditched the empty gun and landed on the collection platform, her sword in hand and ready.

The *oni* dropped down in front of her. "It may be damaged, but it's still going to fire," he said. "It's on automated countdown. You can't stop it."

"We'll see about that," Kiyomi snarled and she launched herself towards the ogre.

Tsukuyomi dodged Kenny's strike with lightning speed and countered with a blow of his own. The sickle blade flashed towards Kenny's chest to carve him open, but Kusanagi whipped around to block the attack. Sparks flew as the steel edge jarred against the ebon staff. The Moon God switched to a reverse sweep, bringing the other blade up to rake across Kenny's legs. All Tsukuyomi had to do was pierce the protective suit. Again, Kusanagi swept around with a low parry.

Kenny kicked against a computer bank and floated upward. Tsukuyomi closed in with a snarl, his cloak fanning out behind.

"You cannot beat me, mortal," Tsukuyomi said. "I have trained for thousands of years with this *ryogama bo*, while you can barely hold a sword."

Kenny drifted down to perch on top of a computer station. "I don't have to beat you. All I have to do is stop you."

"Impudent whelp!" Tsukuyomi slashed the blade down. Kenny launched backward in a slow-motion somersault and the sickle scraped past his boot to stab into the electronic circuitry, where it bit deeply. As Tsukuyomi wrestled to free the weapon, Kenny scrambled to the nearest USB port and slammed home the override chip.

"It's over!" he said. "It's done. Any second now, this

ship's going to correct its course and return to its original position, where it can't hurt anyone."

Tsukuyomi ripped his blade loose, shredding the machinery. "A noble intent, fool, but to no avail. The first thing I did was to encrypt all the command codes. Only I can change the position of this craft."

Kenny's eyes lit on a pair of red handles beside the monitor. "Position, yes, but what about direction?" He rammed the thruster controls forward as far as they would go.

With a low hiss of venting propellant, the solar shield began to rotate on its axis.

Silver vaulted upward to avoid the onrushing blade. Kiyomi skidded beneath him and grabbed hold of the collector platform to slow herself. Thumbing the joystick controls of his jet unit, the *oni* reached into the sparkling cloud of lens fragments and selected a wicked-looking splinter.

"All I have to do is puncture your suit and the blood will boil in your veins," he said, gripping the crystal shard.

Kiyomi faced him, *katana* raised. "Actually, I'll freeze first, but it's the same result."

"*RRRARGH!*" Silver charged towards her, stabbing and slashing with the glass dagger.

Like a matador facing a bull, Kiyomi watched him close the gap, waited till the last moment, then twisted to the side and lashed out with the sword to send the shard spinning out of Silver's grip. The *oni* jetted back, out of sword range, then smiled.

"Hold that pose, Toots," he said, glancing at something behind her.

"Huh? Wh–" The now rotating platform swung up and hammered Kiyomi in the back. "AGH!" The blow felt like a baseball bat to the kidneys, and it was only weightlessness that stopped it from doing more damage.

"Now I've got you!" Silver closed in, smacking the *katana* from Kiyomi's limp fingers. He wrapped one meaty paw around her neck and the other around her helmet.

"Gkk . . . can't breathe . . ." Kiyomi gasped.

"That won't be a problem when I rip your stupid head off," Silver snarled.

Tsukuyomi pounced on the nearest keyboard and began typing commands, his fingers a blur.

"You're too late, mortal," he crowed. "Look."

Kenny blinked up at the wide monitor screen showing the weapon targeting system. The red crosshairs glowed like a branding iron over the Pacific Ocean, to the south of the main Japanese island of Honshu, but moving rapidly towards land.

Text crawled across the lower half of the picture: TARGET ALIGNED . . . FIRING IN 40 SECONDS . . . 35 SECONDS . . .

"You have but delayed me, Kuromori," Tsukuyomi said. "But, like night follows day, my reign is inevitable. Surrender."

"Never!" Kenny roared and threw himself at the Moon God.

Kiyomi squirmed in the huge *oni*'s grasp. The hand around her neck was compressing the metal ring that formed the join in her suit, and the other hand was twisting her helmet with inexorable force. Any second now, the seal would break and death would follow.

Fighting against the throbbing pain in her lower spine and the *oni* voice raging in her head, Kiyomi reached for the only chance she had left, tucked into the small of her back.

Silver leered at her from within his faceplate. "You know, Toots, in a funny way I'm going to miss our little playdates. Still, all good things come to an end. Time to say good-bye, Toots."

Kiyomi's fingers closed round the handle of her *tanto* and she whipped out the short blade.

"OK . . ." she wheezed. "Good-bye . . . Toots." She plunged the sword into the *oni*'s back, punching through the oxygen tank in his Primary Life Support System backpack.

Silver gave a gasp of horror and spun around, slapping a hand over the vent to stem the flow of escaping gas. Kiyomi kicked away and hit her jet pack controller to move out of flailing range.

"My air! My air!" Silver shrieked, grabbing hold of the solar-collector platform to steady himself.

Kiyomi reached for her microphone button. "Kenny . . .?"

Tsukuyomi brought his staff up in both hands, blocking and parrying Kenny's frenzied blows.

. . . 15 SECONDS . . .

"You have courage, mortal, but it is nothing without training," the Moon God commented, switching to one hand to fend off the attacks.

. . . 10 SECONDS . . .

Kenny maneuvered himself around with a step towards the main console. The video screen showed the crosshairs sweeping inward, seconds from landfall. He was out of time.

"It's all I've got!" Kenny yelled and he threw his sword, like a javelin, at Tsukuyomi's head.

"Oh, please." The god swatted the sword aside and it twirled away.

In that second of distraction, Kenny swiveled towards his real target: the red button he had seen Tsukuyomi use before. Stretching flat out, he slammed his palm down on the control.

"NO!" Tsukuyomi roared, as the weapon fired.

40 四十

Kiyomi looked up, feeling a shudder ripple through the space station.

"I wouldn't stay there if I was you," she croaked at Silver, who was still clinging to the wreckage of the collector platform.

"Well, you're not me, so shut it."

The shield flared with a blinding intensity – and a pulse of energy blazed down, striking the hapless *oni* and incinerating him. It struck the two lenses and sizzled towards Earth, far below.

"Oh, no. We were too late," Kiyomi moaned, her voice creaky and disappointment clouding her face.

She sighed and watched the shield slowly rotate. Brilliant shafts of sunlight stabbed down through the holes in the canopy she had made and danced over the windowless control module. She adjusted her jet pack and headed in its direction.

Tsukuyomi stabbed his weapon towards Kenny's heart. Without thinking, the boy's hand shot up and caught the shaft of the staff.

"What new madness is this?" Tsukuyomi said, his nostrils flared and eyes wide.

Kenny tightened his metallic grip and twisted. The head of the staff snapped silently and drifted away.

The Moon God retaliated, lashing the remaining stump across Kenny's helmet with such force that the boy was catapulted up to smash into the ceiling before ricocheting off and slamming into the far wall. Kenny drifted down to land on his backside, faceplate cracked, so that he was seeing multiple Tsukuyomi images bearing down. Air continued to hiss out of his suit.

"You missed," Kenny said. "Fired into the sea. Maybe fried a few fish, but that's all. Now that your Sun Gun's out of action, it's just a matter of time before they shoot this thing down. It's over. You've lost."

Tsukuyomi's eyes smoldered like two hot coals and his teeth flashed white in the shadows of his cowl. His staff shook in his hands, but the sickle blade gleamed.

"I waited thousands of years for my revenge . . . only to be denied by you, a mere child . . ." The Moon God was so incensed that he struggled to form words from his tightly-clenched jaw.

Kenny pressed himself against the wall, spreading the palms of his hands against the metal.

"I wish I had the time to kill you slowly . . . oh, I could torture you for years, so that death would be a sweet mercy . . ." Tsukuyomi gathered his wits and straightened up. "There will be other times for me . . . but not for you, Kuromori. I will have the satisfaction of killing you first."

"You'd better take a ticket and get in line," Kenny said, focusing his *ki*.

Tsukuyomi raised the sickle blade for a final strike.

"Before that though," Kenny said, "say 'hi' to your sister." Power flowed from his hands into the wall behind, transforming the metal to purest glass.

"*NOOOOOOOOOOOOOOOOOOO!!!*" Tsukuyomi screamed as rays of brilliant sunlight lanced through the wall, flooding the control room and blasting him to nothingness.

All that remained was his lingering scream.

Kenny lay on the floor for a few minutes, bathing in the glow of the sun. Spots of light danced and shifted on the ceiling as the light struck his fractured faceplate. The blue disk of the Earth slowly slid into view. Screens began to flash and warning lights blinked. Kenny forced his aching limbs into action and rose upright.

. . . CRITICAL ORBIT WARNING . . . UNCONTROLLED REENTRY IMMINENT . . . CRITICAL ORBIT WARNING . . . was the message scrolling across every screen.

Kenny looked back out through the glass wall and saw the sodium-foil panels buckling and collapsing. A red warning light blinked inside his helmet: oxygen at six percent.

"Ken-*chan*? Are you there?" Kiyomi's voice made Kenny jump.

"Kiyomi?" His heart leapt. "I thought you were de–"

"No, but you will be if you don't open this door. I'm still stuck outside the air lock."

Kenny grinned and floated over to release the door. Kiyomi pulled herself in and joined him on the control deck.

"Well, we won," Kenny said. "High five?"

"You're such a dork," Kiyomi said, grabbing him in an awkward embrace. "This is like hugging Oyama."

"Hah! Listen to you. I thought girls weren't allowed to do *sumo*."

"You're the one wearing the diaper."

Kiyomi scanned the room. Broken electronic components floated in the air; instrument lights pulsed and flashed like a disco machine; one wall was glass with the blazing sun peeking through gaps in the rapidly disintegrating shield. "Where's you-know-who?"

"Tsukuyomi? I don't know for sure, but I figure he's back where he started. Dark side of the moon or something."

"Huh? How come?"

"He said that he was forbidden from ever setting eyes on the sun, and something Genkuro-*sensei* told me before we left . . ."

"What, that you weren't ready?"

"No, about keeping a clear mind and seeking the light.

317

It seemed to make sense."

Kiyomi nodded. "Figures. Creature of shadow. Give him pure sunlight with nowhere to hide."

Kenny spread his hands. "So now what?"

"Now? We wait until our oxygen runs out or we burn up on reentry. He blew up the ATV, so there's no way off this wreck."

"That's nice. Some reward for saving Japan."

Kiyomi pushed herself down to sit on the floor opposite the new picture window. She patted the vinyl beside her and Kenny sat too.

The Earth below was a dazzling blend of blues, greens, whites, yellows and browns; a tranquil disk, teeming with life.

"Wow, what a view," Kiyomi said, watching the curve of the blue planet. "We are going to make such an awesome shooting star. I wonder if anyone will make a wish on us."

Kenny reached out and took Kiyomi's hand in his. "I could make a wish now. Does it count if you wish on yourself?"

"I don't know. Hey, Ken-*chan*, you know that saying 'too young to die'?"

"Yeah."

"What a load of crap. I mean, babies die."

"I think you're taking it too literally. I reckon it's to do with people who aren't ready to die, who haven't really lived yet, who haven't done all the things they wanted to."

318

"Oh. Well, what is it you still want to do?"

"Me? It would be nice to see Newcastle win something. You?"

"I'd settle for not turning into an *onibaba*. That'd be a good start."

A huge section of foil canopy tore away from the structure, twisting and blazing brightly as it burned up in the upper atmosphere. The control module shuddered again.

Kenny squeezed Kiyomi's hand and looked in her eyes. "Same question, only seriously this time," he said.

Kiyomi cocked her head. "You know those three days when you went off in a huff?"

"It wasn't a huff. I told you –"

"Whatever. Anyway, then . . . I missed your stupid face."

Kenny nudged her with his shoulder. "And I missed you."

Kiyomi blinked back tears. "Stupid helmet. It's making my eyes water."

"Yeah, mine too."

More pieces of the solar shield broke off and plummeted through the Earth's atmosphere.

Kiyomi linked her fingers with Kenny's. "At least this way we'll always be together."

"Yeah, and wearing diapers."

Kiyomi punched Kenny on the arm. "You have to go and ruin it, don't you?"

"Tell you what . . . you know what you said before, about maybe fifteen seconds before we suffocate, if we lose the helmets?"

"Yeah."

"Well, what about that kiss I owe you?"

"What about it?" She looked up at him from under her brow.

Kenny swallowed hard. "Well, we could kiss now. That way, at least we'd be in control, instead of waiting for . . ."

"Are you serious?"

"Are you?"

Kiyomi rolled onto her knees and pulled Kenny to kneel opposite. "You see that red warning light in your helmet? That's an oxygen warning. We've only got a few minutes left anyhow."

"So, nothing to lose then."

"OK . . . the trick is to not hold your breath, otherwise your lungs go splat from the inside. Breathe out first. You really want to do this?"

"Hmm, freeze to death locked in a kiss with you or burn to death in horrible agony. Let me see . . ."

Kiyomi reached for the locking catch on her helmet and Kenny mirrored her action.

"This is so dumb. OK, on the count of three?" she said. "One . . . two . . ."

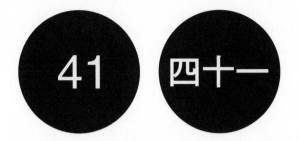

41 四十一

"**T**hree."

Kenny was surprised at how calm he felt, reaching up to undo the latch on his helmet. At least it would be over quickly.

"Calling *Hoshi no Kagami*, calling *Hoshi no Kagami*, do you read me, over?" crackled a man's voice inside their helmets.

Kenny froze and quickly refastened the helmet's locking catch.

"This is . . . the space mirror," Kiyomi breathed into her microphone. "Who is this? I mean, who are you?"

"This is Captain Mike Richards of Virgin Galactic Space Ship Four, on approach for rendezvous with your position. ETA about three minutes," the pilot answered.

"I'm sorry, you're who?"

"Virgin Galactic, ma'am. Commercial spaceflight operator. A Mr. Sato of the Japanese government authorized this mission. Said it was an international emergency. Do you know him?"

Kiyomi laughed, feeling almost giddy with relief.

"Yeah, I know him. You have two passengers to pick up and can you make it quick, please? We're almost out of oxygen."

"Copy that. On our way. Over and out."

Kenny and Kiyomi had ringside seats to watch the sleek white rocket-plane hybrid pick its way through the orbiting wreckage to draw up alongside the control module.

Kiyomi extended the concertina soft-dock tunnel and the Virgin craft fired its small retro rockets to line up perfectly. Behind, the tattered disk of the solar reflector continued to disintegrate under the power of the sun.

"Outer doors open. Ready for boarding," Captain Richards said. "One at a time, please."

"Ladies first," Kenny said, ushering Kiyomi towards the air lock's open hatch.

"No, you go. You're in worse shape than me."

"How about 'rock, paper, scissors' to decide?"

Another tremor rocked the module and sunlight streamed through shielding panels beginning to separate.

"There's no time. This thing's going to – Go!" Kiyomi shoved Kenny forward.

Kenny spun as he fell, but reached out and hooked his fingers into Kiyomi's combat belt, pulling her into the air lock with him.

With a violent wrench, the control module tore loose and the connecting tunnel ripped free, twisting and dangling from the shuttle door. Still holding tightly on to Kiyomi, Kenny leapt through the module's outer hatch, kicked against the metal rim and reached up for the tunnel edge, dangling feet away.

"We're not going to make it!" he cried, watching the sleeve slip past.

"Yes, we are! We have to!" Kiyomi hit her jet pack control, venting the last of the nitrogen gas. She thrust her shoulder into Kenny's back, boosting him forward. His hand clamped on the tunnel rim and he hauled upward, into the passage. Below, the control module blazed like a meteor, fracturing into a chain of glowing stars.

Kenny reached the small air lock on Space Ship Four.

"It's only designed for single entry," the captain's voice warned. "Two adults won't fit, not with all that gear."

The red warning light in Kenny's helmet was now a solid red. He had mere seconds of air left.

"Only one thing for it," Kenny said, pulling Kiyomi close. "Hold your breath."

She nodded and exhaled. Kusanagi shimmered into Kenny's hand. With his arm over his head and the blade pointing downward, he swung the sword in a tight circle, slicing through the bulky life-support-system backpacks. Both units drifted away, propelled by escaping oxygen.

Kenny felt the saliva begin to boil off his tongue and fingers of ice snake around his body. With the last of his strength, he hauled at the silicone sleeve, yanking them both towards the shuttle's air lock.

They cannoned off the door frame and squeezed inside. Black spots danced before Kenny's eyes as he slammed the door shut.

Relief flooded through Kenny when he heard the hiss of incoming air; to hear anything at all meant he was no longer in a vacuum. The inner air lock door opened and eager hands reached to help Kiyomi and Kenny into the passenger cabin.

Kenny unlatched his helmet and blinked up at a uniformed flight attendant, her hair neatly tied back in the microgravity environment.

"Good afternoon, sir," she said with a dazzling smile. "The cabin is fully pressurized for your comfort. If you'd like to take a seat, the captain will begin our descent."

Kenny buckled into a seat beside Kiyomi and leaned over. A strand of her hair wafted up and tickled his nose. "Hey, our helmets are off," he said. "You know what that means?"

Kiyomi reached over and touched her lips to Kenny's. "Mm, you taste good – *and me hungry!*" She bared her teeth and lunged at him.

Trapped by his seat belt, Kenny raised his arms and screamed.

Kiyomi shrieked too, but only in a fit of laughter. "Oh, your face . . . Too funny . . . Ow, my sides . . ." She dissolved into giggles.

*

Hundreds of workers lined the main runway at the Tanegashima Space Center, shielding their eyes in the bright autumn sunshine, as they waited for the delta-winged spacecraft to land.

A tiny dot dropped from the sky, growing steadily larger, twin vapor trails streaming from the wingtips. Landing gear engaged and the nose lifted as the craft touched down smoothly on the tarmac. The avidly watching crowd gave a huge cheer and clustered around the taxiing ship for a better view.

Kenny clumped down the steps, followed by Kiyomi, and was greeted by Assistant Director Ogose and a beaming Ibuki. They bowed, he bowed, they bowed again.

Sato pushed his way through and grabbed Kenny in a fierce hug. "You did it, Kuromori! You did it!"

Kenny grinned. "Did you doubt me?"

"Of course I doubted you." Sato beamed and ruffled the boy's hair.

Kiyomi elbowed Kenny aside. "Come on, Ken-*chan* had me for backup. How could he fail?"

"How indeed?" Sato threw his arms around her.

"Sir?" Kenny asked. "How did all this come about?" He directed a thumb at the Virgin spacecraft.

Sato smiled. "You can thank your father for that. When we explained to him what was happening, he refused to accept it. He said there must be another way. He made a lot of phone calls. He never gave up."

"Like father, like son, eh?" Kiyomi said.

"Come," Sato said. "Let's get you two back inside. You have no idea how much paperwork you've caused me. I'll be buried in it until New Year."

It was another six hours before Kenny was finally able to enjoy a hot shower.

Sato had made him go over everything three times before he was allowed to remove the space suit and undergo extensive medical checks. After more questions, and a hot meal, he was allowed to clean himself up.

Kenny toweled off, grabbed the tracksuit which had been laid out for him, emblazoned with the Japan Aerospace Exploration Agency logo, and dressed himself. He went to the full-length mirror to fix his hair – and saw a tall *tengu* standing behind him.

"At least I didn't throw up this time," Kenny groaned. "I'm getting better at this." He straightened up and saw the sky overhead was streaked with lemon and peach. Early evening stars winked at him. He shuddered at the thought of nightfall.

"This way," the *tengu* said, directing Kenny towards a wooden building with a steep thatched roof.

White pebbles covered the ground and a tall wooden fence enclosed the courtyard. Beyond, thick forest surrounded the site.

"Where are we?" Kenny asked.

"Ise," the *tengu* answered. "Someone wishes to meet you."

Kenny stopped at a set of simple wooden steps leading up to a pair of plain doors. "Are you sure about this?" he asked. "I mean, I'm not properly dressed. Maybe I should . . ." He caught the look of cold menace in the *tengu*'s eyes. "All right, all right . . . I know the drill."

In his bare feet, Kenny ascended the stairs. The doors swung open to greet him and pure white light swallowed him completely. He felt weightless once again, luxuriating in the healing warmth of the sun's rays. Gradually, his eyes adjusted and he discerned the shimmering outline of a female form.

Amaterasu was every bit as beautiful as Inari and Kenny could not tear his eyes away. She was a young woman, with waist-length black hair and golden eyes. A white kimono, with a red *obi* sash and trim, covered her slender frame.

"You are Kuromori, the *gaijin* child, champion of Inari?" she asked. Her voice tinkled like musical notes.

"I, uh, well, um . . ."

"I, and the whole of Japan, owe you a great debt. You have much courage for one so young."

"Well, uh, I . . ."

She smiled. "Such bravery should not go unrewarded, Kuromori. I wish to offer you a gift, as a token of my gratitude. Anything you wish, just name it."

Kenny looked away at last. "There is one thing . . ."

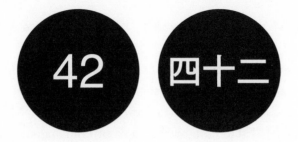

42 四十二

"I thought I'd find you here," Kenny said, stopping on the path which led through the gardens of the Harashima residence.

Kiyomi adjusted the spray of white chrysanthemums she had placed in front of the headstone. "Sometimes I wonder if things would be any better if he hadn't . . ."

"Come on, Taro knew what he was doing. He was trying to make up for a wrong, to put things right again." Kenny knelt beside Kiyomi. "And if he hadn't, then everything else wouldn't have happened. And it would be *eiein no yo* right now: eternal night."

"You're very sweet, Ken-*chan*, but it changes nothing. I have . . . such terrible dreams . . ." Kiyomi shuddered at the thought. "I'm still . . . changing . . ." Her voice was hollow, devoid of any hope, and it wrenched Kenny to hear her like this.

"I brought you a present," he said, rooting around in his jeans pocket.

"I don't need anything."

Autumn leaves drifted like snowflakes all around.

"Trust me, you'll like this." Kenny held out a small jewelry box.

Kiyomi looked at him with suspicion. "Is there a cockroach in there or something?"

"No . . . Open it."

Kiyomi lifted the lid. A small plain ring of red jade nestled inside. "Oh, wow. That's beautiful, but not really my style."

"Try it on anyway. You have no idea what I went through to get that for you."

"It looks expensive. Where did you buy this?"

"Ask no questions. Just enjoy the moment."

Kiyomi shook her head.

"Trust me," Kenny insisted. "Please. Just try it on."

"OK, if it means that much to you." Kiyomi slipped the ring onto her finger – and fainted.

Kenny propped her up in his arms. "Kiyomi? Kiyomi? Wake up. Are you OK?"

The ring itself was gone.

The image of Kenny's worried face faded away as Susano-wo extinguished the light and sent the bronze shield back to its resting place.

"The girl will be well, Kuromori," he rumbled. "Well enough to help you fetch me the jewel. And then the world will be mine!"

His insane laughter echoed in the dark.

Glossary

anata wa? *(ah-nah-tah-wah?)* – and you?
ayashii-ketsu *(ah-yah-shee-keh-tsoo)* – mysterious cave

basashi *(bah-sah-she)* – raw horse meat, sashimi-style
bikkuri shita! *(bik-koo-ree-she-tah!)* – what a surprise!

-chan – term of affection appended to a name
chikara *(chee-kah-rah)* – power
chotto matte *(chot-toh-mat-teh)* – wait a minute

dare ga imasuka? *(dah-reh-gah-ee-mass-kah?)* – who's there?
-dera *(deh-rah)* – temple
dojo *(doh-joh)* – training area for martial arts
Doraemon *(Doh-righ-mon)* – popular children's series about a robotic cat
dorotabo *(doh-ro-tah-bo)* – mud man

eiein no yo *(ay-ayn-noh-yoh)* – forever world; eternal night; everlasting four

ema *(emma)* – small wooden plaque on which *Shinto* worshippers write their prayers or wishes

fukuro *(foo-koo-roh)* – an owl
futon *(foo-ton)* – a thin padded mattress

gaijin *(guy-jean)* – foreigner, outsider
gaman *(gah-man)* – endurance, perseverance
ganko *(gahn-koh)* – stubborn
genkan *(genn-kahn)* – entranceway
gomen nasai *(goh-men-nah-sigh)* – I'm sorry

haiden *(high-den)* – *Shinto* hall of worship
hakama *(hah-kah-mah)* – traditional pleated trouser skirt
hanten *(hahn-ten)* – short padded winter coat
harionago *(harry-onna-go)* – a female monster with barbed hair
honden *(hon-den)* – *Shinto* main shrine; place where holy object resides
hoshi no kagami *(hoe-she-noh-kah-ga-mee)* – mirror of stars

ima, shine! *(ee-ma-she-neh!)* – now, die!
itai! *(ee-tigh!)* – it hurts!

jinbei *(jin-bay)* – traditional summer pajama-like clothing

jinmenju *(jin-men-joo)* – a tree with human-faced fruit

jubokko *(joo-bock-oh)* – vampire tree

kaginawa *(kah-gee-nah-wah)* – grappling hook

kami ga nai! *(kah-mee-gah-nigh!)* – my hair's gone!

kanji *(kan-jee)* – a system of Japanese writing using Chinese characters

kao o mitai? *(cow-oh-mee-tigh)* – do you want to see my face?

kata *(kah-tah)* – a system of repetitive training exercises to master complex, choreographed patterns of movement

katana *(kah-tah-nah)* – a long single-edged *Samurai* sword

kawaii, da ne? *(kah-wah-ee-dah-neh?)* – it's so cute, isn't it?

ketsu ga itai! *(ket-soo-gah-ee-tigh!)* – my butt hurts!

ki *(kee)* – energy, spirit, life force

kinasai *(kee-nah-sigh)* – come

kingumo *(king-goo-moh)* – a metal spider

kitsune *(kee-tsoo-neh)* – a fox

kodama *(koh-dah-ma)* – a tree spirit

Kojiki *(Koh-jee-kee)* – an 8th century collection of founding myths

komainu *(koh-ma-ee-noo)* – lion-dog shrine guardians

konaki-jiji *(koh-nah-kee-jee-jee)* – a monster that cries to lure passersby

konban-wa *(kon-bahn-wah)* – good evening

ko-tengu *(koh-ten-goo)* – juvenile bird-demons
kuchisake onna *(koo-chee-sah-keh-on-nah)* – slit-mouthed woman
Kuebiko jinja wa *(Koo-eh-bee-koo-jin-jah-wah)* – regarding the Kuebiko shrine
-kun – term of affection appended to a male name
kuro *(koo-roh)* – black

mado *(mah-doh)* – magic, sorcery
matte! *(mat-teh!)* – wait!
mayotte shimaimashita *(mah-yot-tay-she-migh-mash-tah)* – I'm lost
me ga itai! *(meh-gah-ee-tigh!)* – my eyes hurt!
miso *(mee-soh)* – seasoning paste made from fermented soybeans, barley or rice
mori *(mor-ee)* – wood; forest
moshi moshi *(moh-she-moh-she)* – hello, when answering the telephone
muri da *(moo-ree-dah)* – that's not possible

nandayo? *(nan-dah-yoh)* – what is it now?
natto *(nat-toh)* – fermented soybeans
ne? – question-forming suffix, like "eh?"
Nihon daigaku e no michi o shitte imasuka? *(Nee-hon-digh-ga-koo-eh-no-mee-chee-oh-she-teh-ee-mass-kah?)* – can you tell me the way to Nihon University?
nihongo o hanashimasu *(nee-hon-goh-oh-hah-nah-she-mass)* – I speak Japanese

nihongo o wakarimasen *(nee-hon-goh-oh-wah-kah-ree-mass-en)* – I can't understand Japanese
nukekubi *(noo-keh-koo-bee)* – a type of vampire with a detachable flying head

obi *(oh-bee)* – a wide sash for a kimono
oishii *(oy-shee)* – delicious
oji *(oh-jee)* – uncle
ojisan *(oh-jee-san)* – uncle
okonomiyaki *(ok-oh-noh-me-yak-ee)* – a Japanese savory pancake
oni *(oh-nee)* – demon, devil, ogre or troll
onibaba *(oh-nee-bah-bah)* – demon hag

ryogama bo *(rio-gah-ma-boh)* – double-ended sickle
ryu no hone da! *(ryoo-no-ho-neh-dah!)* – it's dragon bone!

sagari *(sah-ga-ree)* – a disembodied horse head
sake *(sah-keh)* – traditional rice wine
-sama *(sah-mah)* – term of great respect appended to a name
Samurai *(sah-moo-rye)* – a member of the Japanese warrior class
-san – term of respect appended to a name
sashimi *(sah-she-mee)* – bite-sized pieces of raw fish eaten with soy sauce or horseradish

seiza *(say-zah)* – traditional formal way of sitting; like kneeling with buttocks resting on heels

sensei *(sen-say)* – teacher; master

shinji rarenai *(shin-jee-rah-reh-nigh)* – I don't believe it

Shinkansen (shin-kan-sen) – bullet train

Shinto *(shin-toh)* – the "way of the gods"; native Japanese religion

Shogatsu *(Sho-gat-soo)* – Japanese New Year

shoji *(sho-jee)* – sliding paper screen door

soba *(soh-ba)* – traditional buckwheat noodles

sumimasen *(soo-mee-mah-sen)* – excuse me

sumo *(soo-moh)* – Japanese heavyweight wrestling

sushi *(soo-shi)* – small balls or rolls of rice with vegetables, egg or raw seafood

tahoto *(ta-hoe-toh)* – a two-story pagoda

taisha-wa, doko desu ka *(tigh-sha-wah-doh-koh-dess-ka?)* – where is the shrine?

Taketori Monogatari *(Ta-keh-taw-ree-Mon-oh-gah-tah-ree)* – the Tale of the Bamboo Cutter

tanto *(tan-toh)* – short sword, between 6 and 12 inches long

tanuki *(tah-noo-kee)* – Japanese raccoon dog

tanbo o kaese! *(tan-boh-oh-kah-ess-ay)* – give me back my field!

Tasukeru koto ga dekiru? *(Tass-ke-roo-koh-toh-gah-deh-kee-roo?)* – can I help?

tasukete! *(tass-ke-teh!)* – help!

tasukete kure! *(tass-ke-teh-koo-reh!)* – help me, please!

tatami *(tah-tah-mee)* – rush-covered straw mat

temizuya *(teh-mee-zoo-yah)* – cleansing place at a shrine

tengu *(ten-goo)* – long-nosed bird-demon

tetsubishi *(teh-tsoo-bee-she)* – iron spikes used to slow down pursuers

tomare *(toh-ma-reh)* – stop

torii *(taw-ree)* – traditional Japanese shrine gate

tsuchikurobi *(tsoo-chee-koo-ro-bee)* – a rolling mass of earth that crushes its victims

Tsuki-no-Miyako *(Tsoo-kee-no-Mee-ya-koh)* – the capital city of the Moon

ushi-oni *(oo-she-oh-nee)* – monster with the head of a bull and the body of a spider or crab

wakaranai *(wah-ka-rah-nigh)* – I don't understand

washi *(wah-she)* – traditional Japanese paper

watashi kirei? *(wa-tah-she-kee-ray?)* – do you think I'm pretty?

watashi no nihongo wa warui desu *(wa-tah-she-no-nee-hon-goh-wah-wa-roo-ee-dess)* – my Japanese is poor.

watashi-wa Ken desu *(wa-tah-she-wah-Ken-dess)* – I'm Ken

yakuza *(yah-koo-zah)* – Japanese gangster

yama-uba *(yah-ma-oo-bah)* – mountain hag

Yata no Kagami *(Yah-ta-no-kah-gah-mee)* – the Eight Hand Mirror

yokai *(yoh-kigh)* – any supernatural creature, such as *oni*

Yomi *(yoh-mee)* – the underworld; land of the dead; Hell

yukkuri shiro *(yook-koo-ree-she-roh)* – slow down

Coming soon

THE STONE OF KUROMORI

Sneak preview...

I told you we couldn't trust those meatheads," Kenny griped while Kiyomi gave his equipment a final check.

"Really? You think now is a good time for 'I told you so'?" she fumed. "Put your regulator in and start breathing." Kenny pulled down his mask and waddled to the edge of the diving platform. "Here's where normally you take a big stride into the water, but in this case . . . Eyes on the horizon!" Kiyomi planted a foot firmly against Kenny's backside and pushed.

"AAAAGH!" Kenny grabbed his mask and regulator to hold them in place as he plunged into the sapphire sea amid a cloud of fine bubbles. Water flooded into his mask and he kicked upward, thrashing to the surface before he remembered he could breathe.

Kiyomi splashed down beside him and gave a thumbs-up signal in the direction of the boat. Captain Mike waved in acknowledgment and raised a red flag with a diagonal white stripe to signal to other vessels that divers were down.

Dwayne, the burly special forces diver, jumped in and

bobbed alongside, while Kiyomi showed Kenny how to clear his mask by blowing air into it. She adjusted the air in his buoyancy jacket, and then gave the thumbs down sign to descend.

Grabbing Kenny's hand, Kiyomi released some air from her own jacket and then lowered her head to swim downward. Kenny copied her movements and the divers kicked gently through the clear water.

Kenny forced himself to relax. It took all his effort not to sweep his arms and kick his legs as he would for normal swimming. Here, he was weightless, gliding beneath the tropical sea. The only sound was the hypnotic rhythm of his breathing. Shafts of sunlight lanced down from above, illuminating sparkling shoals of fish. A huge leatherback sea turtle labored upward, close enough for Kenny to see the barnacles growing on its shell, and a glittering curtain of glassfish exploded into mirrorlike fragments as the divers approached, reforming after they had passed.

As they descended farther, Kenny felt an uncomfortable feeling building in his ears. Remembering his training, he pushed air into his pinched nose and waggled his jaw. His ears popped just as a shadow fell across his back. Twisting his head upward, Kenny saw the unmistakable bullet shape of a large shark.

Dwayne continued to lead the way, glancing back from time to time to make sure that Kiyomi and Kenny were keeping up. He pointed and, in the distance, Kenny could see a dark, angular form rising up from the seabed. Even from here he could discern stone blocks and massive terraced steps, like the sides of a truncated Mayan pyramid.

As they drew closer, the features of the underwater ruin became more distinct. Kenny could make out a standing pillar, narrow channels, a road of sorts, platforms, stairs – and more sharks. Thousands of adult hammerhead sharks were circling lazily around the edifice like a slow-motion tornado. Everywhere Kenny looked, he saw stubby, twig-like shark silhouettes revolving, as if on guard.

Dwayne released more air from his buoyancy jacket and sank down to the seabed, gesturing for Kiyomi and Kenny to follow. He glided along the bottom, kicking up sand with each stroke of his flippers, and led the way beneath the sharks to the south side where a crude staircase appeared to have been cut into the rock.

He motioned for Kiyomi to take the lead and in reply she circled a finger to indicate a loop around the ruins. Still holding Kenny's hand, Kiyomi led them in a counterclockwise circuit of the city. They passed a huge star-shaped slab which resembled a turtle, a small triangular pool, twin pillars that looked as if they had come from Stonehenge, and a partly eroded stone face.

By now, Kenny had forgotten everything except the scene around him. He turned his head in every direction, drinking in the wonder of the underwater world. Questions crowded into his mind. Who or what could have built such a structure? Did it sink or was it always underwater? Was it part of an ancient civilization or just an odd natural formation?

He could see why it would be fascinating for treasure hunters, but was there any treasure; if so, what hope did they have of finding it? Yet why else would Susano-wo have sent them here?

Kiyomi gave his hand a sharp tug and pointed upward. Kenny looked. All he saw was the silhouette of the giant turtle still cruising above, a black shadow against the bright surface. And then it hit him: he could *only* see the turtle. Where had all the sharks gone? Kenny's stomach lurched. What could scare off a thousand sharks?

The answer came from the middle distance: a cluster of silvery dots growing larger with each passing second. Kiyomi looped her fingers into Kenny's weight belt and hauled him backward. She pointed to a narrow chasm behind a rectangular boulder and kicked towards it.

Dwayne glided away to take a better look at the rapidly closing objects. Not liking the look of them, he unsheathed two wicked-looking combat knives and held them ready.

The approaching objects sharpened into sixteen-foot-long, metallic-blue cylinders, with stabilizing fins, dead black eyes and gaping mouths crammed with hooked teeth: mako sharks . . .

Kenny took a last look and gasped, almost ejecting his breathing regulator, as Kiyomi yanked him into the fissure. As if a hunting pack of mako sharks wasn't terrifying enough, each predator was carrying some kind of humanoid creature on its back. It was only a split-second glimpse, but Kenny saw gray skin, pointed heads and jagged spears in hands, all bearing down on the hapless Dwayne.

Kiyomi wriggled her way as deep as she could into the dark crevice. Kenny followed blindly, bumping his face into Kiyomi's shoulder and dislodging his mask. Salt water flooded in. He was about to clear his mask when he felt Kiyomi's steely grip on his hand. Squinting through the sea water burning his eyes, he saw Kiyomi holding her breath and stabbing a finger upward. A cloud of silvery air bubbles was rising from his exhaust valve, as obvious as a smoke signal.

Kenny concentrated for a moment, summoning his *ki*, and imagined one large bubble. The rising cluster of individual globules shivered and coalesced into a single sphere. Maintaining his focus, Kenny directed the bubble downward, into the depths of the channel they were hiding in. Now all they needed to do was wait it out until the shark pack lost interest and moved on.

Something brushed against Kenny's head and he reached up to catch a hard, flat object. Peering at it in the near dark, he recognized the blade of one of Dwayne's knives. He turned it in a semicircle, to grasp the handle – and was confronted by a severed hand, still gripping tightly.

"YAAAAGH!" Kenny yelled, losing his mouthpiece and his concentration. The bubbles shot upward once more.

Kenny fumbled for his regulator and exhaled to empty the water from his mask. As his vision cleared, he saw Kiyomi shaking her fist at him and backing away along the crevice, while shooting fearful glances upward.

Shadows converged overhead and one of the shark riders dismounted to stand astride the chasm. It peered down into the gloom and Kenny felt its eyes bore into him. He shrank back, pressing himself against the rock to blend into the shadows. He knew he had nowhere to run.

In its webbed hands the creature clutched a long spear with twin serrated blades. It steadied itself and took aim . . .